The Star Trap

The Star Trap

MARJORIE DARKE

DECORATIONS BY MICHAEL JACKSON

Kestrel Books

KESTREL BOOKS
Published by Penguin Books Ltd
Harmondsworth, Middlesex, England

First published in 1974
under the Longman Young Books imprint
Reissued 1982

ISBN 0 7226 6262 9

Printed in Great Britain by
Richard Clay (The Chaucer Press) Ltd,
Bungay, Suffolk

Part 1

1844

★ ★ ★

THE STROLLING PLAYERS

I NOTHING!
She craned from behind the sheltering screen of laurels to risk a second hasty glance through the scrolls of the tall iron gates to the dusty road beyond. There was no one to spy on her!

Now that the moment had arrived for flight, her courage quailed and dwindled to a pin-point. Insoluble problems rose up; craggy mountains that loomed and threatened until she all but turned and fled back into her plaster prison. She put a hand to her constricted throat and touched the concealed locket. A small seed of stubborn determination, planted deep inside her many years before, put out shoots at the reminder and began to grow. Her thin wisp of a body shook with fear and excitement behind the cramping bushes. Dare she go? She had only to walk a few yards to be free from the octopus confines of the school grounds, but still she hesitated, clutching her carpet bag as if it were filled with comfort instead of clothes. In the distance the sound of iron-bound carriage wheels trundled through the dry spring air. She froze. But the echoes died, leaving only bird-song and the clicking of winter branches stirred by a rising wind.

'Frances Redmayne, what would Mama think? You should be ashamed!'

7

The sound of her own voice knocked around hollows in her stomach, but brought back the necessary impulse. She was outside the gates with one last look at the solid white walls and dead-eyed windows of the schoolhouse. A cedar of Lebanon laid fingers on the high brick wall at one end of the garden as if to check it growing higher still. Frances smiled slightly, remembering this first impression, when her father had brought her to Blackheath eight months before. Eight months! However could she have allowed eight months to pass before deciding how to set about realizing her ambitions? Mrs Harper's Seminary for Young Ladies had weakened her confidence for a time, but now she felt herself to be as before, Frances of Thrushton Hall, living with Papa, her days filled to the brim with riding, the excitement of the new railway being built across the estate, the risk and disobedience of those secret meetings with John Gate.

Little gusts of wind caught her long black hair, blowing the curls up round her chip straw bonnet and across her eyes, momentarily cutting out the view of house and grounds. The letter, tucked inside the silk of her glove, crackled. There was no more time for hesitation. The choice was made. In less than an hour, when the gong sounded for afternoon tea, her absence would be discovered and she must be on the train for London Bridge by then.

She began to walk briskly along the road, still thinking about John. What an ill-assorted pair they had been. A farming lad who could neither read nor write and the Squire's impetuous daughter. Ignorance and arrogance rubbing shoulders! She still felt ashamed of the high-handed way she had offered to teach him to read, in spite of the fact that, in his hunger to learn, he had accepted all her teasing scorn, turning it into respect and friendship. His single-minded patience had been rewarded. Prison doors opened for him when he had gone to learn railway engineering at Mr Hartlipp's works; they had shut behind her at the Seminary. But all that was over. She had escaped! And realizing there was no sense of failure to carry around any more, apprehension was replaced by burning determination.

As the road turned out into the Heath itself, she wanted to run but knew that any casual eye would be attracted to the sight of an unaccompanied girl in such a hurry. She had to be sedate, unruffled; look as if she were out for no more than a stroll, but it was so difficult when every nerve in her body shouted run ... RUN! To be alone on the Heath was odd enough. She must do nothing to draw further attention. Thank goodness the place was empty! Her feet scurried over the grass and stirred up little swirls of dust as she reached the road edging Greenwich Park. She rounded the corner and, passing between dignified Georgian houses, began the descent down Croomes Hill. A man in a top hat and wrinkled trousers followed a wheezing bulldog from one of the houses into the street. He glanced incuriously at Frances. She felt cold beads of sweat start out on her forehead and round her mouth and strove to remain calm and unhurried.

The wind, growing ever stronger, flapped her skirts against her buttoned boots and looped them between her legs. Irritably she straightened them, wishing she could wear trousers. They were so much more practical. If only she had been the boy her father wanted how different life might have been! The world would spread out before her. What would she choose? Help her father run the estate? The idea was far more attractive than having to supervise the domestic affairs of Thrushton Hall, or some other big house when she married. Papa took it for granted that her future lay in marriage. A far cry from her own ambitions. She scowled. Boys had the best of it. They could choose anything ... medicine, the Law, farming, even railway engineering, as John had done. It would be better still to be a director of a railway company, sharing Papa's passion for the new permanent ways: able to say 'This is how things will be' and everyone taking notice. Just as Papa had done on that first journey along the Thrushton and Molesbridge Branch Line. She saw herself staring through the carriage window at John and the navvies standing beside the track; feeling the tension as the train gradually slowed to a halt. The picture was all absorbing, making her blind to the park railings, trees, grass, people ...

'Look out, missie!' a voice bawled, and she came to with a start as a handcart piled with rags, broken furniture and junk of all kinds appeared out of a side street, brushing close to her. She stepped back and the boy propelling the cart gave her a wink from under a tousled bush of dirty hair. 'Bless you, missie ... don't want to 'urt you none.'

She stared about. Where there had been nothing but windswept quiet, all was bustle. The side street leading to the park gates was full of

loaded wagons. The drivers shouted to one another and at their strain-
ing horses. A mangy dog with a bitten ear shot between the wheels of
a wagon that had the word 'RICHARDSON'S' painted along the side
in flourishing letters of scarlet, black and gold.

Of course, it was the Easter fair! She had never been allowed to visit
it, but one of the maids had given a highly-coloured account of the
wild beast shows, dwarfs and fat ladies, stalls selling gilt gingerbread
and penny toys, sword swallowers, fire-eaters and Richardson's acting
booth. She had listened avidly to the detailed descriptions of actors and
actresses pouring out oceans of words, pacing the makeshift stage;
their painted faces weirdly lit by pots of burning fat that served as
footlights. Anything connected with theatre was food and drink.

The wagons, which had momentarily halted, began rolling again.
Frances responded with a feeling of urgency. Good Friday, and the first
were arriving. Easter Saturday in the morning and Papa was to fetch
her back to Thrushton for . . . She screwed the letter into a tight ball
in her fist, refusing to think of the threat it contained. Time enough
for that when she was on the train.

Arriving at the brand-new station she rushed in through the gate
reserved for first class travellers, without a thought for her limited
money. The clerk in the booking office raised his eyebrows at the
unaccompanied young lady who offered a sovereign for her ticket, but
she was too anxious to notice. A train was already waiting. There were
two sets of carriages, closed yellow and black for first class, open blue
for second. With no hesitation at all, Frances handed the ticket to the
collector and climbed into the nearest yellow carriage. She was faintly
relieved that it was empty and settled back against the padded seat, taking off her gloves and arranging them over the carpet bag which she
rested on her lap. A corner of the letter from her father pressed uncom-
fortably into her palm. It typified the way things were between them,
she thought with a touch of bitterness; forever sparring and hurting
each other and yet close . . . or was it all on her side? Old familiar feelings of rejection threatened to engulf her. She fought them back and
was saved by the sound of the guard's whistle and the lurch of the train.
The thrill of the unknown raised sentinel hairs along her arms and nape
of neck. In spite of the misfortune of being a girl expected to obey the
binding rules of convention, she had defied them all! At eighteen . . .

well, give or take a month . . . she had elected to take charge of her own affairs. It hadn't been easy; she remembered conversations with John. Those distant nights, when they met in the derelict hut beyond the village, had been filled with fantasies of engineering and the theatre. She had a high respect for his solid achievement. Time and distance might separate them, but the memory of their companionship, the long serious talks and study, sewn together with warm laughter, remained constantly at the back of her mind. And yet . . .

She shook her head impatiently as if to throw off unwelcome thoughts. There were aspects of their friendship she had no wish to remember. If he could be so determined over his wish to be an engineer, what of his other intentions? No . . . she would not think like that. What nonsense it all was. Nearly a year gone by and there had been no word of John except an arid comment from her father that: 'James Hartlipp tells me Gate applies himself diligently to the work in hand.'

The train was rumbling rhythmically across the long viaduct which cut through rich green meadows peppered with farms and cottages. Frances kept her mind determinedly on watching the view through the carriage window. Occasionally she caught a glimpse of the Thames glittering under pale spring sunlight and saw white barge sails taut in the strong wind. And then the river looped too far and was lost. They had passed through Deptford where an elderly lady in black sateen and an even older man in blacker serge with a well brushed bowler hat joined her. They looked disapproving, Frances thought, but who cared about that? What did they know about her and her private world! If they did, she added to herself with a silent giggle, they would be shocked out of their dull little minds.

In a field below the track some apprehensive cows were making for the opposite side of their field. Buildings were beginning to encroach on the countryside and in the distance the dome of St Paul's Cathedral dominated the uneven skyline. She had heard someone say that before long London would swallow up the country dividing Greenwich from the City and spill over beyond. Ridiculous speculation in her opinion, though she had to admit anything was possible after witnessing the miracle of the growing railways. The excitement of train speed never failed to thrill her, in spite of many journeys with her father.

She opened the letter and smoothed out well-worn creases, reading the words she knew by heart.

Thrushton Hall – March 14th 1844.

My dear Frances,

I have read your recent communication with increasing disquiet. Your several letters indicating dissatisfaction with the Seminary and its mode of life have left me not unmoved. In spite of your head-strong nature, I recognize that perhaps I have misjudged the type of education necessary to you. I have therefore decided to terminate your stay with Mrs Harper and have arranged with Lady Sellinger for you to join her and her daughters, Rose and Emily, in a trip to Europe. I feel sure you will take great delight in this arrangement, especially as it includes a visit to Italy, a country I know you have long wished to see.

I intend travelling by railway from Thrushton to Greenwich (what a triumph to be able to do this). From there I shall arrive by hackney carriage which I have engaged to meet my train. All this on Easter Saturday.

Until then I remain your affectionate father
Oliver Redmayne.

Frances was not fooled by 'affectionate'. She had learned a long time ago to treat such words with reserve, shielding her own tender feelings from his cool appraisal. Deliberately she crumpled the letter in her hand as the train lost speed and slowed to a halt. They had arrived at London Bridge. Her two companions creaked onto the platform. Frances followed, pausing for a moment to open her hand and watch the wind whisk the paper from her palm. So much for that silly twittering pair, Rose and Emily Sellinger, and their opportunist mother! It was a pity to miss touring Italy and especially Naples where her mother had been born, but there would be other times.

There was a leisurely sense of purpose about the half-finished station. Travellers passed through a temporary exit into a forecourt where a network of scaffolding framed a clutter of wagons and carriages, sweating horses and red-faced drivers plying for trade. Bewildered, Frances put down her bag and tried to decide in which direction she ought to go. This first taste of being on her own in busy London scattered her senses.

'Cab, miss?' A grinning driver in a shabby coat with a cape stood at his horse's head not three feet away.

She hesitated, knowing her destination was the Haymarket. An omnibus clattered into the yard. Below the windows on a painted yellow strip were the words 'LONDON BRIDGE ... BANK ... STRAND ... TRAFALGAR SQUARE ... PADDINGTON' in ornate black lettering.

Frances seized her bag. 'No thank you,' she said breathlessly and hurried towards the omnibus.

The passengers had been disgorged from above and inside and others were already climbing in.

'Jump in, miss, brisk and sharp! We'll be off before you can say knife.' A cad, who combined the roles of conductor and salesman, was touting for passengers. He gave Frances a wink and a nod, half helping her with her bag so that she felt herself swept into the omnibus. The cramped interior had a bench either side of a central aisle which was strewn with trampled straw. Choosing a corner furthest from the door, Frances sat down and tried to bring some order into her ruffled composure. Everything was so strange. She felt as if her world had been taken to pieces and put together again in a pattern she could scarcely comprehend. The train had provided familiar and friendly protection but sudden loneliness touched her now. She lifted the small gold watch pinned to her dress beneath her cloak and glanced at the face, more to recapture security than to learn the time. It was five minutes past four. Already she must have been missed at the Seminary. There was plenty of time in front of her but none behind and she longed to be on her way again.

The omnibus was half full by now and smells of crushed straw, stale sweat and musty breath assaulted her. A fat woman in greening black skirts with a rusty shawl crossed over ample breasts and a bonnet covered with shaggy feathers, peered over the basket on her lap.

'You want to take care, dearie.' She nodded towards the watch. 'There's many 'ud like to 'elp theirselves to a dainty like that. On your own are you? Have to be careful . . . there's that many folk with wicked thoughts and straying fingers, I'll tell you!'

The cad poked his head into the open doorway. 'Ready, ladies and gents? Fares in hand when you alight, *if* you please!'

'How much is it to Trafalgar Square?' Frances asked, roused to a flurry by this sharp-nosed attack.

'Sixpence to you, miss,' said the cad and slammed the door.

'And to us all inside,' said the fat woman. 'You won't need to find your money yet, dearie. It's quicker to walk, there's that much traffic. If it weren't for me bunions I'd be on Shanks's pony, I'll tell you.'

Frances took a coin from her reticule and slipped it into her glove, staring through the window beyond the fat woman's hat, trying to avoid further conversation. The omnibus rolled down the ramp from the station into the street below and jolted towards London Bridge. The leaden waters of the Thames frothed up under the paddles of slim-funnelled steam packets and more barge masts spiked the sky. And then they were across and in a narrow maze of streets packed with traffic. The noise was incredible and progress tediously slow. Frances slid into a daydream about the evening to come. Her skin prickled with antici-pation as all the years of tightly cherished imagining unrolled and she was back again in the warm darkness, with the smell of cigar smoke and orange peel mingling with an indefinable something that meant 'Theatre'. Tonight would be her second visit but not the last. The future she pictured for herself lay not in front but behind those magic curtains where different worlds could be created in the blink of an eyelid.

The omnibus rumbled over the cobbles of Ludgate Hill, shaking its way between overhanging buildings where shops and offices crowded and jostled with hurrying people and clattering traffic, as if the whole of living lay in the effort of elbowing a way to the front.

Frances recognized the Strand, then Charing Cross and Trafalgar Square from the days when Papa had taken her by carriage from their Bayswater home for roundabout drives. It seemed a lifetime ago, though it was only three years since her grandfather had died and she had gone with Papa to Thrushton when he inherited the estate.

She got up and pulled the strap, sixpence ready in her hand. The fat woman smiled a kindly warning.

'Take care, dearie . . . and watch out for those pickpockets. 'Ope you finds your friends quick.'

There had been no mention of friends. She had no friends in the world now. Perhaps it was only another good wish. She smiled back and stepped from the omnibus, spending a few hair-raising moments crossing into the wide expanse of Trafalgar Square where more scaffolding surrounded an immense elegant column being built to support an effigy of Nelson.

✷ ✷ ✷

The first touches of dusk had greyed the sky before Frances reached the Haymarket Theatre. A crowd was already bunching round the doors, waiting for the theatre to open. Frances eased towards the playbill pasted on the wall until she could read the flourishing letters: 'THE TAMING OF THE SHREW – BY WILLIAM SHAKESPEARE ... SPECIAL EFFECTS DEVISED BY ...' It flowed on and on, listing actors and actresses, afterpieces, songs and tableaux. Already the glory of it all enchanted her, feeding her impatience with dreams of what was to come.

Under the colonnade the crowd was getting restive and when the doors opened, people pushed towards the booking office in good-humoured mood. A small boy brushed past Frances, worming his way to the front. She envied his impudence, understanding his impatience. The time seemed endless before she was inside, and then the scent, sweet and heady as incense, met her. She bought a ticket for the pit, more cautious this time about her financial position, and made her way awkwardly down the steps with the carpet bag bumping against her legs. Coming into the auditorium she was amazed by its changed appearance. On her last visit the soft glow of wax candles and oil lamps had provided gentle light. Now everywhere was ablaze with the brilliant whiteness of the new gas jets. Settling herself on a hard wooden seat with the bulky carpet bag tucked beneath, she looked round. The theatre was beginning to fill already and the hum of conversation punctuated by bursts of laughter and the calls of women selling ginger beer, oranges and nuts, stimulated Frances' tremendous excitement to the point where she thought she must give it expression ... stand up and shout ... dance between the seats ... shriek out her happiness ... anything ...

Instead she stared hard at the green curtain hanging in the frame of the proscenium arch before the stage, willing it to rise and reveal the mysteries and delights waiting there. Her bottled emotions must have

15

made her look strange because a middle aged woman in a lavender silk dress, who had come to sit next to her, leaned over and asked if she felt faint.

'Oh . . . n . . . no,' Frances was startled.

'Exciting, isn't it?' said the woman, fanning herself with her gloves. 'No matter how much I come it's the same . . . like walking into another world I always think. A good deal better than the one outside. It's not just on stage . . . I like seeing the people. You get a variety of folk come here.'

It was true. In the rising tiers of seats in the circle behind her and in the boxes crowding the stage Frances could see elegant women with men in evening dress, while high in the roof the people packed into the 'gods' were totally different. Workaday folk, who thrashed and jostled one another, whistling and cracking jokes and nuts, the shells of which they shied onto the heads of the audience below. The house lights dimmed, as only new gas could, and a gasp of awe went up in which Frances was included. As the curtain rose in a series of festoons the audience shuffled and coughed into gradual quiet after a cheer for the wiry Sly and the plump Hostess who burst onto the stage, arguing hotly. The scenery was a marvel to behold and Frances was filled again with amazement at the size of the stage. More actors appeared in costumes she thought a miracle of invention, speaking their lines with such conviction that she was lost in admiration. Consciousness of self began to slip from her and she was caught up by one character and then another in a multitude of identities; laughing when they laughed, being scornful with their scorn, witty, arrogant . . . But gradually her involvement focused on Kate, whose rebellious personality struck answering chords that went deeper than appreciation of the actress's performance.

> '. . . I am no child, no babe.
> Your betters have endur'd me say my mind,
> And if you cannot, best you stop your ears.
> My tongue will tell the anger of my heart,
> Or else my heart, concealing it, will break;
> And rather than it shall, I will be free
> Even to the uttermost, as I please, in words.'

16

And it was Frances who was speaking. Petruchio, Bianca and Lucentio filled her world as they argued and wept, laughed and sighed: and all the time she was there on the stage with them. More than that . . . the stage itself melted away and she was *living* in their world.

When the curtain fell at the interval it took several minutes before she could bring herself back into her surroundings.

'Oo that was lovely!' Her companion stirred into life. 'Quite took my breath. What do you say to a bottle of ginger beer?' She beckoned to the seller.

Unable immediately to detach herself from the play, Frances did not respond, until courtesy prodded her into replying:

'That would be nice.'

The ginger beer burned her throat bringing a pleasing glow. Afterwards she bought some cobnuts and shared them with the woman, cracking them between her teeth.

When the play continued her involvement returned as if the break had never happened. In the brief moments when bursts of clapping for principal actors or for particular pieces of spectacle, broke Frances' absorption, she became aware of feelings which almost amounted to ecstasy. It was perfect! Nothing in the world was more desirable than to be part of the magic which bound her. Every rustle of taffeta, voice inflection, body movement, built an illusion so splendid nothing else mattered in the world. There had been no mistake in coming. All the pricking doubts fled. No matter how difficult, she must become part of that astonishing world and share its glory.

Four hours later, when the Haymarket Theatre opened its doors and spewed out the sweating, shouting, singing mob of an audience, Frances moved out in a dream. Gaslight winked from puddles on the rain-drenched street as she was pushed and shoved from one direction to another. Gradually the crowd thinned as the wealthy got into their private carriages, while the rabble scurried on foot through the rain and the reckless hired cabs.

In a haze of limelight and Shakespearian words, with the whisper of silks and clang of striking swords in her ears, Frances was quite incapable of pulling herself back into reality. The rain soaked into the straw of her bonnet and dragged at her carpet bag, but all she knew were the rags of memories whirling inside her exhausted mind. In spite of fatigue and mental indigestion she floated in a world more real to her than the mud-splashed street where she stood. Kate's shrewish words snapped and tangled with a popular ballad that had come ... where? She could scarcely recall ... before the afterpiece which was all about a home-coming sailor. There was a dancer too ... somewhere ... light as thistledown, lit by changing coloured lights, red, blue, green ...

'Good evening, my dear. Walking this way are you?' A hand cupped her elbow and a man with a moustache waxed to fine spikes smiled down at her, tipping his curly bowler hat. In a panic Frances pulled away, the encounter filling her with alarm spiced by all the tales she had ever heard about the fate of unchaperoned girls in the evil city. She looked round wildly. One of the new hansom cabs was standing at the kerbside a short distance away. She ran towards it, scrambling clumsily up the step. The driver was beside her in a trice, helping her in and closing the flaps with a bang.

'Thirty Mortimer Place, off Bedford Square,' she urged in a voice barely recognizable as her own.

'Very good, miss.'

There had been no time for thoughts about dwindling money. Bleak reality was forcing its way into her cloudy dreams. The driver took the cab along the streets at a spanking trot, rain drumming on the roof and bouncing off the horse's back. The unpleasant incident had shaken her more than she liked and for the second time since she had formed her plan, sharp splinters of doubt made the journey increasingly uncomfortable. She was planning on staying one night at least with Miss Pringle, her former governess, who had gone to look after her widowed brother at his lodgings. Would she be there? She must be! Frances gave herself a mental shake. It was stupid to have come so far with no real disaster and to give way to fears about things that might never be. But for once her optimism was not rewarded. She paid off the driver and stood damp and disconsolate in front of a tall narrow terraced house in a dingy street. There was nothing welcoming in the anonymous windows or the shadowy door at the top of four stone steps. In the weak light from a distant gas-lamp she could just distinguish the gleam of a brass knocker in the shape of a lion's head. She climbed the steps and rapped on the door. Silence . . . a second knock; and then the flicker of a candle behind lace curtains. She waited and heard bolts drawn . . . and remembered it was well after eleven at night.

'Yes?' A voice squeezed through the crack.

'Miss Pringle . . . is she in?' Frances did her best to sound authoritative, but it was difficult.

'Who is it wishes to see her?'

'Frances Redmayne . . . she was my governess until a short while ago.' The words tumbled out and she felt another surge of doubt at having given her name.

The door opened a little more and the face of an elderly woman with plaited hair crowned by a nightcap, leaned out for a closer look.

'She's not here, I'm afraid.'

'Not here?' Frances could not believe her ears. 'Has she gone on holiday?'

The nightcap wagged. 'Left . . . after the funeral.'

'The funeral?'

'Mr Pringle's. Died very sudden. Didn't you know?'

Frances shook her head, unable to say a word.

'Got a place as companion to an invalid lady in Kent. Didn't want to go, but there was no money, you see.' A question had crept into the voice. One that Frances understood but could not answer. Her throat was blocked by a lump as big as a fist and inside her head her life had blown up. The rain seemed to be drumming hard in her ears. She was utterly desolate.

'Here,' said the voice, far in the distance, 'you all right? Come inside for a minute out of the rain.'

She felt herself drawn into the darkened hall and somehow she remained standing. There was a hiss and a sputter as the woman lit a gas jet.

'My, you do look peaky, dear. You'd better sit down.'

At the hint of sympathy Frances dropped her bag, slumping onto the proffered chair. The doubts she had experienced in the cab returned with redoubled force. At one blow the perfection of her plan was ruined by the unthinking action of another person! The misery inside her swelled up and burst into a storm of tears.

2

'CUP OF TEA, DEAR?'

Frances opened her eyes to a windy sunlit morning that poked inquiring fingers between the curtains and rattled the window frame of the small bedroom. She stared sleepily at the willow-patterned teacup and then, as memory came rushing in, was wide awake. The bed in which she lay was a narrow iron affair but not uncomfortable and the walls of the attic room were covered with faded wallpaper which had once pictured a riot of cabbage roses. For the rest there was a marble-topped washstand, a chest of drawers and a rag rug beside the bed. A sampler on the wall told her 'GOD SEES ALL' It was a depressing message which reduced her powers of invention. She could think of no convincing answers to the questions she knew were hovering. Last night she had been so overwrought that the nightcapped woman, who turned out to be Mrs Billings, landlady of the lodging house, had asked no questions but dosed her with gin and hot water, tucking her into bed with a generous kindness that Frances was only just beginning to appreciate.

And now here she was again with a face full of kindly inquiry. Waiting! Frances sat up, smoothing the frills of her flannel nightgown, pushing straying curls away from her face. In daylight the enormity of her plight shrank to tolerable proportions. She accepted the tea gratefully. Yesterday's midday meal was a long time ago and the ginger beer and cobnuts had done little to fill the gap.

'Glad to see you feeling more yourself,' said Mrs Billings, still waiting.

Frances decided to tell a section of the truth. 'I owe you some explanation of how I came to be visiting at such a late hour.'

Mrs Billings gave her an encouraging smile.

Frances lowered her eyelids in what she hoped was an expression of demure shame. 'I . . . I have a confession.' She was judging the amount of hesitation needed to sound convincing. 'I'm at school you see. At least I should be, but I decided to make a visit to London . . . without telling anyone.' She risked a direct glance and saw that Mrs Billings was confused. Now for it! Down went the lashes. 'I . . . wanted to see Mr Webster's production of "The Taming of the Shrew".'

Silence!

'At the Haymarket Theatre.'

Mrs Billings was shocked. 'The theatre!' she said incredulously, and left her mouth open.

Frances lost some of her self-possession and sat forward in the bed.

'Oh I know it was foolish of me, especially being on my own (and that is really true, she thought, remembering the man with the waxed moustache) but I wanted to see it so badly. I love Shakespeare with all my heart . . . my mother was a great actress you know, but I expect Miss Pringle has told you all about us, so I can count on you to understand.' The words came rolling out, gathering speed, winding up the pleasure she had in spinning fantasies. There was intoxication in manipulating other people; using the dusky quality of her voice to influence them. It was like weaving a tapestry . . . a thread inserted here and there . . . and the direction of their thoughts could be guided any way she wished. Except for Papa. The thought came unbidden, acting like a splash of cold water. She looked appealingly at Mrs Billings who had just said:

'Alone!' In tones of deep horror.

'I know what you must be thinking, but please forgive me! I felt the same last night and that is why I came here. Miss Pringle was always so kind to me and . . . and I thought she would help me to put things right. Everything was such a muddle! It was too late to return to school, you see. I did leave a note . . . and I intend returning today, believe me!' She managed to make real tears come to her eyes.

Mrs Billings must have believed, despite discrepancies in the story. An hour later, after a substantial breakfast, Frances was on her way supposedly to London Bridge Station in a hackney carriage that smelled of horses and had straw stuffing poking through a rent in the canvas seat. On the way she told the driver to change direction and take her to the Haymarket. Then she felt for her watch, which ought to have been pinned to her bodice. She knew immediately where she had left it; under the pillows in the iron bed. What a fool she was; what an idiot! Now she would have to go back after seeing Mr Webster and that would give the lie to her promise to return to school.

The carriage halted in front of the columns of the Haymarket Theatre. Angry with herself, Frances opened the door and climbed out. Perhaps, afterwards, when her future was decided . . . she would fetch the watch, playing the scene in a friendly hurried way . . . discovery of the error at the station . . . long journey back accounting for time . . . yes, that was it.

The carriage jingled away and she was left staring at a playbill pasted beside the closed door of the theatre. Now that the moment had come she was disconcerted by the blank face of the theatre. Somehow she had expected a flurry of people, open doors, life surging and brimming, drawing her in with interest. There were people about, busy, hurrying, but they were the shoppers, tradesmen, street sellers, none of whom threw her as much as a glance.

Frances turned away, chilled by her own mood rather than the blustering April wind which was blowing up pewter-coloured clouds with the promise of more rain. She stood looking up the street, uncertain what to do, and caught sight of a scurrying figure bent against the wind. As the girl reached the theatre she paused and went to look at the playbill then, with a glance at Frances from a pair of bright blue eyes set close to her turned up nose, she pulled her green cloak more closely round her angular body and hurried on, turning into the side street. There was something in the searching quality of her glance that arrested Frances' interest. She followed the girl at a discreet distance round to the back of the theatre and saw her disappear through a double door. With a thudding heart she went closer, guessing this was the stage door. As she stood irresolute an errand boy swung jauntily past, a pair of gaudy red boots tucked under one arm. With an impudent stare he whistled his way through the door and disappeared into a shadowy passage which Frances glimpsed before the door slammed. Her courage was almost enough . . . only a step more needed and . . . A flare of voices sent her back round the corner where she stood frowning at the dirty pavement. Was she always to be so faint-hearted? Having enough boldness to rush at her dreams, only to become as scared as a rabbit when they threatened to turn into reality.

The stage door banged, and the errand boy passed at a trot, waving as he went. Another crash of the door. Footsteps echoed over the cobbles and a shrill voice called out:

'Boy . . . wait there . . . wait will you!'

But the boy was out of earshot half way across the street, the clatter of a dray covering the shouted words. The girl with the bright blue eyes, bareheaded now and without her cloak, ran towards the corner where Frances was standing, waving the red boots the boy had delivered. Watching, Frances saw what was going to happen. As the dray turned off towards Haymarket there appeared from behind it a brand new hansom cab with sparkling yellow wheels and golden brown varnish. It was travelling at a brisk pace towards the stage door. In her haste the girl misjudged the distance. Frances dropped her carpet bag and lunged forward, snatching at the girl's sleeve, jerking her back from the plunging hooves. So close was the horse that his cloudy breath blew across her face. The girl shrieked as the red boots fell under the wheels of the hansom. The driver swore and hauled on the reins, sliding to a stop some yards further along.

'Gawd . . . oh mercy . . . the boots!' The girl was wringing her hands, apparently unconcerned with her own narrow escape.

Frances retrieved them from the gutter. 'They aren't really damaged,' she said. 'There's a scratch on the leg, but the worst is just mud.'

'Lucky you wasn't crushed to a pulp,' said the sweating driver who had come back to see who had been hurt. Finding no damage, his anger boiled over. 'You wants to look where you're going. Frightened me poor 'oss near to death you did. Look at 'im quivering there!'

A few stragglers had paused to find out the cause of the commotion. A woman with protruding eyes and a round red face, called out to him to: 'Lay orf the gel!'

The driver turned to the rest, opening his arms in appeal, asking them to back him up. He wasn't to blame! There were a few shouts of 'No' and someone called: ' 'E's been at the porter . . . look at 'is nose!' Boos from the growing crowd. The girl, who had been polishing the boots on her sleeve, turned to Frances.

'Come on,' she said. 'Let's get out of this!'

They retreated to the stage door and went inside. The girl turned impulsively to Frances.

'I'm ever so grateful. It wouldn't have been just them perishing boots under the cab if you hadn't acted so prompt, I know that! Me stomach feels all churned up to think of it. I could do with a nip an' all. Should think you could too! Just give me a minute to tell Lady Muck the boy's brought the wrong pair and then we'll have a glass. Stay there!' She was gone into the shadows with a curious bouncing movement that was half walk, half run and Frances was left staring into the gloom where a flight of steps led up to a closed door of heavy oak with a brass handle. Shaken though she was by the near accident, her dominant emotion was one of excited triumph. She was inside the theatre at last, and not in the auditorium, but in those secret regions where the magic was made.

'You waiting to see someone, miss?'

She jumped, turning to see a small man with white hair, coming from a cubbyhole beside the stage door. At the same time the girl reappeared calling:

'It's all right, Bob . . . she's with me. Come on, love!'

She held onto Frances' arm and propelled her through a bewildering number of winding passages that smelled of dust, stale perfume, sweat and an indefinable something Frances could not place. And then they were in a small room piled with a curious assortment of wigs, shoes, gloves, fans, beads and baubles of every description. On a string overhead the thin legs of a row of fleshings swayed slightly in the draught from the door.

'Me hideout, as you might say. Not the wardrobe proper, that's through there,' said the girl, nodding towards a second door. 'Sit down!' She indicated a stool, then taking glasses and a bottle from a cupboard with a missing door, she poured two generous measures. Clinking her glass against Frances' she added: 'Let's drink our own health . . . no one else will! Lizzie and . . .?'

'Frances.'

They drank and Frances nearly choked. When she recovered Lizzie was looking at her shrewdly.

'Tell me . . . you were wanting to come in . . . before I mean?'

Frances nodded, not sure how to explain.

'Thought so. I can always tell.' She spoke confidently and Frances wondered how she had betrayed herself.

'I wanted to see Mr Webster. Is that possible?'

The girl gave a snort of laughter, shaking her head so that the frizzy blonde hair piled on top bobbed about. 'Chosen the wrong day, love. He went to a party after the show last night . . . got back in the small hours. He'd had a merry time, I'm telling you. They all did! Didn't see him myself, but Lady Muck up there had a tale and a half to gossip about. If he does turn up this side of teatime, he won't want to give no auditions.'

Frances looked at her in astonishment. The girl grinned.

'Saw you, didn't I? Written all over you . . . and then when you spoke, that capped it. With a voice like yours anybody would have a fancy to use it.'

Frances blushed with pleasure, delighted by this recognition of her secret pride. 'I could wait,' she said eagerly, ''till he feels more . . . himself.' She was prepared to wait until Doomsday for a chance to speak with the famous Ben Webster, manager of the Haymarket Theatre. It never occurred to her to doubt her own powers of persuasion. When they conversed he would be charmed by her unusual voice, and when she proclaimed the lines from 'The Merchant of Venice' she had by heart, he would be captivated.

'I don't know about that,' Lizzie interrupted her thoughts. 'They are a bit funny about strangers getting into the theatre and I can't really vouch for you, can I? Oh, I know you saved me from getting knocked down and I'm ever so grateful, but . . . well . . . I don't know anything about you.'

Frances felt crushed, but not enough to make her leave. At the sight of her downcast look, Lizzie's doubts seemed to retreat.

'Still, what is there to lose? You'll be no worse off if he won't see you, and as for me . . . I've enough black marks against me name already. One more or less ain't going to make no difference. There's nothing like having a grab at any opportunity that comes along. I'd do the same meself. Just don't expect too much, will you?'

Frances warmed to her. 'Are you an actress?' she asked.

'If wishes were horses, beggars would ride,' Lizzie said obscurely. 'No, I'm a nothing . . . a nobody and an everything rolled into one.

Dresser to one and all, except the principals . . . old Mother Whatsit's skivvy and I fetch and carry for anyone that shouts. But I tell you, one day I'll show 'em. I know how to put over a song and I've a leg as elegant as you could wish. See!' She hitched her skirts to her knees, showing long slender legs encased in soft black kid boots buttoned from knee to ankle. Frances was surprised by such immodesty and when Lizzie kicked high into the air, first with one leg and then the other, she wanted to giggle. Covering her amusement came the sound of voices and doors banging. A scuffle of feet and a loud voice called something she could not make out.

'Here we go again!' Lizzie cast a despairing glance at the ceiling. 'What's wrong this time? Before me dinner too!' She finished her drink in one gulp and banged down the glass. 'Come on, love. If it is him you'd better seize your chance.'

Her heart pounding, Frances followed. They retraced the route back towards the stage door and almost collided with a group of people arguing between themselves. Behind them, the door on the left at the top of the steps was no longer closed. Beyond was a room carpeted, upholstered and decorated in pale sea green.

'The greenroom,' Lizzie murmured.

It was empty except for a man and woman framed in light from a long window. The woman had enormous dark eyes and was dressed in a flamboyant saffron-coloured gown which shone and sparkled with her frequent hand movements as she emphasized her words. Frances was too preoccupied to take in the content of the conversation, which in any case was partly muffled by the talk of the group outside.

'That's him,' whispered Lizzie, pointing briefly to the stocky man listening with some impatience to the tirade of the woman in the saffron gown. 'Your luck's in.'

'Lizzie, you wretched girl . . .'

Lizzie threw Frances a look which spoke a great deal about her feelings, before turning to the speaker, a small witch-like woman with a white face and a penetrating voice. But Frances was not watching. Her thoughts were centred on the problem of how to draw attention to herself as she went into the greenroom. She wanted to make a good entrance and tried hard to remember the exact phrases she had spent months practising for a moment like this. The saffron woman took no notice of her at all and continued to stream out complaints apparently to do with her part in the next production. The stocky man had his back to Frances, so there was no hope of catching his eye. If only he would turn round for a moment she would be able to walk forward, holding out her hand while she spoke the proper words of introduction. But the saffron woman had launched into a fresh grievance, ignoring Frances entirely, though she was now close to them. There was thunder in Frances' ears from her monstrous heartbeats. She had to speak! It was the only way to attract attention to herself.

'Excuse me!' Her voice came out cracked and unrecognizable.

'. . . but my dear Marion, it is impossible . . . quite impossible. If I've said it once I've said it a thousand times.' There was determination in the way Mr Webster straightened his shoulders.

'Excuse me!' said Frances more loudly.

This time she got the attention she was seeking and it blew away the remnants of her prepared speech. The saffron woman stared at her angrily and Mr Webster turned, frowning.

'Who are you . . . who let you in?' he asked.

'Could you spare me a few moments?' Frances faltered, squirming at the meek sound of her voice.

'Can't you see I'm engaged? I've given enough instructions about unauthorized persons being denied access to the greenroom and backstage! There ought to be some hope of my orders being followed.'

Frances was dismayed by his irritation. He looked exceedingly grim. Not at all like the smiling courteous man she had built in her imagination. He seemed prepared to sweep her out into the street without the hope of an interview and Frances grabbed wildly at words . . . any words that would delay him long enough to listen to her.

'I'm Frances Redmayne,' she said, wishing her voice sounded less breathy.

'Can't you see Mr Webster is busy,' interrupted the saffron woman peremptorily.

Her interference seemed to turn Mr Webster's irritation away from Frances. 'Marion, please! Now then Miss . . . er . . . Redmayne.'

The saffron woman drew herself up, turning away haughtily, with an exaggerated twist of her shoulders.

Frances was still searching for her lost speech.

'Come along, miss . . . I haven't got all day. What is it you want to say?'

'I was hoping . . . that is . . . would you accept me . . . I want to be an actress.' She was horrified by the sudden blundering way she had revealed her most precious ambition; with a crude childishness, as if it were no more than a sprat on a fishmonger's slab.

Ben Webster raised his eyebrows, his expression changing from surprise to amusement and back to his former irritation. When he spoke his manner was a little less forbidding.

'So many ladies do. It's an oversubscribed profession.'

The disappointment which showed on Frances' face seemed to make him relent and he spoke more kindly.

'If you were hoping to be engaged by me I'm afraid I can offer you nothing. We have a full company for this season and the next.'

Frances scrambled after her self possession. There must be something she could do to salvage her resolution from the wreckage of a career that seemed to have ended before it began. 'If you could just listen to me,' she begged. 'If I might speak some lines . . .'

There was a snort from the saffron woman and Ben Webster flashed her a look which silenced any comment. He patted Frances' shoulder as if she were a persistent child who needed coaxing out of the way. It was not an attitude that inspired confidence or soothed her shattered feelings.

'Well . . .' he said at last. 'I suppose I could *listen*. Of course you mustn't take that as a reason for hope. A little advice is the most I can offer.'

Before Frances had time to react to this tiny concession, a harassed young man in shirt sleeves and a bottle green velour waistcoat came hurrying into the greenroom.

'Oh, Mr Webster, could you come down to the office? There's a man come about those gauzes you ordered and he's got some tale about money owed on the last order and the bill's to be paid before he will do anything. I've reasoned with him, but he insists on seeing you . . . and Mrs Arthur says the gold epaulettes are a disgrace and can she purchase two dozen more?'

'Not to mention the hem of my burgundy gown in act two . . . trodden on . . . ripped to shreds . . . details I suppose but . . .' The saffron woman was preparing for another attack, but Ben Webster waved silencing hands.

'I'll be along in a moment, Penn. Tell the man to wait.'

'He says if you don't come now he's to close the account,' said Penn a trifle nervously.

Mr Webster looked at Frances. 'You see how it is, my dear. Another time perhaps? Though I can't do anything for you really . . . better try elsewhere . . . in the provinces or at one of the minor theatres.'

He walked briskly out of the room, leaving Frances in a hot passion of shame and despair. As he disappeared into the corridor beyond the door, all her cherished dreams collapsed into rubble. With a last scornful glance, the saffron woman turned away and began gossiping excitedly about the previous night's performance with a small bouncing man whom Frances recognized as the sailor in the afterpiece she had seen. More actors and actresses wandered in, several of whom had taken part in 'The Taming of the Shrew'. There was something agonizing in being confronted by them at such a moment. Frances felt as if she were choking, and longed to get out of the theatre so that she could hide her shame and mortification.

Lizzie came in with a message for the saffron woman and a fur-lined pelisse for the witch-like actress who was no longer there.

'Gone for her usual pick-me-up,' someone said and laughter swelled.

Feeling like an outcast, Frances threaded her way to the door and would have run away without another word, but Lizzie came scuttling after her.

'Just wanted to say not to lose heart . . . it's not easy, the competition is that wicked. I should know, I've tried!' She looked questioningly at Frances' miserable face. 'What'll you do now?'

Frances shook her head. With the collapse of her plans she could think of nothing but the cold knowledge that she could not . . . *would* not return to the Seminary.

Impetuously Lizzie took Frances' hand between her own rough palms in a gesture of understanding for her bruised feelings. 'All the best, love. Can't say more, can I? If you're ever really down on your luck, or just passing, call in. I live with Ma just off Seven Dials near Drury Lane. Five Flower Court . . . take the second passage from the right.'

They reached the stage door just as someone bawled out: 'Lizzie!'
'Gawd!' she said with a shake of her tightly curled hair. 'I'm not taking much more!' And dropping Frances' hand she hurried away into the gloom.

★　★　★

Frances had rashly dipped into another sovereign to pay the driver of the cab. She did not care. In fact her despair was so complete, she was not even aware of the fact. After weary hours of trudging from the disaster at the Haymarket to Covent Garden, which seemed to be concerned solely with opera, and Drury Lane, where she suffered a curt refusal via the stage doorkeeper, she had spent a long time trying to decide what to do. The afternoon was well advanced when she returned to collect her watch. There was no hope now of covering up her falsehood about the promise to return to school. But her head felt like a stone and only the simplest of thoughts registered. What she was to do afterwards, was a question she had given up examining.

As she took the sharp turn into Mortimer Place, she saw a hackney carriage standing in front of Mrs Billings' house. A tiny flicker of suspicion touched her. It surely could not be anything to do with Papa already? There was no doubt in her mind that she must have stirred up a hornet's nest by her flight. It was true she had pinned a note to the coverlet of her bed, but only to say that she had left by her own free will and that she would communicate with her father when everything was settled. In the moment of hesitation the front door opened and to her horror her father emerged. Even at that distance there was no mistaking his poker-straight back in spite of the enveloping cloak. She did not wait to see his stern expression. There was a chemist's shop on the corner opposite, into which she fled. The cool interior smelled of camphor and pine mixed with a sharp tang of ammonia. A grey-haired man behind the counter looked up in some surprise, but asked what she required politely enough.

'A bottle of smelling salts,' was all she could think of, as she listened to the ring of horses hooves on the cobbles outside. She paid for her parcel, knowing there was no watch to collect now. Her father would have it. Outside a sensitive sun dipped behind clouds and fine rain blew in on the wind. With an empty mind Frances stumbled towards the main street, her carpet bag like a lead weight in her hand. She could not think of anything at all. The sounds and smells and sights passed her, blanketed by the fog in her mind. She had no idea where she was going, or in what direction and it was only when the wind swirled round, bringing heavier rain to beat her face, that she became aware of her surroundings.

The street was meaner and more crowded than the quiet squares and gardens from which she had come. A constant flow of traffic passed up and down with a deafening clatter, narrowly avoiding collisions as drivers shouted oaths over the top of the din. Frances looked round, alarmed, searching for something to tell her where she might be, but there was nothing at all. It was a part of London with which she was totally unfamiliar. Panic rose, tightening her throat and making her heart pound. If her defeat at the theatre had been horrible, it was nothing to her situation now; a young girl, alone in this doubtful part of London at the mercy of pickpockets, thieves or worse. The patch of sky grimly hanging onto uneven rooftops turned as dark as her thoughts and the rain came in earnest. Someone pushed past her, knocking her elbow and raising the ghost of last night's encounter.

Oh God above, thought Frances. What am I to do? And then she remembered Lizzie's words . . . there was one place she was welcome and that was five Flower Court, though heaven knew where that was! With courage born of despair, Frances went up to a kindly looking woman who had just come out of a draper's shop.

'Excuse me, could you direct me to Flower Court? It is near to Seven Dials.'

Expressions of astonishment and disapproval chased each other across the woman's face. 'You don't intend going down there, my dear, surely? Not the place for a young girl . . . specially in this weather.'

Frances could not see what the weather had to do with anything, except that it was making her feel damp and uncomfortable, but she was too weary to argue and merely repeated her question. The woman gave her a queer look, but began to explain. It seemed that they were not far away. With a brief word of thanks, Frances began to thread through the crowd, winding along streets that grew progressively uglier and more sour smelling. Houses leaned across nose to nose and blowzy women sat in the windows above, gossiping. Someone threw out slops that missed Frances by inches and drenched a passing urchin. He screamed a string of oaths that another time might have filled her with interest, but now slid past her ears to join the racket of bawling voices and rattling cart wheels. The shadows lengthened as the strip of cloud between the roofs thickened. Fear grew and mastered her fatigue. She began to hurry, darting nervous glances up black alleys and into dim interiors. Suddenly the street ended and she found herself in an irregular open space from which several dark passageways tentacled into obscurity. She paused, feverishly trying to recall which one she was supposed to take, but she could not for the life of her remember. She dared not ask again, for the passers by in their drab clothes, seemed to threaten her with curious glances.

'Why I declare, it's my young lady Frances!'

Frances spun round and saw, with the greatest feeling of relief she had ever experienced, two sharp blue eyes peering at her from under a sodden velour bonnet.

'Oh Lizzie,' she cried. 'I . . . I've come visiting!'

Lizzie smiled, looking at her in the same shrewd way she had done at the theatre. 'Lucky for you I chose this way home. Had to call in and get some oysters for Ma. Come on, it ain't healthy to dawdle in these parts.'

She took Frances' arm and hurried her across the street to one of the passages. They dropped deeper into the heart of the maze and the smells grew to a rotten stench. Patched buildings crowded over them, for the most part clothed in ominous silence, with occasional bursts of raucous shouting or brassy laughter as a door was opened and people emerged from crumbling interiors. Everywhere was dim and ragged with shadows, except for garish lights illuminating the gin shops. As they passed an old woman reeled out and stumbled against Lizzie.

'Spare us a copper for a drink to keep the rain out.'

But Lizzie shrugged her off and, when she turned and snatched at the parcel of oysters, jabbed at her with one sharp elbow.

'Get y'bleedin' hands orf or I'll belt you proper!' Lizzie yelled in a voice that would have done credit to a coster.

The woman shrank into the shadows and Lizzie pulled at Frances' arms.

'Nearly there, love. We're through the worst of the Rookery. Our house is a cut above this lot, I'll tell you.' There was a note of pride in her voice.

They were in another passage, not much better than the ones she called 'the Rookery', but it seemed a little cleaner and the smell, if not pure, was bearable. Lizzie stopped in front of a flight of broken steps leading to a dingy front door that had three screw holes where the knocker should have been.

'Ever such a lovely knocker it was . . . made like a bow of ribbons. Got pinched two nights ago . . . would you credit it!' Lizzie rattled the key in the lock and pushed open the door. Stepping into the darkened hall that smelled of baked apples, fresh soap and beeswax, she called out: 'Ma . . . we've got a visitor!'

3 THE SMALL OVER-FURNISHED ROOM WAS LIT BY THE light of a fire that glowed and twisted under a blackleaded hood. Beyond a table, draped in a heavy green cloth, two women were sitting on a striped horsehair sofa. The thinner of the two got up as Lizzie and Frances came in, holding up her hands in mock dismay at their dripping clothes. In the half light Frances saw her as a replica of Lizzie as she might be in thirty years' time; gaunt, with creased skin, salt and pepper hair screwed into a bun on top of her head, the unrelieved black of her plain dress decorated by a small brooch of curling pinchbeck.

Lizzie pushed between her mother and the table towards the fat woman who was hauling herself to her feet.

'Rosie!' she squealed and threw herself on the mound of a chest, which was draped with strings of jet beads glittering like polished coal.

'Lizzie, me duck!' Rosie enveloped her in a mountainous hug. The echo of their kisses smacked the walls and bounced onto Frances, including her in the emotional welcome. 'Why you're both drenched!'

'Soaked through I shouldn't wonder,' said Lizzie's mother, all concern. She bustled about taking the carpet bag, bonnets and cloaks, in a shower of comment and spray. 'Raining cats and dogs . . . real April weather. Rosie was drenched too . . . spoiled those nice ostrich feathers in her hat, didn't it love?' talking over her shoulder. She turned to Frances. 'Here, get those wet boots off! Lift your skirt a bit, love . . . don't mind us, we're all girls together, ain't we, Rosie?'

'Always were and always will be,' Rosie wheezed with a bubble of laughter.

Lizzie put an arm round Frances' shoulders. 'Ma, this is Frances . . . my Ma . . . and this is our Rosie; Mrs Copperdyce, I should say.'

Lizzie winked and gave a brief curtsy which encouraged more rolls of breathless laughter.

Frances smiled without reserve. Standing there, her skin warming from the heat of the fire, soaking in the kindliness, she felt the fear and misery of the past hours dissolve and vanish.

'Sit down the pair of you and get warm. You look starved. Brought the oysters, Lizzie? That's my girl. Rosie called in at the Angel and got a jug of stout. With them apple cobs I made we'll have a supper fit for a queen.' Still talking, Lizzie's mother disappeared to the kitchen.

No one seemed in the least curious about who Frances was or how she came to be there. Friendly unquestioning acceptance brought blinding tears to her eyes, so that she stumbled and almost fell over a great lump on the hearth rug. The lump rose with a snuffling yelp and became a large dog with a flag of a tail.

'Grit, you old devil,' said Lizzie patting the dog affectionately. 'Why you're as damp as a dishcloth. Look at you steaming!'

'Takes him a fair time to dry out with his overcoat,' said Rosie. She lowered her bulk back onto the sofa.

Blinking away the tears, Frances looked at Rosie properly for the first time. After her size, the most remarkable feature was a head of bright red hair looped and draped in an elaborate style. The abundance was indisputable, the honesty of the colour less so. Rosie settled her three chins and clasped beringed hands across her well-corseted stomach.

'And what's the latest scandal at the Haymarket, Lizzie?'

Lizzie sighed. 'Oh there's enough to keep going for six months without trying. The amount of tittle-tattle you wouldn't believe ... and the service they expect! A bloomin' skivvy, that's what they think I am ... taken all I can stomach and more. Why this morning I nearly got skinned about a pair of boots ...' and she went on to explain about the fate of the boots and how she had been saved by Frances. Her mother came back as she was talking, with a tray loaded with plates, cutlery, food, four thick white mugs and a jug of stout. '... give in me notice I did,' Lizzie was saying, 'before he got in first and sacked me ... else I'd have to be back by now for the evening show. You should have heard Lady Muck! What a carry on ... anyone would have thought I'd left her stranded on a boat in the middle of the Thames, with no oars!'

'Oo Lizzie, you never!' said her mother with more than a hint of dismay.

'Oo Mrs Masters, I did!' mocked Lizzie.

'What'll you do for money? Doesn't grow on trees and the house hardly brings in enough for us both.'

'I'll find something. I've a mind to be on the stage instead of slaving behind it.' Lizzie was suddenly sharp and edgy.

'You could join up with Tom Vaughan,' Rosie suggested. 'Saw him a week back at Lacey's, where I've been helping out in the wardrobe. He told me he was on his way to Tewkesbury to take over old John Packer's company. Dropped dead he did, in the middle of the stage.'

'He never!' Mrs Masters was all astonishment.

Rosie nodded, shivering her chins. 'True as I sit here. He asked after you, Lizzie love, and said to tell you there's always a place in his heart for you and in the company if you want to go. Says he'll be in Evesham next Friday and to ask at the Trumpet for him.'

Frances saw Mrs Masters' sparse eyebrows shoot up. She looked none too pleased. 'He's a cheeky one!'

But Lizzie was sitting up straight, very intent. 'There's a welcome for you! It couldn't have been better timed.'

'I know his sort of welcome!' Mrs Masters inferred fathoms of dark conjecture.

'Go on, Ma, he's a good sort . . . and handsome,' said Lizzie quickly.

'Handsome is as handsome does!'

'And gives his all to it, I daresay!' Rosie gasped with asthmatic chuckles, digging at Lizzie's ribs.

'Well I don't know . . . you ain't serious, Lizzie?' Mrs Masters asked doubtfully.

'It's a chance for me, Ma. Come to think of it, it's a chance for you too.' She looked at Frances keenly.

This rearrangement of her life was so unexpected. 'It all depends,' she said, not thinking about ingratitude until Lizzie's sharp 'On what?'

'A number of things.' Frances tried to be vague.

'Well of course, I don't want to push you into something you ain't happy about,' Lizzie said, a trifle huffily.

'Oh it's not that . . .' But it was.

'What then? Want to go on the stage, don't you?'

She had to say yes, although the answer was not completely true. Trying to find a way to say that it wasn't any sort of stage, seemed ungrateful. But her dreams were of those where great drama was produced; the tragedies and comedies of Shakespeare, Marlowe, Ben Jonson. Would Tom Vaughan's company be playing such things? The words would not come in a plausible way, only boldly as they had that morning, and she was not going to be tricked into making a fool of herself again. If only she had time and privacy in which to think, but Lizzie seemed to have accepted her word as an accomplished fact. It was all settled. They would travel to Evesham next Friday.

'We'll go together as far as Warfield,' said Rosie. 'Me and Grit here have a place at the Queen's Theatre . . . course,' she added confidentially, 'it's Grit they really wants. He's a great comfort to me since I lost me figure . . . keeps me in work. Saves people a treat, big or small it don't matter to him . . . on stage of course. I don't know if he'd do the same in the street! I'll be giving a hand in the wardrobe I daresay. Me acting days are over.' She sighed. 'You wouldn't think as how me waist used to be only twenty inches when me stays were laced. Say it as shouldn't, I was a beauty in me day. All the fellers were after me. Hair down to me waist, burnished gold . . . it's all I have left of them days.' She cautiously patted the hair that Frances felt sure must be dyed.

After they had eaten and drunk to a comfortable standstill, Lizzie stood up with the dregs of her stout held out in her mug.

'Here's to us,' she said. 'Evesham, look out for Miss Lizzie Masters and Miss Frances . . .' She looked down at Frances with a grin. 'Never asked your other name, love . . . got a sieve of a brain.'

'Redmayne,' smiled Frances through a haze of stout and fatigue. She was no longer tormented by doubt. It was comforting to be able to accept at last that fate had decided her future. And what was more, she just did not care! A faint tingling prickled her skin with the thought of experiences to come. Whatever happened she was going to walk on a stage, posing gracefully, pouring out the words, creating characters . . . It never occurred to her that she had not been invited by the man in charge of the company. All she knew now was a drowsy contentment and an immense longing to sleep.

Later, sharing Lizzie's bed, a sharp stabbing dismay at the way the pattern of her life seemed to have slipped from her grasp troubled her, and then sleep came.

*   *   *

The week passed like a strange dream for Frances; slow and yet swift. She discovered that Mrs Masters kept a theatrical lodging house. A curious assortment of people passed her on the stairs or made brief appearances to eat meals in the kitchen. Lizzie was everywhere, laughing, chatting endlessly of theatrical affairs, helping with housework and cooking. From her, Frances got a muddled impression of theatre life as a richly chaotic existence where people stayed up half the night and did not wake until midday. Strange words like 'grooves', 'floats', 'gauzes', 'flies' and 'thunder run' tantalized her imagination. She tried to make her explain, but almost every time Lizzie would break off halfway through in order to refill the coal hod or run an errand for her mother. Frances helped as much as she could, but in the well ordered household there was little for her to do and the gaps in her days were often filled with uncomfortable thoughts about the rashness of having run away.

'You don't want to fret so much,' Lizzie said one night as they lay side by side in the comfortable darkness which encouraged confidences. 'Take life as it comes.'

'It's easy to say that . . . not so easy to do,' Frances replied, adding suddenly: 'It's so dreadful when Papa's angry. I can't help thinking how bitterly he must feel about me.'

'Is he very strict?' asked Lizzie. 'Tell me about him. What does he do?'

'He runs . . . a farm. I suppose you would call him strict.'

'A country girl are you? I'd never have guessed! Did you ever help on the farm, or didn't your dad fancy you as a dairymaid?'

'I rode sometimes,' Frances said, beginning to wish she had not been so open. 'But that's about all. Papa thinks a good marriage is the proper career for all girls.' She deliberately avoided describing her father's position as Squire of Thrushton, or the size of the Hall and estate. She wanted to be accepted for herself.

'Well I'm not against being wed . . . to the right feller that is. But to spend me life as an unpaid housekeeper and never taste the fun of the stage ain't my idea of living.' Lizzie yawned. 'It's a great life . . . the stage. So much variety . . . singing and dancing . . .'

'All those lovely words.' Frances could almost feel them rolling round her tongue, waiting to be spoken.

'With a twist of your hips and a saucy glance.'

'Expressive gestures,' Frances said.

'Oh they likes a bit of suggestion with a song!'

She hadn't thought about that kind of entertaining before. 'Is that what you like doing most of all?'

'Nothing like it . . . out there in the limelight with a good tune and the feel of your body swinging through a dance . . . I'll be a butterfly born in a bower . . .' warbled Lizzie, then: 'Whoops!'

Frances giggled. Somehow Lizzie could make it real. Life overflowed into the things she described, filling them with colour and richness. She was glad in a way that Lizzie's ambitions were along different lines from her own. There was less chance of any jealous clash. Lizzie must have thought so too, because she put an arm round her and gave her a hug.

'We'll get along fine, being so different . . . so long as you don't worry yourself into an early grave. When you've made your name your dad'll be proud of you . . . see if he ain't!'

Frances did not reply. The cold unvarnished truth was inescapable. She had damaged the family reputation, a sin Papa would never forgive. She felt sure he had already ceased speaking of her, just as he had her mother after her death fourteen years before. She turned over in bed. Yet stubborn determination had brought her this far; she was not going to give up now. Papa was not the only person who mattered in her life. She closed her eyes and set about the task of going to sleep.

The day before the journey to Evesham was a whirlwind of activity. In her usual grasshopper way, Lizzie skipped from one job to another as she packed her belongings into a wicker valise, muttering threats when it overflowed and refused to close. Frances had expected to do her own packing swiftly. Most of her possessions had been left behind at the Seminary and she had little more than a change of underclothes, two nightdresses, her locket with the portrait of her mother painted on ivory and a few trinkets. She pushed them into the carpet bag. The locket she wore as always. Lizzie looked up from her knees beside the bulging valise.

'I should have thought, you'll be needing some stage clothes. Fancy me not telling you before, but that's me all over. Regular scatterbrain Ma says. You'll need another dress; black velvet with wide sleeves is all right for some things, but it ain't suitable for melodrama if you're a Utility or Walking Lady . . . and that's what we'll be. Red stuff's the best, with blue ribbons. And there's a cap and apron, and a fan and fleshings and a stomacher and . . . what else . . . oh yes, shoes; silver buckles are best . . . and of course we both ought to have some russet boots and breeches . . .'

'Breeches?' Frances cut into the stream.

Lizzie burst out laughing at her astonishment. 'Sometimes women have to dress up as men you know,' she said.

Frances remembered Viola in 'Twelfth Night'. 'But why do I have to have all those things? Doesn't the company provide them?'

'Oh love, what a greenhorn you are!' Lizzie said, not unkindly. 'The men get some provided but the women have to find all their own things.'

Frances was dismayed by the prospect of having to buy so much. The remaining six sovereigns in her reticule seemed precious little when she thought how long they might have to last. 'How much will you earn?' she asked.

'I don't know. Depends on the takings. After Tom takes his share and the dead shares, that's the four extra shares for being manager, the rest of us get an equal amount. Could be anything.'

'Nothing, more like,' said Mrs Masters, coming in with a pair of freshly ironed drawers and a flannel petticoat.

'Oh don't be so gloomy, Ma,' Lizzie said. She got up. 'Frances and me are just orf to old Gilstein's to get set up with some stage bits.'

'Mind you don't let him overcharge you.'

'What do you think I am?' Lizzie said. 'He'll have to get up early in the morning to get the better of me!'

Old Gilstein's shop was tucked into a crevice between a watch-maker's and a tailor's a few streets from Lizzie's house. Frances had never seen such a weird assortment of garments as those hanging in festoons from nails and hooks and heaped over chairs and counter.

Old Gilstein, balding and bearded, struggled from behind one of the mountains, asking how he could be of service? There followed a long complicated period of haggling, which Frances observed in awed silence. Lizzie was an expert in bargaining and when they finally left, their arms full of musty clothes, neither had spent more than fifteen shillings.

Back in Lizzie's bedroom they surveyed their spoils.

'Not bad . . . do nicely for a tragedy,' said Mrs Masters, turning over a black velvet skirt with a few moth holes. 'I just hope you ain't bought no unwelcome visitors along with this lot.'

Lizzie shrugged. 'So long as there ain't no lice I don't care. Fleas you can catch if you look sharp.'

Frances stared at her in horror. She could almost feel the creatures marching up her spine.

'Don't take on,' said Lizzie catching sight of her expression. 'I was only joking. You take everything too seriously. But it stands to reason you can't go through life without coming across the odd visitor, specially in our walk of life.'

The fact that she was included so definitely in the 'walk of life' gave Frances less pleasure than she might have expected. She felt the first uncurling of suspicion about the adventure.

The second was to come at the end of the journey.

$$\star \quad \star \quad \star$$

'We'll miss it for sure . . . Lizzie, have you got your parcel of food . . . where's that dog . . . Grit . . . Grit . . . Look at him now, cocking his leg as if he'd all the time in the world!"

They were under the arched roof of Euston Station. Rosie Copperdyce flapped and fussed in black bombazine agitation. Mrs Masters and Lizzie were both talking at once, stopping only to fall on each other from time to time with tears and kisses. Frances turned her back, a little disgusted by so much unnecessary emotion. She stared at the long row of chocolate and black carriages and the shining loco-motive blowing off excess steam like frosty breath. She remembered the look of remarkable joy on John's face as he shook the great Mr Stephenson's hand and accepted a ride in the wooden third class carriage of the first train to run through Thrushton. It had been a marvellous day, crisp and sunny like this. The warm velour carriage seat beneath her fingertips and the small disappointment that Papa would not allow him to come in their compartment was in her mind. With a touch of surprise, she realized this was the first time she had thought about her old life for several days.

The guard was slamming doors. There was no more time for reminiscence. Frances hurried forward, Lizzie, Rosie and Grit following in a tumbling bustle. The guard's whistle pierced the air; a lurch and they were on their way. Lizzie leaned out of the window, tears streaming down her cheeks.

'. . . have you forgotten . . . left the hatpins on . . . five shillings under the tea caddy . . . write to you by the penny post . . .'

The space widened between their desperately clinging conversation. Lizzie was waving to the receding figure of her mother, her handkerchief flapping like a single forlorn flag. Then she sat down. With great speed she recovered her spirits and began chattering to Rosie about a play she had seen, where a dog had saved a little girl from certain death when the cottage where she lived went up in flames.

'Sounds like a show I was in at one of them Penny Gaffs down Wapping way, years ago. Not with Grit of course . . . before his time. A big collie called the General . . . it was when my Albert was still alive. Me husband,' she explained to Frances. 'We were having a bad patch. No work, so we took what we could . . . not the blood tubs, me duck, never them . . . but near everything else. Hard grind, but we had some laughs I can tell you. Then my Albert got the cholera and was took. Afterwards . . .' Her eyes moistened and Frances was afraid she would cry.

Now that they were on their way, Frances felt the restless anxiety of the past week disappear and excitement take its place. No matter what the journey's end brought, she was prepared. The very fact that it was all beginning in a railway carriage did much to colour her mood. The constant variety of scenery, people getting in and out, the guard coming along to light the oil lamps when they halted before the long Kilsby Tunnel, emerging the other side into spring country where trees and hedges were already misted with green: all of it thrilled her. Even Lizzie's dark warning to 'Wait and see how you feel after we've been shaken to pieces in a stagecoach for two hours' failed to quench her good humour.

Birmingham arrived, and they said good-bye to Rosie and Grit.

'Take care! If ever you're Warfield way I'll always be glad to see you.' There were more tears and limp handkerchiefs fluttering farewells as the coach pulled out, and then they were on their own.

Walking from the station yard out into New Street, Frances and Lizzie began strolling up and down, glad to stretch their cramped limbs as they waited for the Evesham coach to arrive. They passed an elegant Georgian theatre with three graceful arches supporting a balcony of columns and iron balustrades. At either end, above arched windows, were plaster panels containing medallions of the heads of Garrick and Shakespeare in delicate relief.

'The Theatre Royal is one of the best outside London,' Lizzie said. 'If you tread the boards there you've a fair chance of making a name for yourself. They have all the stars come.'

'The stars?' Frances imagined sparkling five-pointed shapes winking their way across a stage.

'Famous actors and actresses ... Mr Gerard, Miss Kemble, Mr Macready, Mrs Faucit ... people like that.'

Frances was impressed. She looked up at the theatre. One day I'll be back, she thought, and then it will be other people standing on the pavement, not me. I shall walk inside and everyone will be anxious to see *me* act, hear *me* speak the lines.

'There it is!' cried Lizzie, pointing.

A yellow coach with red and black wheels was rolling over the courtyard in front of the station. The broad coachman pulled on the reins bringing the four steaming horses to a halt. Frances could read the words 'TALLY HO!' painted across the side.

'No hurry, love,' said Lizzie. 'They'll have to change the horses first.'

Lizzie had been right about the jolting ride to Evesham. Their joints ached and they both felt queasy from the stale air inside the coach and from its bone-shaking motion. Everyone seemed to be suffering. Hardly a word passed between the passengers packed tight along each seat, and there was no way of telling how far each was travelling. But when they reached the inn fronting the River Avon at Evesham, only

43

the luggage belonging to Lizzie and Frances was handed down. The rest of the travellers were bound for further afield.

They climbed stiffly from the coach and took their luggage from the driver, asking one of the ostlers to direct them to the Trumpet Tavern.

'Over the bridge and keep going to Pig Market, then turn left and carry straight along and you'll find yourselves at Merstowe Green directly. The Trumpet's there.' The ostler eyed these two unaccompanied female travellers with a great deal of interest.

'I'll be glad of a walk,' said Lizzie. 'Me stomach feels like a piece of sour plum duff.'

The distance was not great and they found their way easily enough to Merstowe Green. The Trumpet stood back from the green with a cobbled courtyard in front and an arched carriageway on the left of the tavern itself. They hesitated to go straight in. Raised voices reached them. Lizzie put down her valise as she exchanged looks with Frances.

'I'd recognize that voice anywhere,' she said.

The tavern door opened suddenly and two men elbowed through, arguing hotly. The taller of the two had long corn-coloured hair which flowed to his shoulders, curling its way round his ripe mouth and over his chin. His arms were thrashing the air like a windmill. But the other was not moved by the obvious entreaty. He wiped stubby hands on his leather apron, glaring with bulging eyes in a perfect fury of disbelief.

'You can talk till the crack o' doom, don't alter the facts none. Money is money and where be it, that's what I'd like to know? Come here with your fancy promises! Hard cash in me palm is what I wants.'

'And you shall have it, but give us time.' The tall man swept his hand round to embrace all the minutes and hours in the world, and in doing so caught sight of the two girls. 'Lizzie . . . my darling Lizzie!' Two strides and he had reached her, catching her round the waist to swing her off the ground.

Lizzie clutched at her bonnet, returning his kiss with evident pleasure. 'Tom, set me down you dreadful man!' But Frances could see she was delighted by the warmth of the welcome.

'What a terrible day to arrive . . . terrible!' Tom was lost in a sudden agony.

44

Lizzie, back on firm ground once more, looked up at him with quick alarm. 'The company ain't sneaked orf with the takings?'

'Takings!' Tom gave a shout of mirthless laughter. 'Takings?'

'This'n and the rest of 'em have done naught but eat and swill with not a penny in return,' said the man in the leather apron.

Tom turned on him with rage. 'Haven't I said that you will get your filthy money. We are performing tonight. Two hours from now and the theatre will be transformed. Gay lights, garlands, mystery and murder to delight the audience.'

'Not in my barn you ent!' snapped the landlord.

'Who needs your ramshackle barn. God's green grass is good enough for us. With the span of the sky for a roof and the stars to mingle with our torches, we'll frighten and delight in a way that will be talked about in this benighted town long after your bones have whitened in your grave.'

Frances was delighted by the fluent extravagance of the speech. She looked at Lizzie, expecting her to be smiling, and saw she was worried. Happiness wilted. No theatre, not even a canvas booth . . . what had she landed in this time?

The landlord gave a grunt of disgust and went back indoors. They heard his harsh voice and almost immediately a seemingly endless stream of people, including children, hustled into the yard. They swarmed round Tom, nudging and questioning. Frances felt annoyed at having travelled so far only to be totally ignored.

'Tom . . . listen a minute . . .' Lizzie pushed through to him. 'I want you to meet Frances Redmayne. She's looking for a place, same as me. I knew you wouldn't refuse her, so I brought her along. We've come all the way from London today,' she added as an extra persuasion.

'Two of you!' Tom raised imploring eyes to heaven. 'God, Lizzie, we can't even feed the present company!' Then with a complete switch of mood, with which Frances was to become familiar, he smiled warmly, advancing on her and kissing the back of her hand with a flourish. 'Charming,' he said. 'You are the very person we want. Angus . . . that's your part. Ralph's run off for a soldier . . . taken the Queen's shilling if you please!' He held her by the shoulders, appraising her from head to toe until she blushed. 'Figure right . . . piquant face . . .'

'Who is Angus?' asked Frances.

'And the voice . . . perfect . . . perfect!' He turned to Lizzie. 'You are a genius, my darling. Where did you find this flower?'

Lizzie began explaining, but her voice was lost in noisy conversation as the actors began demanding to know what he proposed doing. Their voices were penetrating and the clamour must have filled the tavern because the door was flung open and the landlord stormed out again.

' 'Ere, get your lot o' ragamuffins out o' my courtyard,' he bawled.

'God and his angels keep me from losing my temper altogether!' Tom said, stretching his arms skywards. 'What will the man have us do? First he demands money, then denies us the right to plan an entertainment which will produce that money.'

The veins stood out on the landlord's sweating forehead. 'I just want a bit o' peace and quiet . . . so do me reg'lars.'

'By all the stars in the universe, man . . . do you want your money or not?'

'You knows I do.'

'Well then, leave us to rehearse . . . and while you're about it, a tankard of ale all round wouldn't come amiss. Acting's thirsty work. Besides, these two young ladies have travelled all the way from our great Capital to give us the benefit of their talents tonight. Evesham should be grateful and honoured to have London actresses gracing its rustic Green.'

'If you think . . .' began the apoplectic landlord.

'Think . . . who's talking about thinking? Action, man . . . action . . . and ale!' Tom's arms described a tracery of lines in the air. 'And while we're about it, the outhouse beyond the stabling will suit us nicely for changing our costumes.'

The landlord spluttered an unintelligible protest.

'He'd have us expose our very skins on the Green!' Tom's voice was full of outraged modesty.

The landlord clenched his fists and took a few steps forward, but the situation seemed to have gone beyond his experience. His hands fell to his sides and for a moment he closed his eyes. Then, without another word, he turned and retreated into the tavern, slamming the door.

'And so are all foes demolished!' declared Tom. 'Now then ladies and gents ... the play! We'll do 'Laird of the Loch'. How's your Scottish accent?' This directed at Frances.

'Och, m'lord, it's nair so guid as it should be,' she replied, with a spontaneity which surprised herself. There was a burst of clapping and Lizzie patted her on the back.

'Splendid ... splendid!' Tom was laughing.

The following two hours were ones never to be forgotten. The play was a melodrama which everyone but Frances seemed to know. Surgrisingly her ignorance was not considered a drawback though her upper-class way of pronouncing words came in for some suspicious plances. Tom Vaughan became a whirling gale of a man, who instructed and demonstrated, speaking lines that Frances and Lizzie must have by heart, listening as they repeated them, at the same time chivvying the other actors, organizing the outdoor stage and even finding time and energy to bully the landlord into producing ale. Frances fluctuated between laughter and despair at her own shortcomings, interspersed with a kind of mild horror at the crudity of the play.

'Exaggerate your bow a little more,' said a large stately woman with dark eyes and coarse black hair, after Frances had made her first wooden entrance. 'You need to bend low like this ...' and she pushed Frances' shoulders hard.

'Give over, Clara! You'll have her on the ground. You don't know your own strength. Muscles like a bargee's woman!' The young man who spoke looked much too cheerful for the villain he was supposed to play, but Frances was grateful for his support.

Clara's husband, a grey-haired man with a nose like a beacon, was less pleased. He waved the tankard he was holding:

'I'll thank you to show my wife a bit more respect, Len Goodridge,' he growled.

'All right ... let it pass, Arthur,' Tom interrupted, 'No time for argument. The light is beginning to fade. Take the handbell, will you, and do your impersonation of Town Crier. It's the best way to draw a crowd. Jack (speaking to a moon-faced youth leering at Lizzie and Frances), prime the pots of fat and set them in a circle with a gap here and here, for exits.' The instructions flew about like the rattle of grapeshot, leaving Frances giddy and bewildered.

Lizzie had already made friends with most of the company and was gabbling and laughing as they moved baggage into the outhouse, which the landlord had finally agreed to loan after a second verbal battle with Tom. Frances followed in stunned silence, too confused by the speed of events to sort out any more of the rabble except one – a small girl with a sharp pale face framing a pair of beady eyes which seemed to be doing their best to bore a hole in Frances. She came to her, holding out a bundle of clothes.

'Ma said to give you these,' she said in a voice pinched with dislike. 'Our Ralph's . . . so don't you make no holes in 'em. He'll want 'em when he comes home.' And she disappeared into the gloom and clutter of the outhouse that smelled of mice and cobwebs.

Frances examined the breeches and shirt which the vanished Ralph had left along with his identity. There was no time for false modesty. She and Lizzie helped unhook each other's petticoats. A rough curtain had been rigged, but it provided little privacy, and halfway into the breeches Frances turned to find herself being stared at by the youth called Jack, who smiled broadly at her blushes and gave her a slow wink.

As the sky darkened and the first stars appeared, a few people strolled idly round the green. Tom came in like a whirlwind.

'Gabriel, would you take the hat round? Jack, you can give him a hand. Two of you ought to be able to make sure there are no back-sliders. A free show is definitely out . . . we need every farthing we can get. The rest of you, places please. Jenny, what are you at? The audience is restive and here you are still in your petticoats!'

Pouting full lips, a plump, peaches and cream woman twisted away from the cracked mirror where she was applying the final touches to her gaudy make-up. 'Don't be such a bully, Tom.'

'Bully? My darling, I shall become a second Genghis Khan if you don't hurry . . . two minutes *precisely*, do you understand?' And he was gone with a whirl of tartan kilts, leaving an odour of chalk and lavender hair oil in his wake.

Arthur had done his work well. A crowd was building up outside and someone shouted:

'We'm waiting then!'

There was a terrible void in the pit of Frances' stomach. Her throat was blocked and she went over and over her lines, forgetting some and inventing others.

'Don't fret, love.' Lizzie saw her look of desperation. 'All you've got to do is run on when your name is called, like Tom told you. Don't forget to bow low with a big sweep of the hand, like this!' She demonstrated, knocking over a basket of props in the confined space. 'I'll give you a shove if you miss the cue.'

A cheer went up as the company assembled on the green. The flaming pots of fat reminded Frances of the descriptions of Richardson's booth at Greenwich fair. Was this what her dreams had come to?

'Look at that, would you!' said Tom in exasperation.

A small urchin standing close to the ring of light had peed into one of the pots, putting out the flame. He grinned satisfaction until Tom reached him and smartly clipped his ear. Howling, he hid behind the skirts of a woman who called Tom a string of ripe names.

'Madam, if it had been your hearth, would you not have done the same?' Tom asked, performing an elaborate bow, adding: 'Beauty often screens a hard hand!' He left her giggling, and strode into the centre of the green, kicking a straying dog out of the way as he went. 'Ladies and Gentlemen ... I call for your attention! Tonight we present for your entertainment, a play of gripping power and ferocity that I promise will stir in your breasts laughter and fear, joy and despair. It is a piece of arrant daring that taxes each actor to the utmost, wringing every last drop from their creative skills ...'

'Get on with it then ...'

A burst of laughter and more calls to 'Stop yer prattle and show us summat.'

Tom acquiesced with another flourishing bow of enormous grace, announcing in a hollow voice that boomed and bounced from the buildings ringing the green: 'The Laird of the Loch!'

Frances' attention had been wandering amongst the crowd as they pressed around the arena. She could see Gabriel and Jack still weaving in and out collecting money into a battered top hat. The audience looked a cloddish lot and an argument developed as a broad beefy man protested he had already paid. He offered to fight Gabriel to prove the point, but he was no match for the two players and Jack emerged waving the top hat in triumph.

The play began; there was no time now for anything but a constant battle to remember the sequence and make sure she did not miss her cues.

'Where is that scurvy rascal who was to bring my sword. Ere the sun sets I'll have his liver for my dogs to eat. Angus . . . ANGUS!' Tom's voice rose to formidable hugeness and Frances, feeling ready to vomit, bounded between the lighted pots and swept a bow so low she almost toppled over. Her hair, which she had secured flat against her head, shed hairpins and a long curling strand tumbled over her face.

'Agnes yer mean . . . can't yer see she'm a girl!' A ripple of laughter greeted the invisible joker.

Frances felt ready to die of shame, but Tom merely gave her a quick wink and nodded encouragingly. Somehow she blurted out the words and played the small scene, thankful to get out of the light afterwards, to hide her blazing face.

'They're a right bunch of stirabouts,' said Len, coming close to her. 'You see . . . they'll be on to any little slip, not only yours.' He smiled at her, patting her arm. 'Didn't forget a line and that's something to be proud of.'

Feeling better, Frances strained for her cues, twice going on too soon in her anxiety not to be late, and hearing cackles of derisive laughter. The third time she never got there at all, having rushed back to the outhouse to collect a cloak she was supposed to take on for the ageing Laird. When she got back to the green, Arthur was striding about.

'Where've you been, for Gawd's sake?' Lizzie pounced on her with a screechy whisper. 'Arthur's had to babble on to thin air instead of to you.'

He was declaiming that his cloak would keep the bitter winter chill from his bones at that very minute, flinging the imaginary article round his shoulders. Frances covered her face with her hands, appalled!

'Give it me,' said Lizzie. 'I'll take it on when I makes me entrance. Don't worry, I'll invent something to explain things away.'

Frances could not imagine how she could do that when the cloak, imaginary or not, was supposed to be on Arthur's shoulders. Even less was left to her imagination when Arthur finally came off and set about her in a penetrating whisper.

'Where did you get to? There I was like a prize idiot, talking to a lump of space. Flaming marvellous ain't it when a member of the company is so dozy she don't know when to come on! By God, I shouted loud enough . . . my throat'll be sore for a week. I've had some odd things happen on stage in my time, but I've never been abandoned altogether . . . someone's always turned up before.'

'Shut up, Arthur!' whispered Len. 'Everyone's listening to you instead of the play.'

'Not surprised,' Arthur grumbled. 'There's more off stage than on.' But with this parting remark he drifted into silence.

Frances stood there wishing she could become invisible. Her misery and embarrassment were so great she felt everyone must be looking at her and quite expected the rest of the company to tell her off when the chance arose. But the play churned on with several fast and flashing sword fights and a great deal of abandoned grief, which somehow turned into smiles and embraces as the hero won the love of the heroine, the villains were killed, and all lost people returned to their grieving parents. If the clapping was anything to go by, the crowd was satisfied, and apart from one or two jokes at her expense, no one made any comment about Frances' mistake.

'We didn't do so bad,' Lizzie said much later that night as they lay on a makeshift bed of straw in the tavern barn. 'Eighteen shillings and a barrel of cider.'

Frances did not reply. The remark was a thin whispering sound on the edge of her consciousness. With her hand resting over the locket containing the miniature of her mother, she drifted into a sleep of utter exhaustion.

4 'IF YOU WANT A REAL INSTANCE OF JEALOUSY, I CAN give you an example from my own experience,' said Clara, leaning across the wagon for a better look at Freddie Knight.

'Go on, Clara . . . what a nerve, with Arthur sitting next to you! It ain't kind to take advantage like that.'

Freddie's remark had more than a grain of truth as Arthur had only two loves, his ale and his wife. Acting came a long way behind. Clara looked ruffled. She tried to assume a dignified posture but the lurching of the wagon defeated her. Instead she treated the assembled company to one of her slow cultivated smiles which was supposed to blend with her Latin looks into a suggestion of mysterious knowledge.

'If you are going to make fun at my expense,' she said, 'then I have nothing more to say.'

'Oh go on, Clara . . . take a chance!'

'Shut up, Freddie!' Frances murmured.

'Why should I? She ought to make sure her wig don't slip instead of coming over all high and mighty.'

Freddie grinned with superb unconcern and took the opportunity to wriggle along the wagon seat closer to her; a movement that was not missed by Arthur, whose sharp eyes made up for his deafness. Frances heard him muttering something about: 'Makin' a fool of himself over that stand-off miss.' She inched towards Lizzie and pushed away Freddie's straying hand from her lap for the umpteenth time.

'For goodness sake can't you stop playing the Juvenile Lead?' she whispered fiercely.

Freddie attempted a dazzling smile, displaying large gappy teeth. 'How you like to tease a feller!'

She frowned as he tried to capture her hand. 'Leave me alone!' But Freddie was irrepressible. He elbowed her ribs, slyly nodding at Clara.

'It'll blow off if she don't tie her bonnet strings!'

Clara put a nervous hand to her coarse black hair.

'It's not as tempting as yours,' continued Freddie, winding one of Frances' curls round his finger.

'Freddie!' Frances almost shouted in her despair at ever making him understand she did not want his attentions.

Everyone looked round, even Arthur. Tom, at the other end of the wagon with his arm round Jenny Love, called:

'Don Juan up to his tricks again?'

'Not the only one,' Lizzie muttered, giving Tom a killing look.

Frances wished with all her heart that the journey was over and she could escape from the packed wagon. They were on their way to Wyching-under-Wood after several months in the Cotswolds, moving from one small town and village to another; playing in barns, taverns and even on one occasion, a disused cowshed. It was not the type of theatrical life she had visualized for herself at all and her disappointment was made worse by the suspicious resentment many of the other players showed towards her. Apart from Lizzie and Tom, Len was the only one who was friendly. She wished he was beside her now with his cheery smile and endless strings of funny stories that always made her laugh. But he was perched by Jack Peach in the driving seat and Frances was not going to stare in case she met Jack's goggle eyes. Even after all these months, when modesty had worn thin with the routine life of a strolling player, the memory of Jack watching her over the curtain brought a flush to her cheeks.

Freddie slid his arm along the wagon rail behind her and put his hand on her shoulder. Trapped close to Lizzie and with no spare seating, she began to think seriously of asking Jack to halt the wagon so she could get down and beg a lift in the Croft's donkey cart which creaked behind. Even the prospect of putting up with the children, Bella pinching, Mary-Ann and little Tom snivelling, was preferable to Freddie's ceaseless pursuit. She looked back at Harriet Croft who was holding the reins. It wouldn't be long before she had to give up her regular part of Old Woman. In spite of her worn face, no audience was going to accept her immense pregnancy. The idea of another little Croft in the company had its drawbacks. Frances had never had much to do with children and the young Crofts were not likeable. She felt more sympathy for their father, Gabriel, who had taken a lift with a carter to Wyching-under-Wood the day before, to paste up the playbills: a temporary escape from his brood which he observed with daily astonishment and which yearly increased. Lizzie said that Harriet had lost count of her babies; most dying at birth or shortly afterwards. Frances had been horrified, but had later come to regard it as a blessing in disguise.

'Before we get to Wyching-under-Wood, can I remind you all that we shall be giving them "Laird of the Loch", not "Maria Marten and the Red Barn" as originally planned. We will do "Sicillian Romance" as an afterpiece and Lizzie can fill in with a song and dance, can't you darling?'

Lizzie frowned, not so much at the alteration in programme as the affectionate way Tom was cuddling Jenny.

'Oh but Tom, I've got my role of Tim Bobbin down to a fine art; words, movement, everything!' Freddie was genuinely put out. 'And you know I can't stand that dreaming Scottish halfwit, Hector!'

'Come on, Freddie, where's your spirit?' Tom grinned.

'Spirit be damned . . . it's my backside that counts! I spend half the play chained to that spiky rock. You ought to try it sometime!'

Frances leaned back against the curved rail of the wagon, glad of the relief from Freddie's pestering.

'Now I wonder whatever made you change your mind, Tom? It wouldn't by any chance have anything to with Miss Love's juicy part in "Laird of the Loch"?' Lizzie asked sarcastically.

Jenny's voice was trimmed with spite as she said: 'You're just greedy for applause. Who's been with the company longest, I'd like to know?'

'It's talent that counts, love, not age!'

'You bitch! Tom, are you going to sit there and let her insult me?'
Another dispute coming to the boil! Frances withdrew into herself.
Let them argue as they please, over the months she had grown adept at
stopping her ears. The warm September sun made her drowsy.
Tamberlaine had dropped into an easy plodding gait as he picked his
way over the rutted lane. What an unlikely name for such a placid
horse! Beyond the hedge she could see reapers at work on the golden
wheat; steady and rhythmic, their scythes glinting. She shut her eyes,
firmly refusing to think of the past which had a nasty habit of rearing
up when she was least prepared. It was a waste of time going over and
over all that had happened and comparing it with her earlier dreams.
The only hope now lay in the future. It might look bleak at the
moment, but that was not to say every last vestige was gone. Despite
forced optimism, Frances could not escape the hollow feeling she
carried most of the time. Even Lizzie's friendship seemed an inade-
quate consolation. Stop wallowing in self pity, she said to herself. Sink
or swim by your own efforts, there's no alternative! The babbling
argument was still in full swing with no sign of abating, but instead of
distracting, the sound acted like a sleeping draught, and more worn
than she realized by a succession of late nights, Frances slept.

She was jarred awake with the wagon rail banging hard into her
back. There was a harsh rending of wood: squeals from the women:
curses from the men. She scrambled to her feet and almost fell as the
whole wagon listed and settled at a steep angle. The actors were thrown
against one another and everyone was in a turmoil. When Frances
finally clambered over the side, she found that Tamberlaine had hauled
the wagon over a boulder baked hard in a setting of mud. Squatting
beside one of the rear wheels which was splayed out in an unnatural
way, Tom slapped both palms on his forehead.

'That's all I needed ... after that lumpish lot at Stope, with their
tight fists, we have to break an axle! More money ... money ...
MONEY!'

'Hark at his impersonation of a miser,' said Lizzie, acidly. 'I'd like to
know who spent our savings on that orgy in Begberrow!' Her irritation
over Jenny's favoured position in Tom's esteem, made her shrewish.
She flounced a little way down the lane.

'We're almost at the village,' Len encouraged them. 'Get your walk-ing-sticks out, ladies and gents. It's everyone for themselves. Don't drink the tap dry. Tom and me'll join you at the inn before you can say "the bailiffs are here"!'

Lizzie nudged Frances. 'Miss Love ain't going to like that one little bit. Still, it'll help fine down her figure!'

'And what about our luggage? I suppose we have to carry that,' Jenny said petulantly, choosing to ignore Lizzie.

'We'll just have to pile it all in Mrs Croft's cart, if she's willing,' Tom muttered. He gathered the rags of his talent and swept her a bow. 'Gracious lady . . .'

'The heavy baggage and no more. I'm loaded down as it is,' Harriet said curtly.

While everyone else muddled through the redistribution of bags, baskets and theatrical props, Frances stood silently on the grass verge, her carpet bag at her feet, waiting for Lizzie. She had learned to accept these regular hazards with resignation.

'Bain't yer coming then?' Jack Peach had left the wrecked wagon after unharnessing Tamberlaine and tethering him to a gate. He was shambling towards her with a grin like a segment of melon. 'Goin' ter fetch a wheelwright.'

Peach? Turnip would be more apt, Frances thought. With his shabby leather jerkin, concertina trousers and hair like a corn stook, he made a fair imitation of a scarecrow. She looked at him warily, trying to guess what trick he had in his mind this time. After having had a mouse stuffed into her carpet bag and the strings of her black velvet overskirt loosened just as she stepped onto the stage, she preferred to keep a safe distance.

'I'll wait for Lizzie,' she said, and was relieved to see him clump away.

'I'll never know why he left farming,' Lizzie said, panting under the weight of her valise. 'Regular farmer's boy.'

'Stage struck!' Freddie took it from her and would have lifted the carpet bag, but Frances pulled it away. 'Saw our late lamented John Packer as the Demon King in a local barn and gave up all for the boards.'

After trudging half a mile, Frances thought longingly of Mistral, the little brown mare she used to ride in Thrushton. Not since the Christmas holiday had she been in the saddle. She wrenched away from the memories for the second time. The door into the past was shut . . . hope lay in the future, and faded and patched though it was, she would not give up that hope. One day she would have her name in big letters at the top of the playbills in all the big cities in the world . . . she would be a star!

'Oh joyous sight!' Lizzie was saying.

They had come into a straggling village, in the centre of which stood a small weathered church with a squat tower. Beyond the village green an ancient inn had settled over the years to corpulent complacency. The bulging walls looked friendly. The windows, slipping in their sockets, seemed to wink an invitation. From the open door an equally corpulent host came out to catch a first glimpse of the actors.

'I feel like royalty,' Lizzie murmured, as cottage doors opened and people stared and waved.

'Or one of those freaks from a sideshow,' Frances said.

'Go on, you do have some funny ideas!'

Later, in the lofty kitchen, with hams hung high above a great fireplace and Mrs Allport, the breezy innkeeper's wife, plying them with tea from a stoneware pot, Lizzie commented again.

'Lately you seem to be sorry you joined up with Tom and the rest of us.' She was unbuttoning her boots, easing them from aching feet. 'Must be so different from your prim school life. I should have thought anything was better than *that*!'

Frances was drinking tea thirstily, listening to the rest of them joking with the innkeeper in the taproom. A wheelwright had been found, rooms provided, baggage stowed and a great meat pie was already cooking in the oven beside the fireplace. The fragrance made her mouth water. It was not the time for disturbing temporary security by talking of personal things. She was not in the mood for confidences.

'It's a beginning,' she said. 'What more can I expect?' She recognized faint antagonism in Lizzie's glance, but had no opportunity to soothe it by further explanation, as Tom came striding through the doorway. Jenny was with him and they linked arms.

'Ah . . . so this is where the feast is prepared.' He sniffed with closed ecstatic eyes, then sliding his unoccupied arm round Lizzie gave her a resounding kiss on the cheek and waltzed both girls round the flagged floor. 'What more could a man desire ... beautiful women, ale in plenty, food of distinction and the promise of entertainment to come. Not to mention a handsome hostess for good measure!'

Mrs Allport put a hand up to her mouth and giggled, her cheeks aflame.

★   ★   ★

'... Do not despair, my master and mistress. There is but a short step to reach the cave of the wise woman.'

'My child ... my child ...' Groans!

'... and where is this hag who calls herself Alida?' Rustling of impromptu foliage. Silence!

'... this hag who calls herself Alida?' Louder, more urgent tones.

'Gawd!' whispered Lizzie behind the curtained recess. 'That's me cue ... where's that flaming shawl?' She pushed past the curtain and scrambled up the box-steps onto the makeshift stage, with a screech that made Frances jump. So much for Jenny Love's scheming! Frances guessed that Lizzie was going to put her heart and soul into the night's performance, words or no words. She heaved at the waistband of Ralph's breeches. Why had she eaten so much pie? But she had to admit her spirits felt the better for it.

'My child ... my lost abandoned child!' Clara cried, in her most heartrending tones.

Frances squinted through a hole in the curtain, waiting for her cue. Rushlights, propped in kegs, threw a smoky glow over the rough walls of the barn. A packed village audience sat on wooden benches, scratching, shuffling its feet and nudging at every marvel. Pots of burning fat, arranged as footlights, nagged at Frances' unfulfilled dreams. She could just see Jack Peach crouched beneath the stage, struggling to boil a kettle of water on a depressed fire he had built from damp straw and green wood. The kettle had a rubber tube attached to its spout, the other end of which poked between two of the stage planks. He was blowing desperately with distended cheeks, eyes streaming. The forest mist was rising all right ... a blue haze from the fire, but no steam from the kettle ... it set the cast spluttering and the audience wiping its eyes. After beating her breast a few times, Lizzie hitched up her skirts

58

and climbed down the steps propped at the side of the stage. She peered between the supporting trestles and thumped Jack's rear.

'Stop it, you great gooby, or we'll all be suffocated!'

Alarmed by the urgency of her whisper and plagued by smoke, Jack's slow wits tangled. He loaded more of the green wood onto the fire and started fanning it, stirring up bigger clouds of smoke than ever. There were murmurs from the restless audience.

'Not like that, you loony!' Lizzie snapped.

Thoroughly confused, but anxious to oblige, Jack seized the kettle and emptied the contents over the fire, which spat and sizzled, throwing up a perfect fog of acrid smoke.

'Fire . . .' someone yelled.

'They'm burning . . . under the stage . . . fire . . .'

Tom strode to the footlights, trying to calm the frightened audience. 'Ladies and gentlemen, please . . . nothing to be alarmed about.'

But he was wrong!

Arthur Woodlock, already fuddled by too good a meal, dropped the scroll he had been holding. It fluttered straight into one of the pots of fat and burst into flame.

'Fire!' The scream was real this time.

Tom stamped out the burning paper, but Jack, half blinded and choking, panicked and stood up, heedless of the cramped space, knocking against one of the supporting trestles with such violence that it tottered and twisted.

Harriet, who had risked a last performance as an Ageing Crone, had the misfortune to be positioned over the wrecked trestle. For one endless moment Frances saw the whole structure tremble . . . then collapse.

Pandemonium broke loose. Some people rushed towards the ruins of the stage, others jammed in the barn door, struggling to get out. Those actors who had not managed to scramble from the stage were thrown in a heap. Someone was still shouting 'Fire', though all that remained was a sour smell of wet ashes. Frances pushed past the curtain and ran to help. She could hear Jack's voice moaning somewhere beneath the remains of the stage and saw his legs thrashing about. Lizzie was helping Clara to her feet and Tom was trying to sort out heaving bodies from splintered planks, torn backcloths and the sad remnants of the forest foliage. Gabriel emerged from somewhere, frantically shoving and elbowing:

'Harriet . . . let me through . . . Harriet!'

Harriet was lying on the floor clutching her stomach and moaning.

'Ma!' Bella was there too, her black button eyes wide and her sharp little face like a ghost.

Gabriel knelt by his wife. 'You hurt bad, love?'

But Harriett had her eyes tight shut and only moaned.

'Better get her out of here and into bed.' Tom looked worried. 'Tell Mrs Allport, Lizzie.'

Harriet screwed herself up and let out a sharp gasping breath. She opened her eyes as if in appeal.

'Ma!' Bella beseeched.

'Reckon this has set her off,' Gabriel muttered.

Frances felt alarm at the thought that the baby was to be born, which changed to cold relief that Harriet's groans were due to nothing more than a natural condition. She had not been hurt.

Tom and Len Goodridge helped Gabriel carry Harriet to the inn. Frances followed a few minutes later and found a white-faced Lizzie coming out of the kitchen.

'Gabriel says the baby is to be born,' Frances said.

'Oh the poor thing!' Lizzie looked so scared that Frances said tartly:

'I should think she'd be glad to get rid of that great lump she's been carrying.'

'And have another stillborn baby? She's six weeks to go yet . . . and Lord knows what the fall will have done.'

Frances stared at her. Anxiety taking hold with dawning understanding. Gabriel was coming down the stairs, his face drawn with worry.

'Someone's to go for the doctor. It's not right. She's in too much pain.'

'There's no doctor for fifteen miles. It 'ud be all over before you could get one here, if he'd come! She's all right. 'Tisn't her first.' Mrs Allport had followed him down.

Gabriel looked at her with stark despair. 'That's how I know. I've been through it all eleven times. Never had a bit of trouble before. Dropped them like peas from a pod.'

The image was comic, but Frances was too busy fretting at her helplessness to notice.

Mrs Allport frowned. 'There's Mrs Biggin. She goes to every laying in . . . lays 'em out too. But she's gone to her sister's at Fensham and won't be back till Monday. That's three mile away.'

'I'll take the cart,' Gabriel said.

'No!' Frances butted in. 'I'll go. Have you a good horse?' she asked Mrs Allport.

'Not in our stable.'

'Well is there a farmer round here who would lend one?'

Mrs Allport shook her head doubtfully. 'I don't know . . . they'm a close lot when it comes to their belongings.'

It would have to be Tamberlaine. Slow, weary Tam. Well she would make him gallop if it was the last thing she did. At least he was faster than that donkey and more willing. As the relief of action took hold she failed to notice the astonishment in their faces. She was giving orders, assuming that everyone would comply as the servants had done at home. 'I'll ride Tamberlaine. He's big enough to take two.'

'But we haven't a saddle . . . you might fall,' Lizzie said.

Frances almost laughed at the idea. She thought of the long tough hours she had spent mastering Bastion, and the times she had ridden Mistral to the hunt. She was hardly likely to come to grief with Tam!

'But Mrs. Biggin won't ride back with you. She's never got on a horse in her life,' said Mrs Allport.

This had not occurred to Frances. She stamped her foot in frustration.

'Dad . . .' Bella had come to the top of the stairs. 'Mam says to come. Little Tom's crying something chronic and Clara can't quiet him.'

Gabriel took the stairs two at a time and Lizzie ran after him, seeing the tears on Bella's face.

'I'll harness Tamberlaine to the cart. I'll get there faster than with that wretched donkey. Which way do I go?'

When Mrs Allport had explained the route, Frances, still in her costume shirt and breeches, her face larded with stage make-up, went into the courtyard. The donkey cart stood near one wall and as she was leading Tam from the stable, Len joined her.

'I'll come along with you,' he said, when she had explained her errand.

They sat side by side in silence as Tamberlaine plodded away from the village. Len seemed unusually serious, though Frances was worrying about the speed and hardly noticed.

'What a day!' Len said at last. 'I reckon I've had me fill.'

Frances, who was wondering whether it would help if she were to get on Tam's back to give him more sense of urgency, came out of her thoughts.

'You mean you want to give up acting?' she asked.

'I didn't say that.'

'What d'you mean then?'

He shrugged. 'It's the whole thing . . . the company, staggering from one disaster to the next with never a penny to show for it and old Tom trying to bamboozle everyone into thinking we're doing fine.' There was a steely edge to his voice that Frances had never heard before. The change worked on her already sensitive feelings, undermining her security. She relied on Len to cheer her up.

'But what else can we do if we want to act?' she asked.

'Well we can't go on like this, that's for sure. But I was thinking of other work.'

'Oh Len, no!' She knew he had been a journeyman weaver before he took up with Tom Vaughan, so he would not lack for work. But the company would not be the same without him. She shivered. His simple statement of truth brought her face to face with all the fears she had been harbouring since that first awful performance in Evesham. She had progressed since then, that was true . . . but to what? The answer was one she was loath to accept. In the mellow dusk it forced into the front of her mind. She was no more than the majority of actors from all she had heard; struggling clumsy pretenders who hung on to existence by their fingernails, wrapped in the struggle to survive, with no hope at all of achieving the heights for which she hungered. Oh, she was sick of the whole thing. She didn't want to talk about it, and this damned horse was like a snail!

'Stop!'

Len looked at her in surprise but pulled on the reins.

Slipping from the cart, Frances went round to Tamberlaine. 'Come on, you old wreck! Get some of that muscle power working.' Wearing breeches was a tremendous help in mounting. The only drawback was the unresponsive horse, but she would alter his ways! With a kick of her heels she concentrated hard in overcoming Tam's reluctance. The cart began to rattle and bump along the lane at a sharp pace.

Mrs Biggin was more than a little astonished by the strange couple who had come for her services. Neither of them had removed their make-up and had forgotten all about it until they saw her goggling eyes. But she was a good-natured woman and agreed to ride back with them, recounting tales of her cases to pass the time. An entertainment Frances could have well done without.

Lizzie had been watching for them from a window and came running into the yard holding a lantern, as the cart clattered over the cobblestones.

'How is she?' Frances asked.

Lizzie shrugged in mute despair. 'I'll take you up,' she said to Mrs Biggin.

Frances and Len unharnessed the sweating Tamberlaine, rubbed him down and left him munching contentedly in the stable. Then they walked back to the inn, all in complete silence. Freddie came out of the taproom as they entered. He had obviously been drinking.

'Fanny, light of my life . . . here give us a kiss . . .'

'Don't call me that!' Frances snapped, and hit him across the cheek with all the force of her pent-up misery and frustration. Then she ran up the stairs to the small room she was to share with Lizzie and sat on the edge of the straw-packed mattress.

She was still sitting there staring out into the night when Lizzie came in much later. She looked up. Lizzie was crying.

'The baby's dead.'

'Harriet?'

'She's going to be all right.'

Frances shivered with relief, unable to feel anything at all for the unknown baby, except a second-hand grief for Harriet in her loss. She unlaced Ralph's shirt and breeches and, taking them off, folded them into a neat pile; finding solace in the mindless routine of undressing. In her flannel nightgown with a shawl round her shoulders, she propped a small hand mirror against the window and began to remove her make-up. Perhaps in the future they would all be able to understand it was another blessing in disguise.

5

'... QUICK, QUICK, SEIZE THE CHILD.'

'I'll see you dead before you harm one hair.'

'Draw then!'

'No ... no ...' Frances screamed, covering her face with her hands, taking a step forward only to cower back as Hero Tom and Villain Len clashed their swords together. Through her fingers she could see the blades flash in the flickering stage-light. Len had done a marvellous job on his make-up. Under his black wig his face contorted in a devilish grimace and she was caught up in terror and hatred. There was a long haunting scream. Tom lunged and Len flung up his arms in an outsize gesture of agony. His sword clattered on the floor. He clutched his wounded chest, groaned, rolled his eyes towards the roof, groaned again, pitched stiffly back, twitched convulsively and was still.

'So die all such villains,' Tom declaimed.

'Father!' Mary-Ann ran forward to be lifted high.

'My child!' He turned towards Frances, who now stood with her arms crossed over her breast. She went to him as he held out his free hand, but kept her eyes downcast as she allowed him to kiss her brow. 'My love, my true and only love,' said Tom, putting a great deal of husky passion into his statement.

'Who has remained faithful to you throughout all these bitter months and who will remain so evermore,' declared Frances, and together they formed a charming tableau.

Roars of approval from the audience. Frances floated on a tide of clapping. The rest of the cast came forward to take a bow and she swept a deep curtsy as farming boots drummed on the wooden floor. Again the company bowed and a fresh wave of clapping greeted them. Hero and heroine stepped forward, hand in hand. It was a sweet moment and one that Frances enjoyed to the full. But as she left the stage, in a mystifying way some of her elation died.

'You did splendid, love,' Lizzie said, giving her a hug.

The sincere warmth in Lizzie's praise cut through Frances' flattened mood. Lizzie was a good sort not to be sore at missing the lead part. With Harriet ill again, they had all had to shift their usual parts. Clara, reluctantly taking the Old Woman, left the Mature Woman's part to Jenny who had more experience. At rehearsal Lizzie had begged to keep her original character of Comic Country Lass, which left the Heroine for Frances. At the time Frances had taken the request at face value, knowing Lizzie excelled as comedienne. Now she was not so sure. It was possible that Lizzie had provided her with a chance she would otherwise never have had. She felt suddenly closer to Lizzie and humbled by her generosity.

'You didn't forget a single line,' Lizzie said, when they were in their cramped hole of a dressing-room in the stable.

Frances greased her face with pomatum and wiped away the carmine and antimony powder with a much stained cloth. In spite of Lizzie's encouraging words she felt drained of energy and flat as a tankard of beer left standing a week. She untied her velvet overskirt and stepped out of it. From outside the sound of a horse and cart rumbling over the frost-hard mud of the inn yard, mingled with the comings and goings of the audience, many of whom were going inside to drink a toast to Christmas Eve.

The company had left Wyching-under-Wood ten days after Harriet had lost her baby and had been constantly travelling ever since; only pausing for one night stands until arriving here in Elmshill. The baby's death had been an omen, Frances thought, gloomily examining the hole in the sole of one of her boots. Since then their fortunes had declined, with Harriet frequently unwell and audiences so thin on the ground that Tom had been forced to sell Tamberlaine and the wagon at Stowe on the Wold in order to pay their debts.

'We can't go on like this much longer,' she said, echoing the words Len had used when they went to fetch the midwife.

'It's better tonight,' said the ever cheerful Lizzie. 'We must have taken a fair amount. Things have a way of looking up at Christmas. It's the Season of Goodwill ... what's going on out there?' She ran towards the stable door buttoning her blouse as she went.

Frances shivered. The night was bitter and an icy draught blew through a hundred cracks in the tumbledown stable. All she cared about was having something warm inside her and then for bed. Slowly she collected her belongings and stuffed them into her carpet bag. Since the mysterious loss of her lace-trimmed petticoat during one performance, she had been meticulous about putting everything away. The petticoat had reappeared as mysteriously as it vanished. The morning after she had gone to fetch the midwife for Harriet, she had woken to find it lying across the foot of her bed. She suspected Bella, who had always born a grudge because Frances had stepped into her brother's part, but she had no proof.

Outside in the yard a bunch of people clustered round a small yellow cart. Tom was in the middle arguing with a crabbed little man in a round hat.

'One silver shilling and not a penny more,' Tom boomed.

Frances felt despair pluck at her. He was never going to change! The sight of a pedlar drew him like a girl after hair ribbons, with money burning a hole in his pocket. He was probably buying Christmas presents for everyone, which didn't make it any better. He ought to keep some on one side for bad times, but that sort of far-sighted planning was foreign to his flamboyant nature. Some of the money he was handing to the pedlar was her hard earned share she reflected bitterly, and was spurred to call out to him. Waving a handful of lace, he crossed the yard.

'For the ladies,' he said. 'I couldn't let Christmas pass without token gifts at least.'

If it was only to be a length of lace it wasn't so bad, Frances thought. Perhaps he had decided to turn over a new leaf.

'Let me salute your performance tonight, my dear. You played the part splendidly . . . splendidly. I can see your name top of the playbill yet, and at Drury Lane too, I am convinced. ''MISS FRANCES REDMAYNE in the Romantic Leading Role in William Shakespeare's Soul Searching Tragedy 'ROMEO AND JULIET' ''. And the moment when the gaslights are lowered in the auditorium . . . I see it all: the footlights glow, the lime stick burns, casting a brilliant pool of light on your rich black tresses. The audience gasps and holds its breath as your slender figure, draped in pure white, lies apparently lifeless on a bier under a shadowy canopy of roses. Suddenly there is a sound . . .'

'I've ordered pints all round . . . that suit you, Tom? The ladies are having port.'

Len's timing was so perfect that Frances burst out laughing. He looked at her in surprise.

'What's the joke?'

But she only shook her head, unable to explain.

A burst of warm air came like a promise of better things as Tom opened the taproom door. Frances wished she had enough nerve to go in, but women were not encouraged in this men's sanctuary and she went into a small room beyond, where most of the company were huddled round a shallow fireplace. Frances shivered violently. Her throat was rough. She felt hot and cold by turns and suspected she might have a fever.

'Here she is . . . the lady of the moment.' Arthur Woodlock, already in a mood of alcoholic well-being, waved a tankard at her.

'Light of my life . . .' Freddie began.

'Well done, love . . . You were grand . . . Never forgot a word . . . And the way you rolled your eyes and tore your clothes . . . Real despair it was . . .' A tide of compliments swept in and she flushed even more hotly with pleasure now that the barrier of suspicion seemed to have crumbled at last.

'Just a mite more fire in the love scene and it would have been a real performance,' Jenny smiled with cat's eyes. 'Considering how little experience you've had though . . .' She did not finish the sentence, but her intention was clear enough.

'Don't listen to her, she's jealous because of all the applause you got.' Clara was overwhelmingly motherly.

'That I'm not,' Jenny snapped. 'Didn't I give a fair criticism *and* praise with it?' She appealed to them all, eyes wide now.

'Hark at the innocence! Butter wouldn't melt in her mouth the way she is,' said Lizzie.

Frances began to wish no one had mentioned her mediocre triumph. The last thing she could face was one of those backbiting rows that had been an all-too-frequent pastime these last weeks. The moment was retrieved as Tom and Len came in carrying two vast trays, one covered with tankards and glasses, the other stacked with hot loaves, a crock of butter and a whole round cheese. A cheer went up. Tom put down his tray on the table and held up his hand.

'One moment my friends, hold your appreciation in check . . . there is more to come.' He went out of the room under a murmur of expectation which burst into further cheers when he reappeared with a side of ham on a board. 'A morsel to keep you from starving until the real Christmas feasting begins.'

Watching Tom carve the ham, Frances experienced the same cold apprehension she had felt seeing him haggle with the pedlar. All this food would cost a fortune, and there was sure to be more extravagance on Christmas Day. She was seized with another fit of shivering, thinking she had come a long way since she celebrated Christmas in unappreciated luxury at Thrushton.

'You look perished,' Lizzie said. 'Here, come along to the fire. Mind yourself, Arthur.'

Meekly, Frances allowed herself to be shepherded to one of the padded fender seats. The warmth of the fire was blissful. Lizzie thrust a brimming glass into her hand. 'Drink it down and get the ice out of your bones.'

The port oiled its way down her sore throat and spread a warm glow round her stomach. She accepted a plate of ham, cheese and warm bread, but found it impossible to eat because of her throat. The drink soothed her, though her head felt heavy and the conversation and laughter reached her as if from a great distance. She let herself drift on the sea of noise.

'. . . to us all, so raise your glasses!'

Frances felt herself nudged. She blinked hard and heard Lizzie saying: 'Get up, love. It's a toast.'

Freddie was refilling her glass again. It was a struggle but she managed to stand. The room seemed somehow unstable, but at least she was warm . . . too warm! Her cheeks were on fire. She wanted to sleep more than anything, but it seemed as if the festivities were getting under way. There was something forced about it, she thought. Christmas should be celebrated on the proper day. But nothing was ever done according to convention in Tom Vaughan's company. She looked round the room, seeing the actors very clearly and was reminded of a picture book she had at home with drawings of marionettes hanging from strings. That's what they all were . . . puppets! If they could be made to understand that this lay at the root of their ill fortune, then they would see how to put things right. She must tell them. Stand! But someone else was proclaiming another toast. Frances drank with resignation. Now tell them! But again she was forestalled. Arthur was calling for a sharing of the night's takings. Tom was laughing . . . expansive . . . what was he saying? Frances drained her glass. Something about 'tomorrow would do . . . a Christmas treat'. She must tell them about the marionettes. Stand up, then they would see she had something to say! The walls were very tiresome the way they moved about. She waved for silence.

'Listen . . . listen . . . listen . . . listen . . . listen everybody . . . listen . . .'

Why were they all laughing? And why were they dancing, swaying as if they were waltzing . . . but there was no music? Freddie was a nuisance, leaning over her. She wished he would go away. There was a wart on the side of his nose that she had never noticed before. It was a very small wart, about the size of a pin-head, but it seemed large.

Lizzie loomed in front of him. 'Gawd, you're squiffed,' she said, and the room tilted. 'Look out!'

Frances felt her arm clutched. She shook it impatiently. Clara had come into view now. And Bella was standing on a stool, her eyes popping. What were they all staring at? Her acting talents weren't that unique. If only the room would settle down. What was it Lizzie said? Squiffed?

Frances felt her knees buckle and her senses swam with shame. She half fell, was half lowered by Lizzie onto the fender seat.

'Bed, Liz?' she managed to plead.

'Put your arm round my shoulders. That's it. Can you stand d'you think?' Lizzie braced herself, taking Frances' weight. 'Give us a hand the other side of her.'

Not Freddie! She didn't want his help. But it was Len smiling encouragement. All she wanted to do was get away from the grinning faces. Oh the shame of it . . . the shame! Frances allowed herself to be guided from the cosy room into the draughty passage and up the cliff of stairs to an icy bedroom.

'I'll manage now,' she heard Lizzie say.

Len said goodnight, but she could not bring herself to answer. In the struggle to undress she appealed to Lizzie:

'How did it hi . . . happen?'

'You should have taken a bite first before drinking that port. Anyone would get muzzy on an empty stomach, especially if they were chasing a fever as well. D'you still feel cold?'

Cold ? Hot? She was both at the same time. In bed, she took Lizzie's hand. It was easier to speak now she was lying down.

'You are a good friend, Liz.'

'Get on with you!' Lizzie's voice was rough. 'It's a poor look-out if you can't help one of your own when the need comes.' She became brisk as if to cover her feelings. 'Shivering again! You've got a fever playing in that draughty barn. That place hasn't seen a hammer or nails since the day it was built, and that's going back a few years. There was a draught like knives under those doors. I'll get a hot brick for your feet.' And she hurried away.

Hazily the words revolved in Frances' mind, 'One of your own . . . one of your own'. Her ears were buzzing with remembered laughter and the echoes of applause. When Lizzie returned with the brick wrapped in flannel, she was fast asleep. Tucking the brick under the bedclothes near Frances' feet, she stood looking at the flushed face with an unguarded expression, tender and maternal.

*　*　*

Frances woke up, shifted, then lay absolutely still as her head pulsated and hammered. Her eyes felt bruised and sprinkled with sand. She sneezed violently which was a cruel trick.

'Oh, God!' she moaned, and sneezed again.

Lizzie came in at this point and went to the window, rubbing away the moisture that had misted over the panes, letting in a little more light from a sullen sky. Rain began to scratch on the glass. Frances shrank under the sheets, trying to escape back into sleep.

'Brought you a mug of tea, love. How do you feel this morning?'

'I'm dying,' Frances said in a muffled voice.

'Oh, that's not so bad then.' Lizzie sounded relieved and yet tense at the same time.

Frances came up from the depths and regarded her coldly. 'Thanks for the sympathy.'

'Now don't take on,' said Lizzie, handing her a steaming mug. 'I meant you can talk and aren't just groaning and carrying on like you did all last night.'

Frances had no recollection of anything but a blank period of sleep and looked at her in some surprise. She took the mug and swallowed some tea gratefully. Her throat was still painful but most of the trouble lay in her streaming nose. She sneezed again, slopping the tea.

'Seems no more than a bad cold,' Lizzie said.

Frances remembered it was Christmas Day. What a present, she thought! All she wanted to do was lie back on her pillow and quietly sink into oblivion. 'Happy Christmas,' she said, more as a formality than anything else.

'Is it?'

Frances looked at her with a rapid movement of her eyes that sent pins of pain darting in and out. 'What's the matter?'

Lizzie had her back to the bed and was staring out into the cloudy morning. From the rigid position of her shoulders, Frances had a suspicion she was very close to tears. She eased herself up in the bed, suddenly apprehensive.

'Lizzie?' Still no response. 'Are you upset? What's happened?'

A dam seemed to burst in Lizzie. She swung round with tears pouring down her cheeks and rushed to Frances, flinging herself on the bed, choking and gulping with sobs.

Frances forgot her headache in a rush of alarm. She put her hand on Lizzie's shoulder, which was jerking convulsively. There seemed no end to Lizzie's abandoned grief. Frances put down her mug and tried to soothe her, stroking the mat of fair curls, patting her back. At last she got really scared and shook her with some violence.

'Stop making that row and tell me what's wrong,' she commanded.

The effect of her strident voice seemed to bring back Lizzie's control. 'Tom . . .' she managed at last. 'He's gone orf . . . with all the takings . . . and that . . . that . . . bitch.' Her voice cracked and leaked venom. 'Jenny Love . . . LOVE!' A universe of emotion went into that final word.

Frances was stunned. 'Gone off?' she repeated.

Lizzie was mopping her ravaged face with her sleeve. 'There's a horse been stolen from the stables too. It belonged to a gent staying here. Of course no one saw, but it don't take much brains to add them together. He'll swing for horse thieving and I'll be glad!' Lizzie clenched her fists and pounded the bed. Then she stopped and gave Frances a look that made her ache with pity. 'No I won't,' she said. 'I'll be miserable for the rest of me days. I'm that much of a fool I'd take him now if he came back and so much as offered.'

Frances leaned back against the wall and closed her eyes, over-whelmed by the news and quite unable to make any sense of this new disaster. She remembered her unease from last night. There was a reason for the festivity; it had been meant as their Christmas feast after all. There would be no celebrating today. There was nothing to cele-brate with. The cold truth smacked into her apathy. They were penni-less, except for her last sovereign and any coppers the others might have. It was not going to get them far and anyway, where would they go?

Painfully she got out of the warm bed and began to dress, shivering at the damp cold of the room. Lizzie did not protest as she would have done had it been an ordinary day. They both knew that a council of war must be held.

In the cheerless morning light of the room which yesterday had held their laughter, the remains of the company were already sitting round a table laid with the scraps from a spare meal. A new fire had yet to generate heat and the sheeting rain made the air dank and chilly. There was a buzz of conversation. Lizzie and Frances sat down at the table, but neither had any appetite. The babble increased and edged round a quarrel which snagged Frances' frayed nerves.

'Have you heard what that rat has done? Gone off with that little vixen if you please . . . and all the takings!'

Frances nodded wearily, thinking Clara's description of Tom and Jenny bordered on the absurd. 'Lizzie told me what's happened.'

'What are we going to do . . . what are we going to do?' Clara's voice rose higher and higher.

'Stop panicking for a start,' Harriet snapped. She had little Tom on her knee and was feeding him a mush of bread and milk. Bella had her eyes fastened on Frances, and Mary-Ann was squatting on the floor playing with one of the cats belonging to the inn.

'I reckon we should close the company,' Len said.

There was a stupefied silence and then a scrambled chatter of voices. 'You can't mean ... how'll we earn ... senseless ... props ... tramping to ...'

'It's by far the best way,' Len went on, in the same matter of fact voice. 'We've been getting no decent houses. You all know it. Now we've been left with a debt to pay off here and little prospect of finding anyone to take Tom's place.' He did not mention Jenny. There seemed to be a tacit understanding about her that precluded discussion. 'For myself I'm going back north to my old job ... and Jack says he's going back to farming.'

'We can offer you a lift along the way,' Harriet said. 'Gabriel and me are set against this life. It's more than I can do with since my last was took. Gabriel is a fair carpenter and we fancy going back home to Huddersfield before...' She did not complete her sentence and it hung in the air, an unnamed threat. Gabriel looked at her like a beaten dog.

'But we've got to pay off the innkeeper first,' Len said.

'Pass the hat round and see how much we can raise,' Freddie suggested.

'Oh I don't think we need do that.' Clara was confident now. 'He'll listen to me, don't you fret. There won't be any trouble.'

Arthur, with a hand cupped to his ear, caught her words. He jerked to his feet and shouted: 'There will if I have anything to do with it! That jumped up piece of half cooked Cotswold mutton ... if he so much as lays a finger on you I'll black his eye!'

Frances was startled. She had seen Arthur's jealousy at work before but never quite so blatantly. Clara seemed unperturbed.

'How you do go on, making a perfect fool of yourself. He's offered me a job as barmaid, that's all. It's a good inn ... plenty of trade. We shan't lack. Course I'll say yes on condition he takes you on as cellarman.'

Subdued, but not satisfied, Arthur dropped into a grumbling mutter.

'So that leaves us three,' Freddie said cheerfully. 'Could be worse things to face than taking off with two such beauties.'

Freddie's banter was the last thing Frances wanted at the moment.

73

'Lizzie and I have made our own arrangements,' she said positively. 'We weren't going to tell you until after Christmas, but as things stand you might as well know now. We've been taken on at the Queen's Theatre in Warfield.'

Lizzie was staring at her open-mouthed. The others hovered on the edge of disbelief, but there was something about Frances' authoritative tone that made them hesitate to scoff. Let them imagine what they like, Frances thought, her head pounding. I'm not going to have that oily creature hanging round us. There was the sovereign. It would get them to Warfield. Surely Mrs Copperdyce would help them. She pulled out the strings of her reticule, which she always carried, looking for the comforting gleam of the sovereign. There was a handkerchief, her small tortoise-shell comb and the piece of lace Tom had given her, but the coin was nowhere to be seen. She hunted desperately, then looked up and met Bella's frightened eyes.

'My money . . . where is it?' she demanded.

'Not me . . . not me! I gave back the petticoat and I ain't touched a single thing since!'

So she had been right in her guess about the petticoat! But there was a ring of truth in Bella's voice. If she had not taken the money then . . .

'He's been round the lot of us I reckon,' Len said. 'I had ten shillings worth of silver in a pouch that's gone.'

Frances could feel the weight of the locket hanging round her neck. It was her last remaining asset, but how was she to part with such a treasured possession; sole link with her mother and something she had come to regard as a charm, protecting the fragile dreams she had nursed for so long? Lizzie was looking at her with a mixture of bewilderment, anguish and despair. She couldn't let her down! It didn't have to be the locket; the chain must be worth something and could be replaced when she got the chance.

Frances leaned across the table and put her hand over Lizzie's. 'Don't worry . . . we are still going,' she said. 'I've got something in reserve.'

Part 2

1845

*   *   *

THE STOCK COMPANY

6 RELIEF WAS FRANCES' FIRST REACTION AS THE stagecoach rolled into the courtyard of the 'Goat and Compasses' in the town of Warfield. Pleasure followed at the sight of such a comfortable bustle of people thronging the street. And in quick succession to that, an awful lost feeling, simply because there were so many people and she was a stranger amongst them.

'Thank Gawd it ain't raining!' Lizzie said. She was taking her valise from the coachman. 'Here, get hold of your bag.'

If it wasn't raining it would soon be snowing, Frances thought. An east wind swept down the street ballooning skirts and threatening hats. Above the buildings a dimming sky already had an edge of leaden cloud. She shivered then sneezed twice. If they didn't find the Queen's Theatre rapidly she would be in bed again. Her cold had turned to a fever after the appalling revelations of Christmas Day. She blew her nose on a square of cambric, trying not to think about that catastrophe. It was enough to know it was over. Clara had been surprisingly human in her concern and had persuaded the innkeeper at Elmshill to allow them to remain for a further week. Lizzie had paid for their keep by doing all the washing up and giving a hand with the cleaning. Frances felt increasingly in her debt. It was not an entirely agreeable reaction.

'We'll have to ask the way,' she said, but Lizzie had thought of that too and was already inquiring from one of the ostlers who had come to change the team of horses. It was like Evesham all over again. But it *couldn't* have such a disastrous end!

They pushed through the crowd, passing houses and shops, until they reached the corner of the street where a hot potato stand spread a warming glow. The fragrant smell of baking potatoes made their mouths water.

'I fancy a nice hot spud,' Lizzie said, looking hopefully at Frances.

'There's sixpence left between us and destitution,' Frances replied. 'If we buy potatoes there'll be even less.'

'At least we shan't be starving!'

Frances bought four leathery potatoes and gave two to Lizzie. The heat soaked into her cold palms in a most comforting way. They stood close to the small fire which burned under an iron oven, and bit into the waxy potato flesh. Since leaving Elmshill they had eaten nothing but a portion of bread and cheese and a glass of porter bought at a coaching inn on the way. With the food, fares and a present of a flask of lavender water for Clara, the ten shillings Frances' gold chain had fetched, had dwindled rapidly.

The Hot Potato man was working briskly, customers coming and going.

'Doing a good trade,' Lizzie remarked.

The Hot Potato man nodded. 'Allus do on race days and market days, and when the Assizes come.'

'No wonder the town's full,' Lizzie said to Frances. 'Rosie knew what she was doing when she came here. The theatre ought to be drawing 'em in . . . horse races, market days *and* Assizes . . . we're going to be all right, love! You could have knocked me down with a feather when you came out with that tale about us being taken on at the Queen's, but it was a stroke of genius. I thought Flirting Freddie's eyes would drop into his lap! He was all but ready to ask if he could come too. Don't know what stopped him really.'

'He'll do better as a soldier,' Frances said. 'He'll enjoy parading his smart uniform in front of the girls.'

Lizzie finished her first potato and licked her fingers. 'I'm keeping the other to warm me poor hands. Come on, let's find the theatre!'

They left the main street, turning into a narrow cobbled lane which curved in a semicircle past a cattle market. Fifty yards further on they saw the shabby theatre. Approaching the faded green double doors they noticed a playbill pasted there. It looked a lengthy entertainment:

QUEEN'S THEATRE

Lessee and Manager Mr. ALFRED BOWSTOCK

This Present MONDAY, January 6th, 1845

Mr. & Mrs. Charles HAMPTON'S BENEFIT

The Performance will Commence with a CHARMING BURLETTA
Especially Composed for the Occasion by Mr. ROBERT WELKIN,
Entitled

SUSANNAH'S DREAM

Which is Entirely Acted in the FOREST OF ARDEN in Years Gone Past.

Susannah–a Young Lady of Beauty but Little Sense–Mrs. Elinor HAMPTON
Her Widowed Mother - - Mrs. BURBAGE
Wheatley Fanshaw - Susannah's Aspiring Suitor - Mr. Charles HAMPTON
Cropper - a Farmer of Ill Repute - Mr. Alfred BOWSTOCK

The SIX Charming SONGS to be Sung by Mrs. HAMPTON,
Mr. HAMPTON and FULL CHORUS

To be followed by

THE FOLLY OF DRINK!

In Which GRIT The DOG of DARING!!
SAVES His MASTER From CERTAIN DEATH!!

Charlie Grimes - A Sailor - Mr. Robert WELKIN
Wyley - a Desperate Character - Mr. Kit COX
GRIT - AS HIMSELF

To be followed by

THE BABES IN THE WOOD

With GHOSTS and DEMONS Rushing Through the FIRES of HELL, a
REAL SNOW STORM in the KINGDOM of ICICLES, MAGIC in the
WITCH'S COTTAGE and MANY MORE DELIGHTS with a FINAL
CELESTIAL TABLEAU!!!

'Told you Rosie knew what she was doing. Good old Grit!' Lizzie tapped the item on the playbill.

Frances was staring up at the theatre. It looked anything but prosperous. Paint was peeling from the plaster façade and a hungry giant had bitten a piece out of the parapet.

' 'Course we ought to make ourselves known to the prompter first . . . it's expected,' Lizzie said doubtfully.

'But we *aren't* expected,' Frances answered, studying the playbill. 'I know that a Burletta's any piece in three acts including at least five songs, but what is a Benefit?'

'What it says.'

'You mean all the takings go to Mr and Mrs Hampton?'

'They can do, but then they'd have to pay all the night's expenses, rent, wages . . . everything. It's safer to go shares with the manager . . . take a percentage.'

'I think,' said Frances, going back to the problem Lizzie originally raised, 'we must ask for Mrs Copperdyce.'

They found the stage door down an alley at the side of the theatre. An old man, perched on a stool, chewing his gums, mumbled directions for finding the wardrobe. But one dark musty passage led to another with doors that opened into dressing-rooms, greenroom and a small turbulent office . . . but no wardrobe. In the end it was Grit who found Lizzie and Frances. He bounded up to Lizzie like a flying doormat, uttering falsetto barks that hardly matched his size.

'Get down you old fiend!' said Lizzie, alternately hugging and pushing at him.

'Grit . . . Grit, hush your noise . . . why LIZZIE!'

Frances shrank against the wall as Rosie materialized from the gloom and enveloped Lizzie in a smothering embrace.

'Rosie!'

The two of them hugged and wept and hugged again. In the background Frances watched. There was a larger-than-life reaction to every detail of living in the theatre. It was ridiculous and yet unavoidable she supposed; all part of the business of illusion. She had to admit being guilty of exaggerations herself, sometimes.

'And Miss Frances too!'

Frances was swept into the soft cushion of Rosie's arms that smelled of old sweats and gilliflowers. Frances felt an unbidden response. There was something comforting about Rosie. Motherly in a way that her real mother had never been. Her treasured memories looked across the years with assumed perfection: an elegant silhouette against a summer windowpane; a deep voice singing a lullaby; the lingering scent of blown roses as her mother bent over the bed, with dark eyes reflecting the diamonds that swung from her ears. There was nothing to match the warm, human animal contact that spoke in a language no words could express.

Grit was bouncing again, hungry for his portion of the lavish affection.

'Get down you sloppy old lump! Like a great baby you are.' Rosie pushed him away. 'Come along out of these draughts. I've a drop of gin that'll take the frost out of your bones.'

'I'd rather have a cup of tea, if you can make one,' Lizzie said, as they followed her into a little box of a room with a sloping roof. In one corner a small black iron stove crackled. Rosie moved the kettle directly over the flames.

'It'll be boiling in the twinkling of an eye,' she said. 'I hotted up the water to add a drop to me gin. Nothing like it in this weather to give you a glow. Now sit yourselves down and tell me all about everything. I don't want to miss one snippet.'

And Lizzie began. Silent at first, Frances found herself drawn into the tale, ending, to her surprise, by talking just as much as Lizzie. The hot tea was good. Steady warmth from the fire pushed through her boots and the layers of her skirts. Rosie wheezed oo's and ah's with bouts of laughter.

'That Tom,' she said at last. 'A Casanova if ever there was one . . . and not a mite of conscience.' She sighed like mewing kittens. 'But he had a way with him. Charm a barnacle off a ship's bottom he could. But don't you lose any sleep over him.' She patted Lizzie's knee, with shrewd assessment. 'There's plenty more fish . . . I reckon he's done me a good turn, because you've come at just the right moment.'

'Is there a vacancy?' Lizzie asked eagerly.

'Not as I know of for acting. Mr Bowstock's hired enough super-numeraries for the panto. 'Course he *might* take you on . . . I'll ask him when he gets in . . . but I was meaning I could do with a couple of extra dressers. There's only me and old Ma Shakespeare. She may have the right name for theatre work, but she's too fond of the bottle to make much of it! Sent word that she's got a touch of the colic and won't be in tonight ... and we all know what's brought that on! So you see, if you hadn't turned up I'd have been in a pickle and no mistake.'

'At least it's something,' Lizzie said flatly.

'Oh I know it ain't got the glamour of stage work, but y'never know. You'll have your foot in the door ... and you've got experience.'

Frances had none of Lizzie's misgivings. It was enough for her to be inside a theatre building, knowing she was to take a vital part, if a hidden one, in the night's performance. Riding on the crest of her relief that they had shelved destitution for the present, she would have cheerfully swept the theatre floors.

Grit had rested his juicy muzzle on her knee and was gazing through a curtain of hair with hopeful eyes.

'Look at him! He's after your tea, me duck. Loves his drink, he does.' Rosie bent with a creaking of stays, and poured some into a bowl under a long table. Then, putting down the teapot, she sorted out needles and thread. 'If you would give me a hand with some repairs I'd be grateful. It was like Bedlam last night, I'll tell you. The Good Fairy trod on the King's cloak and ripped off some of the trimming, then Harlequin knocked off *her* wings, and to cap it all two of the chorus got hooked on the same nail sticking out of the Witch's cottage and tore great holes in their skirts. Charlie Hampton's a sound carpenter, but his mate is that careless.'

'Hampton?' asked Frances, taking a needle, threading it and knotting the end of the cotton. 'Is he the one to have a Benefit?'

'That's it, me duck. He doubles acting with making stage scenery. Ever such a clever man. Elinor Hampton is our leading lady, Nell we call her. Ever such a nice couple they are. Two nippers they've got ... Charlotte and Bradley. Made their stage debut in the panto. They're the Babes. Before that they've had little walking parts, but never any lines to say.' Rosie rambled on as they stitched at the torn costumes. 'There's a nice atmosphere about this company. 'Course folk have their tiffs ... who doesn't? When you get a threesome like James Sullivan and his wife Celia and her dad Grimsby Jerrold, the sparks fly now and again. You should have heard them the other day. "Hogwash" James says to his Pa-in-law . . . they was talking about his performance . . . "What" says Grimsby "You have the affrontery to insult me? Behind my back you may think you can get away with it, but to my face . . . NEVER!' '. He shouted so loud poor Mrs Burbage dropped her glass of stout. He was all ready to set about James with his fists . . . would have, if Alfred hadn't come in. I think James was quite relieved. He's not much of a man, between you, me and the gatepost . . . a bit like one of them clinging vines I always think. What Celia sees in him . . . but there, everyone to their own taste . . . sew these buttons on again will you, me duck?' handing a padded multicoloured waistcoat to Frances.

Around them the hum of theatre life began to grow. The door kept opening and actors and actresses leaned in asking for new boot laces, the loan of a bit of jewellery, or to collect freshly washed fleshings. Frances was nodding and smiling, returning greetings as if she had been part of the theatre for months. She hunted for red ribbons in Rosie's 'Bits' box and gave a nervous-looking supernumerary her mended skirt. In the scarce unoccupied moments she longed to wander round the theatre and learn where everything was, absorbing the sight and sound and smell of it all. After the abortive months of playing hack melodrama in draughty barns, she had at last been accepted into the life of a real theatre; even if it was by the back door. The strange feeling of bursting joy haunted by the fear it might all come to nothing, must be the same that John experienced when she gave him his first reading lesson. But there was no time to go exploring. More last minute repairs were given to her, and then it was time to go down with Rosie and Lizzie into the wings and hang costume changes on the rail, and see that all the props were in place, ready for the performance. The odour of size and dust greeted them, and the hot sickly smell from the new gas jets, one on stage, another in the wings.

'Ever so bright and shiny they are, me duck. Don't know as if I like them as much as candlelight . . . not so romantic, if you take my meaning, but there's a brilliance and you can do ever so many clever things with coloured glass slides in front . . . and the lime stick burns a treat.' Rosie was puffing and sweating as she worked . . . and talking, all the time talking! Grit came ambling up and pushed his wet nose into her hand. 'Go on you dafty ... it's a good job I don't have to find costumes for him. A couple of swift brushes with the theatre broom is all he needs.'

Frances edged towards the stage. A dog-eared script lay on a table close to one of the scenery flats. A little further and she had a clear view of the stage with the shadowy auditorium beyond. She had an impression of curved galleries decorated with flying cherubs and acanthus leaves, as the flickering light from the stage glinted on gilt paint. In the pit below, dark lines of empty benches breathed anticipation across the dead footlights. There was a heightened air of expectancy as people hurried about doing last minute jobs. Another half-hour would see the doors open and the house fill with noise and excitement. The stage itself was dressed for action; the flats already pushed into place along grooves which stretched across the boards like inverted railway tracks. Above Frances' head corresponding grooves were cut into wooden beams. A small wiry youth came on stage carrying a bush painted on a flat board, which he propped in front of a square trap door in the corner, close to the curtain. There were other traps, she noticed, at least three, including one of very curious shape made from triangular sections, the apex of each meeting at a central point. As she was about to move away there was a sudden rumble, the triangular flaps snapped back and the body of a man streaked several feet into the air, landing with a grace surprising in such a large person. Before Frances had recovered from her astonishment, the man knelt beside the trap and pulled up one of the flaps which had closed behind him.

'That's cured the star trap, Charlie. Just a bit more soap on the pulley for smooth running, then I want you to check the left corner trap.'

He stood up, a long oddly-proportioned man, dressed from head to toe in a tight-fitting black costume that emphasized his big-boned frame and gave his sallow black-moustached face a satanic air. Frances backed into the shadows as he left the stage and passed between two flats into the wings.

'Oh, Mr Bowstock, can you spare a minute?'

The man paused, frowning, then seeing Rosie his expression turned to a broad smile. He came across and slapped her bottom. 'Do anything for you, love, but make it sharp. I've got a man chewing his fingernails to the quick in my office, waiting for me to sort out some financial tangle. Think I'm a mathematical genius, these tradespeople.' He gave a mock groan, slapping the back of his hand on his forehead.

Rosie introduced Frances and Lizzie, explaining their plight and their hopes. He immediately assumed the cool matter-of-fact character of manager. 'Enough supernumeraries . . . parts all filled . . . next season perhaps . . . or even when they toured the circuit in the summer season . . . meanwhile if Rosie could do with the help he would pay them five shillings a week . . .'

It was a convincing performance. Frances saw that this was his real self, though with actors it was always difficult to tell when they were being themselves. She wondered if she was beginning to be like them. Papa was fond of telling her she was a self-opinionated minx. But it wasn't true. Underneath the mask of brusque arrogance, she hid the vulnerable part of herself which bruised as easily as moth wings. What else could she do but put on a bold front? Only with John had she been able to reveal a little of her real thoughts and desires. She felt a passing twist of pain for this lost friendship which took the edge off her pleasure at the offer of a job. Then there was no time at all to think of anything but carrying out instructions, putting last minute stitches into costumes. It was a whirl of buttons and hooks, painted faces, last minute panics as a string broke or someone could not find a slipper. Voices were pitched ever higher and higher until the musicians, unnoticed as they slipped into their pit, struck up a few rasping chords and burst into a polka.

'Sh . . . sh . . .'

Frances could hear the audience like an animal waiting to be fed. The curtains were down. Actors hurried to their positions, pulling at their fleshings, adjusting bodices and breeches. The prompter sat with the script issuing last minute instructions. A climactic chord from the band – full blast! The curtains were scooped to the top of the proscenium arch and the many-throated animal roared its pleasure.

7

ALFRED BOWSTOCK ROLLED THE ENDS OF HIS moustache between thumb and forefinger and tried a disarming smile.

'It's a most sympathetic role, m'dear ... and with your sensitive approach you will be able to make a little jewel of the part.'

'No!' Celia said firmly.

'And the costume ... great possibilities in that for those clever personal touches which you do so well.'

'No!'

'Rosie and you together can achieve great things ... great things.'

'No!'

'The tag ... Robert will change the script I'm sure, so that you can round off the play and be the centre of a final tableau.'

Robert looked anything but pleased by the bland way Alfred was altering his play. 'I really don't see ...' he began frostily.

Celia turned on him. 'I daresay you don't. You wrote the trashy thing and you deliberately omitted to write in a proper part for me. It's spite, that's what it is ... sheer pique! Ever since I got more curtain calls than you did that time in "Maria Marten", you've had it in for me. Don't deny it!'

'I wouldn't dream of contradicting you at any time, madame!' Robert said crisply.

Two spots of red burned on Celia's rounded cheeks. 'Don't start getting at me or I'll tell all I know about the way you carry on.'

James Sullivan, absorbed in his own thoughts until that moment, came out of the clouds and frowned at her. 'What do you mean "Carry on"? Carry on with whom ... you?'

'If he was it might be a more fruitful union. I've waited long enough for grandchildren,' said Celia's father.

'Now for it,' Lizzie whispered to Frances. 'Hackles up and claws out. Old devil . . . sitting there like a white-haired apple dumpling as if butter wouldn't melt in his mouth! I do declare he's going to make it even worse!'

Grimsby was leaning towards Mrs Burbage, apparently looking at her script, his nose polished to a red glow by endless glasses of porter. Pitching his voice to carry, he added:

'He's not a man, he's a great bag of wind blowing off his own praises!'

'Father!' Even Celia was outraged, and Mrs Burbage examined her script with intense care.

They were gathered in the greenroom of the Queen's for a reading of Robert Welkin's new play 'Castle of the Owls'. At this rate, Frances thought irritably, they weren't going to get further than allotting the various parts, and even that seemed doomed to failure. Celia was a little blonde bitch and why James kept up these bursts of jealousy when he ignored her the rest of the time, Frances could not understand.

'Grimsby's a trouble maker,' Lizzie whispered. 'He's the one that's jealous if you ask me.'

'Of his own daughter?'

'Who else?'

Frances sighed. It was all such trivial nonsense and such a waste of time. They were still bickering and looked as if they would go on for some time. Across the room she could see Kit Cox building a house of playing cards to amuse young Bradley. There was more sense in doing that than arguing. Kit looked up, caught her eye and grinned wryly. Frances smiled back, thinking how much he reminded her of Len, with his cheerfulness and wit. She missed Len. It disturbed her to think she might never see him again, or any of the old company for that matter. There was something rootless about theatre life that left her feeling unsteady, as if the ground was made from constantly shifting sand.

'Come now . . .' Alfred was trying to cajole everyone in order to calm the tension.

But Celia, once started, was away on a waterfall of words that splashed and rushed around the company, threatening to drown any-one foolish enough to try and cut in. Frances wondered if it was ever going to stop. Alice Douglass was working herself up to a dogmatic pronouncement, spreading like a ship in full sail into the centre of the room.

'Are you going to allow such petty trifles to stand in the way of our work, Mr Bowstock? We've been here now for at least half an hour and all we've heard is a selfish bandying of unimportant emotionalism. The play's the thing, not this slipshod stumbling over the worn carpeting of certain people's private affairs. I've been in the theatre now for a good many years and I'm not one to throw my great experience into everyone's face, but on this occasion it would seem that someone has to make a stand.'

'Mrs Douglass . . . please!' Alfred waved his hands up and down in a gesture that suggested she ought to sit down.

'It's no good trying to placate,' she trumpeted. 'Gone is all reason. The time has come for plain speaking . . .'

She was well into her Heavy Woman role now, spilling words as liberally as Celia. Frances had a sudden picture of John laboriously writing on his slate. He respected words and never flung them about in the careless way Alice and Celia did. Odd that she should be constantly reminded of him these past eight weeks at the Queen's. More than she had been for months and months. What would he be doing at this moment? Probably working over some part of a locomotive with great care and efficiency, steadily learning his trade, while she sat and listened to ludicrous statements that had nothing at all to do with acting. There were times, of course, when learning was painfully fast, like that dreadful occasion in Evesham. The ghost of that fiasco was still enough to make her shudder.

Alice had reached a crescendo, which included acid comments about married couples who were too prone to air their matrimonial difficulties in public, so shaming themselves and showing up their inadequacies.

'No one asked for your opinion, you old cow!' Celia shrieked, and Frances was back in the seedy greenroom.

Alice turned, an injured duchess. Her brown eyes opened wide, her very hair seemed alive with indignation. She poured her talents into the part of Juno insulted. 'Never been spoken to in such a way . . . going to stand here and . . . Mr Bowstock, are you allowing this trumped up bit of . . .'

Alfred Bowstock lost his temper. 'I've had enough,' he bellowed. 'SHUT UP!'

The silence that followed was almost painful in its completeness. Even Alfred's poise was slightly shaken. He cleared his throat and adjusted the stock round his neck. 'I've come to a decision,' he said in tones laced with enough severity to prevent argument. 'As Mrs Sullivan is so adamant about refusing the part of "Millicent", I withdraw from the battlefield and offer it instead to Miss Redmayne.'

If the silence had been complete before, it was stunned now. Even Lizzie's jaw dropped. Frances' wavering concentration was walloped into attention. She must have misheard! It was barely two weeks since she and Lizzie had been accepted as more than backstage skivvies. Three Walking Lady parts, one as a village maiden, two as part of crowd scenes . . . and now she was being presented with the Juvenile Lead. Celia might consider it no more than a minor part, but she, Frances, was overwhelmed.

'Well?' Alfred Bowstock was looking at her quizzically.

'Thank you . . . very much. I . . . I'd like to play "Millicent",' said Frances in the voice of a stranger.

A babble of protest broke out with the voices of Celia and James high in complaint. Alfred ignored them.

'Good, that's settled then!'

Robert Welkin crossed to Frances and bent over her with a sly smile. 'I'm delighted . . . delighted. You will do the part more than justice. To be frank, I had you in mind all the time. Mrs Sullivan needs a jolt. Her performances have been a trifle dull of late.'

Frances caught Celia's look full of malice and hatred, and knew she had heard every word. A chill of apprehension filled her. She knew enough about the close-knit life of the stock company to understand that her good fortune would not be allowed to pass without attack.

'Now then ladies and gentlemen, that leaves three more parts unspoken for . . .' Alfred thumbed through the script. ' "Patty", you Miss Masters. Plenty of comedy there, suit your talents . . . "Grider", Kit Cox. A lovely scene in Act Two, Mr Cox. Scope for your tumbling ability . . . more of that when we rehearse.'

Somehow they got through it all with Celia sitting in martyred silence beside her husband, as if she were Saint Joan at the stake.

'Do her good, blown up little baggage,' Mrs Burbage whispered, after they had skimmed through the play and were moving away. She tucked the script under her arm and patted Frances' hand. 'There may be some spitefulness beforehand, but when it comes to the performance you'll be all right.'

Nell Hampton was the only other one to remain undisturbed. In her usual placid way she smiled at Frances as she folded her darning. 'Don't worry. It's all a storm in a teacup.'

'Alf's set them by the ears this time,' Lizzie said and grinned.

Alfred came over to them. 'Word perfect by Friday,' he said.

'You do go on!' Lizzie giggled, looking at him from beneath her eyelashes.

Partially absorbed in her script, Frances realized Lizzie was flirting again, and frowned. It was an intrusion. She wanted to get away somewhere on her own to study the part and to bring some coherence into her feelings. There was an emptiness inside her that she could not seem to fill. With a mumbled excuse, she slipped from the room and, collecting her cloak, ran out of the theatre towards the lodgings she shared with Rosie and Lizzie.

*   *   *

Standing in the wings, Frances tried desperately to still the madly fluttering butterflies in her stomach which kept rising up her throat and threatening to choke her. Between the flats she had a narrow view onto the lighted stage. She could see Charlie Hampton's shoulders bowed over the prompt script and her stomach turned over. Nell ('Helen' in the play) was already on stage in a frilled white nightgown, sitting in front of a dressing table, brushing her long blonde wig. The cue was coming. A few more words and gestures and she would hear her name called.

'Millicent!'

She had been concentrating so hard, listening for her cue, that now it had arrived she couldn't remember a single line. Oh God, what was it she had to say? Rosie was pressing something into her hands . . . a bunch of paper flowers. That was it . . . the flowers . . . present the flowers.

Coming out of the workaday wings into stage brilliance, Frances hurried a few steps, paused to arrange the flowers and sniff their scent, then held them out with a smile.

'For you, Miss Helen. A messenger brought them not ten minutes since.'

Behind her, in the back grooves, were the painted flats of a gloomy castle interior. A draped bed stood upstage left with an ottoman at its foot and a thick rug beside. The dressing table stood right centre stage. Footlights hissed steadily; a wall of light that blotted out those eager faces in the audience. 'Helen' stood up at 'Millicent's' words and came forward, arms outstretched, smiling. Frances felt the burden of anxiety fall away as the character of 'Millicent' stole her identity.

'Millicent' busied herself preparing the bed for her mistress, turning back the coverlet, a pause to exchange confidences, then more stage business, and all without flaw. Coming out into the wings, Frances saw Lizzie's pert face with the crooked grin.

'You're doing a treat, love. Keep it up . . . just fix these tapes for me, will you? I'm on in a tick.'

Frances dealt with the tapes in a dream, trying to line her real self beside the assumed character of 'Millicent'. It was something she had yet to master. Time and again she had watched the actors leave the stage laughing and gay to switch into curses about the way their shoes pinched, or else come off weeping to crack a joke with Rosie or Ma Shakespeare waiting to help them change costume. Frances had time now for the butterflies to take hold as she waited for her next cue. Lizzie was on, the words streaming out in cracked cockney. Audience laughter drifted over the footlights and into the wings. Kit had joined Lizzie and was flirting with her. She inched up her skirt and aimed a kick at his ankles: he tumbled and rolled to delighted clapping.

'Don't miss the cue,' James Sullivan said, pushing Frances aside and positioning himself for his entrance.

Frances was furious. The whole week had been full of nasty remarks and spiteful acts. Her new fleshings disappeared and a pair full of holes substituted; her hare's foot vanished and she had to make do with a rag to put on her powder, until it reappeared in Rosie's 'Bits' box several days later . . . now this! He thought she would be late on stage, did he? Her mouth tightened. She would show him!

Charlie Hampton's mate and a casual hired help were in charge of scenery and were pushing forward half of a scene change behind the cover of gauze mists and dimmed lighting. Not long now before 'Millicent's' first exchange with her lover 'Harry'. The forest scene was in place. Tree wings slid forward. The ghost would rise through a trap behind the gauze.

Kate was fluttering about like an agitated moth, asking everyone if they had seen a letter she had mislaid, describing it with vague gestures. As if it mattered *now*! Robert was saying something . . . 'A little more carmine, you look pale.' Well she felt pale. Pale green! If they didn't leave her alone she would be sick. She had to go closer. James was well into the soliloquy over his painful lot, waving his arms as if he were demented. Every time it was different. There was no proper cue, just a pause and a sharp watch for his beckoning hand. There! A shorter time than she remembered, but perhaps that was her nervous state.

Frances ran between the flats. She saw James pause mid-speech. Oh God, she had mistimed her entrance! She had come on too soon. Sweating with horror, she looked at James. No help there! The glance he gave her was so barbed and venomous, she longed to sink through one of the traps into the dark underworld of stage machinery. But it wasn't her fault, it was his ever changing signals! For a suspended moment she could not move.

'Hark! A sound in the bushes . . .' invented James, jabbing towards the floor with his finger.

She crouched, listening to him slide back into the lines. Her real cue came and she stole between the bushes. But the illusion was lost for the whole scene. Even the ghost looked damp and depressed, rising through a swirl of mist.

'Can't you do anything right?' James snarled, following her into the wings. 'Flaming little amateur!'

'If your movements were more precise it might help,' Robert Welkin retorted in her defence.

'My movements? I did enough to signal a bleedin' army forwards from two miles away.'

'The flapping of a dying bat!'

'That's right . . . fight for your little protégée. She might pay you with a couple of kisses if you ever melt the iceberg round her. She's a . . .'

'Hold your tongues, can't you! The whole house can hear you.' Alfred Bowstock loomed over them, his black moustache bristling threats.

There was no time for injured feelings. Battered but determined, Frances ploughed into the second scene. Footsore and weary after their long trek through the forest, Hero 'Peter', 'Millicent' and Lover 'Harry' emerged and turned towards the castle which stood in all its ancient splendour: massive portcullis below grey stone walls, supporting two turrets on either side the parapet; one a sturdy construction with conical roof and flag flying, the other . . . a galleon in full sail?

James swore under his breath. 'That bloody halfwit . . . he's used the wrong flat that side!'

' 'E's gone to sea,' shouted a voice from the audience, and there was a burst of laughter. 'Where's yer sailor's 'at, Pete?'

Frances could see Robert quivering with suppressed rage, but he managed his lines through catcalls and the rumble of the flat being changed. Inwardly she thought it would have been much better to leave it there and ignore the whole thing. She went through the motions of sinking down exhausted against a mossy bank, trying to put over 'Millicent's' despair.

'Sh . . . give 'er a chance,' a woman's voice called.

'Sh . . . sh . . .'

The theatre quietened, then a cheer went up for 'Helen' the heroine, followed by booing as 'Helen's' father pursued her through the bushes.

'At last I have caught you,' Grimsby boomed, stumbling over the the wedge of wood supporting a bush and almost falling into Frances' lap.

The smell of porter hit her full blast as he launched into his speech:

'You ungrateful unnatural child! The scourge of your ageing father.' He raised imploring arms to the heavens. 'My life is withering . . . blighted by your treachery.'

The silly old fool thought she was 'Helen'. It was that last drink in the wings before his entrance that had pushed him over the edge. Frances raised herself on one elbow, every nerve tense.

'Sir, I am but the maid, Millicent,' she interrupted.

'You wants to look over by the tree, dad . . . first on the right past the log . . . don't trip over yer feet!'

Grimsby swung round, hunting for Nell. 'Aha . . . there you are, madam . . .'

The audience was getting into its stride: 'Have a nut and get yer strength back!' A handful of shells rattled onto the stage.

It was chaos. A living jangling nightmare! Frances strove to make a real performance of her part without being able to lose herself, and swung between tears and hysterical laughter. As the actors moved to and from the stage in a hectic bustle, sprinkling the air with curt references to anything round which they could curl their tongues, there was time for nothing except the bare bones of routine. Underneath the busy surface of costume change and listening for cues, Frances was aware of seething weighted despair, ready to spring up and consume her as soon as the play was over.

The last scene had begun. Rosie gave Frances the metal-studded box which she had to carry on stage. It supposedly held papers referring to the hero's birth, parentage and other resolving matters. Charlie had passed on his prompter's job to Alice Douglass because he could not trust anyone else to control the gas lights or the limelight for the storm. His mate was up in the roof, already sending the first metal ball down the thunder run. Charlie was creating a splendid lightning effect. Frances listened hard. Whatever happened, she was not going to mistime her entrance again!

Alfred was poised centre stage, halfway through a speech: '. . . and the proof of it all I have told you lies in this box!' A wave of his arm towards the wings.

That was it! Frances swept on stage, her long skirt flicking out with the movement of her body. The exterior of the castle had been replaced by flats representing a gloomy hall, with stairs curving from the right. Passing the stairs she felt a tug at her skirt and twisted in reaction. The actors were waiting, so was the audience. She grabbed a handful of skirt and pulled.

'. . . this box which you see before you,' stalled Alfred.

'What's up?' Nell whispered from behind her fan.

'A nail . . . I'm hooked on a nail!' Frances tugged and succeeded only in becoming more securely trapped.

'Aha . . . the box . . . I see it now . . . all will be resolved.' Alfred was ad libbing frantically.

Frances thought of keeping on walking and risk ripping her skirt, but the nail had clawed into her petticoats with such firmness she would have had to put down the box and wrestle with both hands to have any effect. It was Kit Cox who saved her. With one of his comic skips and a wink at the audience, he crossed the stage, took the box and, with a flourishing bow, offered it to the waiting 'Earl'. Under cover of all the movement involved in working out the conclusion of the play, Frances was able to bend down and wriggle herself free of the nail. For all the havoc, the audience seemed well pleased. Under much clapping and whistling, the cast bowed and bowed again. Frances and Robert, hand-in-hand, were given a special ovation, but she could not recapture any of the elation she had experienced during that first attempt at a leading role in Tom Vaughan's company.

Afterwards her deep despair had to be restrained still further because she had promised to wait in the wings to help Lizzie in her next act. There were two quick changes of costume. Rosie had to be in the other wings at the time and Lizzie said she wouldn't trust anyone except Frances to hook up her bodice quick enough. She could see Lizzie on stage; the provocative swing of her hips; the fluttering eyelashes . . . warbling towards a chorus:

> '*I . . . told . . . him . . .*
> *Courting down below stairs*
> *Or flirting in the street,*
> *He'd never find a wench with airs*
> *Or ankles half so neat.*'

A twist of her body and she had her back to the audience, skirts whisked up enough to show the length of her elegant legs encased in the high buttoned boots of Italian kid that she prized more highly than anything else she possessed. In spite of the vulgarity of her songs, she knew just how to put them over to summon cheers and clapping from an audience. Frances listened for it, the fresh bodice ready in her hands, waiting for Lizzie to come off stage. Hurry, Lizzie, please hurry, she was begging inside. But Lizzie seemed to be lingering over her acknowledgements. And then she was off, panting and swearing as she struggled to get her sweating arms into the long sleeves of the bodice. With a brief: 'Thanks, love,' she was back on stage and Frances was free to run and hide in the dressing room, and indulge in a waterfall of tears.

She wept for the tumbled wreckage that had been tonight's play, for her own crushed illusions about being an actress and, dropping further into nostalgic self-pity, she wept for the loss of her old comfortable life, her father, and above all the image of her talented actress mother whom she had betrayed by her own inadequacies. In her despair she felt trapped by everything and in particular her own ambition to become a star. When Lizzie came into the dressing-room she was still hiccuping automatic sobs.

'Lord, what a sight you look, love! Don't take on so. I've seen many a worse hash than that. Why you quite took their hearts out there in the audience. Clapped you fit to bust . . . and an admirer waiting outside right now.'

'Oh no . . . tell her to go away. I can't see anybody,' Frances snuffled into her handkerchief.

'Him, not her, and he says he must see you . . . it's very important.'

'No . . . no, I can't!' Frances raised her head, her face smeared with the ruins of carmine and lamp black. The door of the dressing-room was half open and as she turned on her stool she saw a figure standing diffidently half in, half out of the room. He was a familiar stranger, boy turned man, in a neat dark suit that was quite unlike the rough country clothes she remembered.

'John!' she said, with such a multitude of emotions rushing in from all sides she did not know whether to push past him and run away down the corridor, or fling her arms round his neck and hug him.

She did neither, but stood up and offered him her shaking hand.

Lizzie, after one shrewd look, collected her belongings, said how pleased she was to meet Mr Gate when Frances introduced them, then tactfully withdrew, leaving John and Frances alone.

8 'IT'S GOOD TO SEE YOU, MISS FRANCES,' JOHN SAID, clasping and unclasping his large hands, which Frances noticed were well scrubbed but stained with black on the pads of his fingers and thumbs.

'You too,' she replied, made ill at ease by his formality. 'Please won't you sit down? I have to take off this make-up. It's all run ... such a mess. I should have done it before, but ...'

He interrupted her nervous chatter: 'You've been crying!'

'Oh!' she said and sat down abruptly at the dressing table, putting her hands over her ravaged face. 'The play was awful ... awful!'

'It was nothing of the sort. Don't you say any such thing! I've been out there and seen for myself. We clapped, didn't we? And whistled!' He was almost scolding her in his anxiety to cheer her up.

She knew he was wrong. It had been a bad performance, but the rush of warmth she felt, made her look up and smile. He smiled back and the time separating them shrank and vanished as if it had never been. She caught hold of his hands, repeating with emphasis:

'It is good to see you.'

For a second the reserve that had been in his expression even when he smiled, fell away. What she thought she saw recalled vividly that marvellous frightening moment when they had been discovered together in the hut by one of the villagers out poaching. Clinging to John for protection she had torn away the covering over his true feelings and surprised the same devotion in his eyes that she recognized now. She stiffened only a fraction, but it was enough to bring back the screen. With mixed feelings she tightened her hold on his hands, striving to keep the balance from slipping back into awkwardness.

'Tell me how you came to be here? What brought you to Warfield? Is Mr Hartlipp here too? Heavens! I hope not or he will tell Papa and then . . .' She looked so appalled that he had to reassure her.

'Don't worry so. Mr Hartlipp won't tell Squire. I'll see to that.'

Squire! She had almost forgotten that title. It seemed like years and years since she was living at Thrushton. There was so much she wanted to know.

'Mr Hartlipp is here in Warfield, but he didn't come to the theatre. He's dining with a gentleman . . . the one we came to see on business. I was to have gone too, but I asked leave to be excused. I'd seen the playbill with your name on it, so what could I do but come?'

She felt better already, seeing him sitting on the stool Lizzie used. Amid all the squalid ruins of this terrible night he was the one hopeful thing that had happened. A rock in a storm.

She began greasing her face with pomatum, interspersing apologies with questions about his work, his sister Polly, his parents and a host of other things until he began to laugh and shake his head:

'Stop . . . stop!'

She looked at him in surprise. 'What's the matter?'

'You haven't changed one little bit. You're just as demanding as ever!'

'And you are just as much of a comfort.'

'Am I?' A touch of colour came into his cheeks and she realized that his freckled weathered skin had paled; the jaw line was more clear cut; the neck thicker, and though his untidy straw hair was the same and the deep-set blue eyes, he was taller and more close packed. With a little stab of doubt, she realized he had grown up. There were changes in both of them in spite of his words; not all surface changes. Inside herself she knew that the brash arrogant girl of two years ago had been hammered into someone she had yet to discover. Whatever her final identity, it would be a humbler, more sensitive one. Good things did come out of depression and defeat: greater understanding of other people. And if it hadn't been for John, she concluded, she would still be wallowing in self-pity instead of considering deeper things.

'You've stopped me from being a complete fool, and that is a real help. My nose is still blocked up and I daresay it will be another half-hour before my eyes stop being puffy, but at least I've come to my senses. Now while I finish taking off all this mess, tell me the news, starting with your work.' As she talked, Frances without thinking began to unhook the bodice of her dress, so that she could remove all the make-up from her neck.

'Perhaps I ought to . . .' John stood up.

'Oh!' She had forgotten conventional modesty. 'What must you think of me! Look, I won't bother changing for a minute. It's just that I wanted to wash because I feel so sticky.'

'I could wait outside,' he offered. 'Have you had any supper? Perhaps we could have something to eat at a tavern, though I don't suppose . . .'

'That's a splendid idea. I'm used to taverns by now. Don't look shocked. I'll tell you all about it while we eat.

* * *

'So there we were, stranded! No money, no company, no prospects! And on top of everything else I had a fever. If it hadn't been for Lizzie, I don't know what would have become of me. It was the worst Christmas I've ever experienced,' Frances said.

John put down his fork and looked at her across the deal table with great concern. 'Whatever did you do?'

Frances smiled, seeing the familiar lines develop at the corners of his mouth. She explained how Lizzie had worked and cared for her, and how Clara Woodlock had turned out to be far more kind-hearted than anyone had suspected, and how they had raised the money for the coach fare by selling the gold chain from her locket.

They were sitting in the Pheasant, a small tavern not two hundred yards from the theatre, eating a welcome meal of mutton and roast potatoes, with porter to wash it down. Frances discovered she was ravenous. She had eaten hardly anything since breakfast because of the tension of waiting for the performance. She filled her mouth again, relishing the food and the warmth coming from a great log fire in the open hearth.

'I'll say this for you, Miss Frances, you've a tough spirit. Reckon Squire never guessed how much. It makes me fair cold to think of all the risks you took and how things might have turned out.'

'Well they didn't,' she said sharply, pricked by conscience at the mention of her father. 'Though you could say tonight's flop was hardly a turn for the better. But that's enough of me. Tell me about your doings.'

'That's a big order,' he said, smiling. 'Where should I begin?'

'With the day you left to go north when it was raining and I only just managed to get to Thrushton Halt in time to wave good-bye. You were allowed in the first-class compartment then.'

'Only because I was travelling with Mr Hartlipp. A rare treat I can tell you! Me decked out in Sunday best with shoes that pinched.' The smile broadened. 'It was fair murder . . . but I forgot the discomfort when you came. What were pinching shoes compared with the thought that I wouldn't be seeing you again for a long time . . . perhaps never.' He looked down at his plate as if he wanted to hide whatever feeling showed in his eyes. 'That was a great day, though,' he owned. 'Travelling all the way to Lancashire and me never having gone further than the ten miles into Molesbridge before. Train and coach the whole day long, and all the days after so strange. The works . . . crammed with such machinery it were like . . . like . . . what can I say?' He appealed to her.

'I know,' she said softly. 'Dreams coming true. Like living outside real life . . . afraid that you'll wake up and find it *is* only a dream.'

He was looking at her again. 'It were a marvel. I never knew life could be full of so much pleasure. Learning all about them great locomotives, studying till I knew every part, working the metal, using the forge to heat it white hot, beating out with the hammer, bringing the skill into me fingertips.' He looked down at his stained hands, then added ruefully: 'And the dirt!'

They laughed together, and it was like being back in the Thrushton days. She was riding again through lush Worcestershire countryside where buttercups sprinkled the grassland with gold stars and John was working first in the cornfields and then in the smoky candlelit hut, crouching over his books and slate, grave and contained, then laughing and talking with her; the warmth of his presence colouring her with lasting contentment. All those times, those moments of companionship and she had never once recognized them for what they were! How could she have been so blind? But perhaps it was not so much blind as the ignorance of a green girl. The hard life of a strolling player had scraped off her thick-skinned preoccupation with herself like an old coat of paint. Her mind was opening.

'It's something to be proud of,' she said impulsively. 'A badge of all you've achieved. In fact if anything is a marvel it's you. Not every illiterate farmer's boy could have got as far as you . . . or boys born into opportunity either.'

The colour rose in his face. 'I owe it all to you,' he said, obviously moved.

'A little,' she admitted. 'But definitely not all.'

'You took so much trouble and such risks meeting me, bringing books and spending hours and hours over spellings and numbers and maps and . . .'

She was laughing again, experiencing the old friendship in a way that dispelled the last shadows of gloom left over from the night's chaotic performance.

'. . . helping me read about railway engineering and roadmaking and bridge building.' He went on with the list. 'A wonder it were! D'you know I sometimes used to nip meself real hard when I was out in the fields hoeing or some such thing, just to see if I would wake up. And when I walked over to the common and saw the old hut like silver in the moonlight, I'd tell meself not to be a fool . . . that I'd dreamed it all up and the hut would be empty.'

'But it wasn't.'

'No, it wasn't.' He was silent for a moment. 'If Squire had sent me to prison, it 'ud still have been worth every minute.'

'Oh, but he never would have done that. After all, you hadn't done anything really wrong.'

'He thought I was one of them that fired the navvy camp,' he reminded her. 'He'd have been within his rights to put me behind bars. He didn't have to believe my story that I was trying to put out the fire, not start it.'

The fact that he left unspoken the revelation of his love, which happened on the same night as the fire, left her relieved and yet disappointed. He must have thought about it, but he could be embarrassed by the memory if his feelings had altered.

'It were long ago and it's as if it were today,' he said. 'In spite of all between . . . Lancashire and now Birmingham.'

'Birmingham?'

'Of course, you don't know that part. Mr Hartlipp's bought a partnership in a much larger firm in Birmingham, owned by a Mr Cowper-Donkin. It's more in the manufacturing line on a large scale . . . bigger workshop and better equipment. It's in the Soho district too, not far from Boulton and Watt's.'

Not wanting to betray her lamentable ignorance she said: 'That must be very convenient.'

'Oh it is!'

Was there a hint of dry humour? Hurriedly she turned the conversation asking about Polly, and discovered that she was married at last to her faithful Wilf and was expecting her first baby.

'She'm plump as a piglet, Wilf an' all. You'd scarce recognize him, he looks that content, with a belly on him that near matches her'n . . . or that's what I tell him. It ent true of course. He'm just pleasantly rounded.'

She could not help laughing. John looked at her, puzzled. 'Now what have I said?'

But she could not explain that her laughter had been triggered by his broad speech. To say so would come as an insult and that was not what she wanted at all. Try as she would to compose her face, her lips kept on trembling, letting out the suppressed mirth. She had not enjoyed herself so much for months. There was something a little alarming in recognizing the fact, suggesting that she was finding theatre life a disappointment.

'And your father, has he forgiven you?' she asked.

'Not me, nor Joe when he came back from America. You'd think a man would welcome his first-born after a journey like that.' John sounded bitter. 'Wouldn't so much as let either of us set foot in the cottage. Weren't so bad for me. I'd only gone to support Joe; besides I had me work waiting.'

'And what did Joe do?' Frances' curiosity was roused over this reappearance of the brother she had never seen.

'Came back to Birmingham with me. He's been at the work-shop ever since, but he ent too happy. The land's what he were born for, not machines. We'm about different as chalk and cheese that way.'

A chill wind blew in cooling their happiness. Frances thought sombrely that they were both loaded with the burden of fathers who opposed them. 'Your father and mine are the same in one respect,' she said. 'They'd like to wipe us out of their lives.'

'Dad maybe, but not Squire. You'm fooling yourself if that's what you think. Since you ran off he's aged. Polly says he walks like a man carrying a great weight.' Course the village folk don't have his confidence, but you know how gossip goes round. Everyone knew he'd had the Peelers after you in London. It's a wonder you slipped through their fingers, though I daresay it's a big place. I've not seen him. Since he told me to keep away I've only been back the once, but from what I've learned I'd say the opposite. You'm more in his thoughts than you ever were before.'

The mood was changing. A steadily rising tide of muddled emotions threatened to drown her altogether. She looked at John, wondering if change was in him too. Did he really love her? It seemed unlikely, in spite of that earlier moment in the dressing-room. As for her feelings for him . . . it was impossible to determine their nature. The whole day had been a series of shocks, leaving her in a turmoil. In a bid for stability she asked him to tell her in detail about his work and what special things he was engaged in doing at present. It was an inspired question. For half an hour she did not have to say a single word. She felt slightly demented, sitting there, part of her listening as John progressed to technical details about smoke boxes and brake systems, while the other part swirled and eddied with a rich mixture of restlessness and random uneasy happiness. She must have looked dazed because he began apologizing.

'I'm sorry! Once I get started on braking systems there's no stopping me. You must be in a right confusion.'

'I'm not,' she said indignantly. 'Perhaps some of the details are above my head, but I understand the principles. You are experimenting with brakes for locomotives, because you think that carriage brakes aren't sufficient.' She smiled triumphantly. 'Am I right?'

'Absolutely!'

'I wish I could see you at work. After all, you've seen me at mine, so even if your experiment were to fail while I watch, it can't possibly be any worse than the dreadful mess I made.'

He leaned across the table. 'Could you come? It would be a pleasure to show you round the workshop.'

She caught some of his eagerness. 'On Sunday . . . no, there's no coach. Monday then . . . no, I'd never be back in time for the performance.' She gave a great sigh. 'See how I'm placed!'

'Like most working folk. They've no time to call their own.'

She had never thought of it like that before. It gave her a curious feeling of fellowship with the ordinary people around her, here in the tavern. She looked at them through the smoky haze and then back at John. He had done it again; given her another foundation stone to shore up her unsteady castle in the air.

'In a couple of weeks there will be a small break. Only two days. Mr Bowstock has to go to London on business in preparation for the circuit tour, and he's said we can close the theatre Monday night and open again on Tuesday. Monday never has much in the way of takings.'

'In two weeks then?'

'Two weeks.'

Birmingham and back in that jolting coach all in a day. The thought made her bones protest, but the pleasure stamped on John's face was worth the prospect. Besides, she felt like a change of scene.

*   *   *

'Very good to see you again, Miss Lizzie,' John said, gravely offering his hand.

'She is to be measured for a new pair of boots,' Frances hastened to say. 'So we thought it a chance to travel to Birmingham together.' She hoped he would accept the explanation which was basically true. 'We can go to the shoemaker's first and then to your workshop.'

'There's no need to trail after me,' said Lizzie.

'Nonsense! How would you find your way to the workshop on your own? You might get lost and spend the day in Birmingham's back streets,' Frances said firmly.

Lizzie was astonished. 'What do you take me for? I've travelled up and down England and know London's ways like the back of me hand. Do you think I can't make head nor tail of a small place like Birmingham?'

'It's not small and you haven't been here before, except passing through as a traveller, so don't argue!'

Frances knew she was not being honest with either of them. When Lizzie had talked about buying boots, it seemed obvious that they should travel to Birmingham together. Lizzie was determined to have the best she could order and the shoemaker in Warfield was not good enough. At first, Frances agreed, then felt doubtful about leaving Lizzie on her own. It seemed unkind and she suggested that Lizzie might like to visit John's workshop. After *that* she felt worse, as John was expecting her on her own. The only solution was to put on a bold front and sweep everyone along with her.

'It's no trouble,' John was saying in his usual obliging way. 'Mr Hartlipp's given me a couple of hours off on condition I make them up at night . . . seeing it's a special occasion. So there's plenty of time. We can go by omnibus to the workshop. There's one that travels close to the bottom of the street.'

They found a shoemaker's not far from New Street who could have the boots ready in one week and promised to send them by carrier for very little extra charge.

'White kid,' Lizzie said dreamily as they climbed into the omnibus. 'It's what I've always longed for . . . with mother o' pearl buttons.'

They trundled through streets cluttered with workshops and factories that made everything from buttons, jewellery and toys to components for sewing machines and every kind of heavy engine, even complete locomotives. At last John stood up. They had arrived at the junction of two roads and climbed from the dank smells of the omnibus into sharp March air tainted with the odour of smoke belching from a tall chimney at the top of the street. The workshop lay behind two high wooden gates about halfway along. John pushed open a smaller door cut into one gate. Coming through into a yard paved with blue bricks, Frances and Lizzie were confronted by a large building made of red brick and corrugated iron that resembled a warehouse. John spoke to the gatekeeper, who nodded and smiled. A few men came and went, throwing them curious glances.

'Mr Hartlipp said he'd be glad to see you,' John said as he led the way across the yard.

All the implications fell into place like lead weights, pulling Frances down into an icy sea of anxiety. Mr Hartlipp knew she was coming . . . knew, presumably, that she was working at the Queen's Theatre, Warfield. He also knew Papa well. She was betrayed! There was nothing she could do to escape from Papa when he came to take her from the theatre. But John had said Mr Hartlipp would not say anything of her whereabouts, and she trusted John. On the other hand, was Mr Hartlipp to be depended upon? He might have feelings of responsibility towards Papa rather than her. She was back again amongst the boiling realities of living which made her feel so helpless.

'Through there!' John pointed to tall double doors, one of which stood open, allowing a cacophony of clanging iron, rumbling machinery and sporadic shouts to spread out into the yard. Inside the building the noise increased and a blast of hot air met them from two hooded forges at the far end. Under the skylights, heavy beams hung with a complex of chains and pulleys to help in lifting the weightier machine parts. Along the outside wall, large windows lit work benches, which to Frances's inexperienced eye seemed to be piled high with a confusion of metal pieces, though the tools were carefully arranged in racks. There must have been at least a dozen workmen in caps, shirt sleeves and leather aprons, their hands blackened with grease, bent over benches or hauling machinery along the length of the shop. Over it all hung the powerful smell of oil and hot metal.

'That's the metal casting shop through there.' John raised his voice and pointed to a doorway on the left. 'You'll see where the pattern making goes on when I takes you to see Mr Hartlipp. But before we go, there's someone I'd like you to meet.' He stopped at a bench where a man was working with his back to them, and put a hand on his shoulder. 'Joe!'

Frances looked at him with great interest. It was John and yet it was not. He was smaller and more stocky, with a broader face that had less intensity of expression. But when he smiled the likeness became marked.

'This is Miss Frances Redmayne, Joe . . . and Miss Lizzie Masters.'

Joe was obviously embarrassed and Frances did her best to be friendly and unpretentious, knowing the gulf of social position that still separated them. Although he had been away in America all the time she lived in Thrushton, in his eyes she was still Squire's daughter, a strange remote being who had no place in his private world. His discomfort spread to include John and herself, but Lizzie seemed blithely unaware of any tension and saved the situation by showing a great interest in Joe's work and getting him to describe exactly what he was doing.

'Come and see my famous brakes,' John said to Frances, and skirted a trolley stacked with long metal strips, picking the way least littered with swarf for her sake. Workmen grinned and winked as they passed. Frances smiled back tentatively, feeling none of the fellowship she had in the tavern. Yet she was a worker too . . . an entertainer. Surely her profession was equally taxing if totally different from the work here? It was a new concept. Ever since he had first entered her life John had opened doors into worlds she had known existed but never understood.

He had stopped by another bench which had beside it a locomotive wheel, roughly two feet in diameter, resting on a wooden rail. The wheel was supported by an axle and a system of chains, connecting rods and levers which in turn were driven by an experimental steam engine. A metal device, looking rather like two clamps, clasped the wheel. John began explaining how the experiment was to work, pointing out the various parts with his capable hands.

Lizzie joined them. 'My, that looks impressive,' she said. 'However do you remember what everything is for?'

'However do you remember all the words you have to learn?' he replied with deceptive seriousness.

'Can you show us how it works?' Frances asked, half expecting him to pull a lever and set the whole thing in motion there and then.

He shook his head. 'Not at present, but if you'd like to stay on for a while when I'm working, I shall be trying it out then.'

'Of course I would.'

John patted the wheel gently, affectionately, at the same time frowning.

'What's wrong?' Lizzie asked.

'Difficult to say as yet . . . but I reckon there'll be too much sway. Can't tell finally until it's tried on a proper locomotive, but there's something not quite . . .' He bent over the wheel and for a moment seemed lost in contemplation.

Frances observed him with a suppressed smile. He certainly hadn't changed where his work was concerned. She remembered the way he used to pore over books and slate with the same frowning concentration that held him now.

'What's a pattern shop?' she asked, to remind him of her existence.

He seemed to return from a distance and straightened up with an embarrassed smile. 'The pattern shop . . . it's where new metal parts are first carved out in wood so that moulds can be taken from them, ready to pour in the molten metal. Skilled work it is . . . real craftsmen the fellers that work in there.' He had begun walking away from his bench as he talked and led them out into a small corridor. Through a half open door Frances saw a man carving a piece of wood clamped to a bench, his movements precise and delicate.

'We won't go in, he doesn't take kindly to interruptions,' John said. He led the way to a second door and knocked.

'Come in!'

Frances' heart contracted at the familiar voice. They entered a small room with rough wooden walls lit by a single sash window and furnished austerely with a sloping desk, two stools, a series of shelves and a small stove. A tall man in a peacock-blue waistcoat, cambric shirt and well pressed trousers, turned to face them. Frances saw that the abundant hair and mutton chop whiskers were greyer than she remembered, but Mr Hartlipp's mode of dress had not changed. Even without his coat he was as dapper as ever.

'Frances, my dear! What a pleasure this is. And how well you look.

Your father will be relieved to know you are in good health.' Mr Hartlipp grasped her hand in both of his.

Frances looked at him in dismay. 'Oh please . . . you mustn't tell him where I am.'

'Why ever not? John did tell me you were apprehensive, so I waited until I could speak with you, but you must know that your father was deeply upset by your flight.' He looked at her with a touch of disapproval. 'A letter would have done much to relieve his anxiety.'

'But if he finds out where I am he will come and take me home.' Even as she spoke, Frances wondered if it was the truth. Papa might very well not want her home. Actresses were hardly candidates for polite upper class society. But he might do something equally drastic that would drag her away from the theatre; a prospect she did not relish. She wanted to explain in depth how she felt, but the words would not come. This meeting was in danger of becoming another situation over which she had no control. She must have appealed to John with her eyes because he said:

'I think Frances would rather tell him herself, when she feels ready.'

She felt grateful, realizing he had explained to her the way things should be. The previous idea of never having anything more to do with her father was wrong. But any reconciliation must come in her own good time. She caught sight of Lizzie hovering in the doorway, waiting to be introduced, and turned, glad of the diversion. In the middle of all the handshaking and smiles, a small stout man in a light grey suit came in. He beamed at them, his cheeks and nose like Victoria plums.

'Mr Cowper-Donkin,' said Mr Hartlipp, and the introductions began all over again with a concoction of words about the weather, the latest addition to the royal family, the fantastic boom in railway shares and a few oblique remarks about the interesting occupation of acting, which could be taken in more than one way, and drew a peppering of giggles from Lizzie.

'Don't mistake me, m'dears. I'm a devotee of the theatre. And to show you I mean every word and don't subscribe one jot to the nonsensical gossip that surrounds actresses, I have arranged for my housekeeper to prepare you a meal, which I hope you both and James too, will do me the honour of partaking. I'd ask you as well, Gate, but I know you have work waiting.' He wheezed out the words and dissolved into a powerful fit of coughing which made the veins stand out on his forehead.

Frances was undecided about the invitation. On the one hand she was here at John's request, while on the other she had a curious longing to learn more news of her father. The food was another attraction. It was such a long time since she had indulged in the luxury of a well-cooked meal.

Mr Cowper-Donkin was pulling out a large silk handkerchief from his pocket to muffle the spasm. 'It's me tubes, m'dears. Lost their stretch . . . got slack in old age. Can't be sure, but that's what my medical friend tells me. Country air, he says . . . get away from the smoky town, he says, and you'll be cured. I've not had time to test that theory yet, but I daresay I'll be driven to it. Time was when I'd no more swallow the town than think of taking a trip to Persia . . . country born and bred. Father a miller over Cheadle way in Cheshire. But there you are . . . I got the iron disease like our young friend here, and it's been with me ever since.' He paused, mopping his perspiring face, then added: 'Well what do you say to a nice morsel of pheasant washed down with some fine madeira?'

'That is very kind. I'm sure we would be delighted,' Frances began, and then felt uncomfortable at having committed herself. This brought a backwash of irritation. Why should she feel awkward? It was a kind thought on Mr Cowper-Donkin's part and he had been at some pains and expense to provide the meal. It would be rude to refuse. Besides, judging by her observation of John's immediate and total absorption in his work, it would make little difference whether she was there or not.

'You don't mind, do you, John,' she added, expecting him to be gravely agreeable, and was confronted instead with blank restraint.

'Good . . . good . . .' Mr Cowper-Donkin was obviously delighted. 'There is just one small matter I have to deal with before we go. You will excuse me?' He turned to Mr Hartlipp. 'James . . . show me these new track chairs . . .'

The two men went out and left Frances, Lizzie and John standing in a shifting silence, which John shattered by saying:

'I'd best be getting back to my work.'

Frances allowed her private guilt to turn into resentment at this abrupt termination of her visit.

'Oh, your work ... nothing must hinder that!' The echo of her former self flashed out before she could catch the frosty words.

Lizzie eyed them both and quietly went to see more of Joe at work.

Frances was raging inside. She knew she was in the wrong, one glance at the shuttered expression on John's face told her how wrong, but pride would not allow her to apologize.

'I don't know whether there will be time after luncheon to see your invention at work,' she went on, making matters worse.

'It doesn't matter.'

Now he was being martyred. 'Of course it matters,' she said in a snapping voice.

'Don't concern yourself, Miss Frances.'

It was the 'Miss' that did it. With anger already building up, his retreat behind the barrier of class came like a slap in the face. It stung as no angry words could. She was furious to a degree that was out of all proportion to the trifling matter that had been the root cause. It was a speck, she thought fiercely, a nothing and he had made it a mountain. The temptation to make his mental slap a physical one in return was so strong she had to fight herself to control it and in doing so felt hot tears rise. She was caught in a spiral of expanding anger that grew because of its very stupidity.

'Don't let me keep you,' she said tightly. Then, thinking it would be humiliating to be left alone in the drawing office, added: 'I'll walk along with you and find Lizzie.'

They left the drawing office in silence. As they reached John's bench Mr Cowper-Donkin and Mr Hartlipp were there with Lizzie. Mr Cowper-Donkin smiled, waiting for Frances to join them. She hesitated, already experiencing a cooling shame. The prospect that she might have closed their friendship, threatened the future. In an attempt to bring things back to normality she said:

'Thank you for showing me round.'

'It were nothing.'

She felt rebuffed at this offhand reply and with her stormy anger still shrinking, wondered where the close understanding that had flowered between them at the theatre had gone. He could not possibly have read her mind and she was sure she had managed to conceal most of her feelings.

'Will you be visiting the theatre again?' she asked.

'It's hard to tell. I've a lot of work on hand and not much leisure!'

'Good-bye then, for the present.' Frances offered her hand.

He took it and for a moment there was more than formal contact. Then he let go and she hurried out of the door into the yard feeling utterly confused.

'He's a well set up feller,' Lizzie murmured as Frances joined them by the gates.

'Who . . . John?'

Lizzie giggled. 'Plain to see where your heart lies,' she said. 'I mean that Joe.'

'What rubbish you do talk,' Frances replied tartly and put her hand through Mr Hartlipp's proffered arm.

9

'LACE ME UP, FRANCES!'

Lizzie hung onto the brass rails of the bed they shared in the cheap lodgings in Cheltenham. It was the end of the summer circuit which had taken them from Warfield across to Hereford and the Welsh Border and then back to Cheltenham for the final three weeks. It had been an up and down tour that left Frances sceptical about her future. But today she felt happier than she had for some time because they were returning to Warfield by the first coach, and she realized with some surprise that she was looking forward to being back at the Queen's. She wriggled the tapes of Lizzie's stays and pulled.

'Go on . . . tighter!'

'It's not healthy. You'll make yourself faint,' said Frances, seeing the whalebone mark the thin flesh and Lizzie's small breasts rise and bulge.

'Oh don't talk silly!' Lizzie turned to appraise herself in the spotted mirror over the washstand. 'Another quarter of an inch and I'll be satisfied.'

Frances sighed and tugged again, tying a secure knot.

'Old straight-lace!' Lizzie said affectionately. She pulled on her stockings, stroking her legs. 'There's nowt like a good pair o' legs to catch the men.' The north country accent sat oddly on her cockney tongue. Seeing Frances' disapproving face, she laughed. 'Well you have to please the men or where would you be?'

Frances turned her back, not wanting to betray the depths of her disapproval. It was not the first time she had come up against Lizzie's cynicism.

'You're a dreamer, love,' Lizzie went on, well aware of Frances' reaction. 'I've got me feet planted on the ground. Good luck to you, I say, but I like to have me meals regular and you can't always be sure of that in our profession.' She began pulling on her long boots, polishing them lovingly with the ball of her thumb. 'Did I ever tell you me Dad was a saddler?'

Frances shook her head, only partially listening.

'Came from Yorkshire. Met Ma when she came with the lakers, that's what they call strolling players in those parts. Fell head over heels in love and walked all the way to London looking for her. It was her legs that did it . . . so he used to say. Augustus . . . Masters . . . father . . . of . . . the . . . celebrated . . . Elizabeth . . . liked . . . a . . . good . . . leg!' She spoke in an assumed bass voice, a word for each button as she hooked them through. 'How's that for a handle? Course he was never called anything but Gus.' She smiled brightly, sweeping away Frances' annoyances.

In the coach, wedged between Nell Hampton and Charlotte, Frances felt her pleasure at the thought of returning to Warfield growing stronger, though the mood of disillusion that had hung around her all summer showed little sign of budging. She looked round the coach; Lizzie and Alfred side by side; Rosie, hat knocked over her eyes, snoring, with Grit lying warm on her feet. At least they were getting a respite from the never ending quarrels that bounced Celia between husband and father . . . they were travelling by the later coach. Kit Cox, on the other side of Bradley, began rattling with laughter.

'Heard this one?' he asked. 'An Englishman, an Irishman and a Scotsman were walking through a wood. The Englishman turns to the Irishman and asks . . .'

She had heard and didn't want to listen. In spite of her improved spirits, a dreadful echo of those fears that had been her constant companion in Tom Vaughan's company, crouched like a cat ready to spring. She wanted peace from all these doubts. Something or someone who was unchanging. A picture of John came into her mind and swung away. Since her visit to Birmingham the rift in their friendship had remained. She had not seen him again. Mr Cowper-Donkin had accompanied Lizzie and herself to the Warfield coach with jovial courtesy, and there had been no opportunity to put things right. The summer circuit had intervened . . . four long months of aching silence.

Laughter cracked into her thoughts. Laughter over Kit's joke. Laughter in which she had no share. It was appalling, this feeling of living all the time on the outside. Solitary freedom that was worse than any prison. Cold comfort remembering how she had thought of the Seminary as a gaol worse than anything in the world. She knew better now. Prisons were places made by your own inadequacies. Sometimes she thought she was beginning to lose her reason. There was nothing but muddle in her head, that tormented her with unaccountable longings for things she could not identify. The only escape came when she shed herself by taking on the personality of the character she played. Even then the black shadow hovered, waiting for her in the wings.

Rosie snorted in her sleep and came to, yawning. Light rain began pattering on the coach windows.

'Oo, me pore feet . . . raining is it? Get orf you great lump?' Rosie heaved at Grit. 'Can always tell when there's a change in the weather . . . me bunions give me gyp. Won't please the farmers, getting rain at harvest time.'

And if the harvest was poor the money would not be about, so there would be less spent on entertainment. The season looked off to a bad start.

'I've been thinking,' Alfred said. 'About the pantomime . . .'

'Putting on your skates a bit, aren't you?' Lizzie ribbed him. 'That's four months away.'

He was not to be put off. 'Planning! That's the essence of a well run theatre. Panto needs a deal of planning . . . all those costumes. Rosie knows, don't you, love?'

'I do that,' said Rosie with feeling. 'Plenty of sewing for me and everyone else.'

'I heard they are putting on one called "Guy, Earl of Warwick" at Birmingham,' Alfred continued. 'Knights and chivalry, plenty of opportunity there for ambitious scenes. I can imagine a battle in the snow with white flakes falling and blood dripping red on the ground . . . through the left corner trap comes the Good Fairy and in a twinkling all turns to a summer's day with flowers blooming, sunlight reflected on cottage windows and a chorus of village maids dancing round the Maypole . . . but all is not well . . . thunder rolls, lightning flashes and through the star trap shoots the Demon King himself . . .'

'But you're talking about the Birmingham panto . . . what about ours?' Lizzie reminded him.

'I've started writing one round the Sleeping Beauty. Seems to me it's got all the vital ingredients for a successful panto; Prince and Princess; castle surrounded by thorns; ... a great contrast with the village scenes. The Prince could be disguised at first; a village boy who had been stolen at birth by a wicked witch ... that's good. I like that.' He searched in the pocket of his frock coat and produced paper and pencil, making notes.

'You could play Prince and I'll be Princess,' said Lizzie.

Frances wished she wouldn't flirt so much. Regular meals couldn't be worth such a game!

Alfred slid his arm back round Lizzie. 'Now I ask you, do I look like a hero?' He twirled his black moustache with his free hand.

'If you ask *me* ...' began Lizzie, then dissolved into squeaks as her ribs were tickled.

Frances went back into her mind and shut the door. Outside, under the lowering skies a few harvesters were hurrying to complete hay stooks before the rain came down too hard. The uneven road shook the coach and her body ached with tiredness. How many miles to Warfield? She searched for landmarks and was rewarded with the sight of a spire which she recognized as that belonging to St Mary's Church on the outskirts of the town. Rosie yawned again, sat up and began to straighten her hat, stabbing with long black hatpins. Mud roads changed to cobbles with a metallic rattle of coach wheels. Frances put up a silent prayer of gratitude that she had not been compelled to wait for the next coach. She would have time to unpack before gathering at the theatre for a play-reading.

Scattered houses crowded to include shops and offices. They passed the horse racing track and were in sight of the Goat and Compasses where she and Lizzie had first arrived destitute but hopeful. She inched forward, preparing to leave as the coach turned into the inn yard jerking to a sudden halt that threw them against one another. In the bustle to get out Frances trod on Grit's tail, making him yelp and scoot for the door almost knocking Rosie's feet from under her. She would have fallen but for John standing there. He caught her and propped her up again.

Frances' heart began thundering so loudly she felt sure everyone must be able to hear it. Looking at John she could not speak because the same unpredictable organ seemed to have taken up lodging somewhere in her throat. He took her bag from the coachman and put a hand under her elbow.

'Hello, Frances,' he said, as if meeting her off a stagecoach was an everyday occurrence and the troubled Birmingham visit had never happened. There was a touch of cold water about the greeting which put her heart back where it belonged.

'You do seem like a jack-in-the-box, springing up at the most surprising times,' she managed to say.

'I came with the carrier. We had a cartload of rails to deliver. The railway is coming to Warfield, did you know that?'

She shook her head, afraid to ask if that was the only reason for his visit. The answer might not be the one she hoped for . . . that he had manœuvred the trip just to meet her. What an extraordinarily calm person he was!

'I shall be coming now and again,' John said casually. 'Mr Hartlipp wants me to follow through the whole procedure of track laying. Of course I know the navvying side like the back of me hand, but I've been helping with the survey this summer, while you were away.'

'That's splendid, John,' she said, trying to bring sense into her fast disappearing wits. 'And how is Joe?'

'Did I hear someone mention Joe?' Lizzie had left the coach and coming up to them, gave John's hand a hearty shake. 'He's a broth of a man.' She pinched Frances' cheek. 'Almost as handsome as your beau.'

Frances could have kicked her. She felt colour flame in her face and for the life of her could think of nothing that would smooth over the gaff. She risked a fleeting glance at John, who looked unperturbed. Lizzie had skipped away and was chattering with Kit Cox as if nothing had happened.

'She's a terror,' Frances said. 'Takes first prize for stirring other people's puddings just for the fun of it.'

'Lizzie's a good sort,' John said with surprising warmth. 'Our Joe thought her a stunner.'

Walking back towards Frances' lodgings they exchanged words about John's work, Joe's uneasy place in the workshop, Frances' circuit tour and a hundred other ordinary things, always edging round the brink of their unspoken quarrel. She had the strong feeling he was waiting for her to say or do something, but because she was so unsure of herself she held back, wanting to preserve the brittle friendliness which was the only bond she could recognize.

They reached the lodging house tucked into a narrow street behind the theatre. All the time they had walked through fine rain not noticing, but now it began to fall more heavily.

'I'll have to go in, John. I wish we could talk more, but Alfred wants us at the theatre this evening and I have to unpack.'

'I see.' John turned up his coat collar. The rain had flattened his yellow hair and was running down his nose. He brushed it away with the back of his hand. 'Good-bye then. I'll be in Warfield again from time to time.'

She could not let him go without a word about their misunderstanding and her own ridiculous anger, and yet the very fact he had bothered to meet her must mean everything was all right. Perhaps it was better to leave spoken apologies unsaid. As she gave him her hand the first clear idea of the day came into her head. She would have preferred to give him an affectionate hug. He shook hands gravely. And there was nothing more to do except unpack, so she went in and closed the door.

*   *   *

John had been right. As the autumn weeks passed, browning the trees through shades of liquid gold and orange, railway workings gashed the quiet pastureland, branching from the London to Birmingham route, on its way to Warfield and beyond. A little flurry of interest stirred the back rooms of the theatre. The same tales about the navvies were spun and embroidered like those Frances had heard in Thrushton. But they remained remote. No burned hayricks, no barren cows, not even a brawl was reported. An occasional appearance in the town was all anyone saw of these rowdy men or their tattered women and children. For Frances the biggest impact of the excavations was John's regular visits to Warfield. He never missed seeing her if it were only for a brief few minutes. Once they spent a whole gleaming afternoon walking in the leafy lanes, talking and talking. But for the most part ties of theatre and the railway made the meetings short. Frances openly recognized how much she had come to rely on these visits. There was nothing dramatic about them, no revelations, just a steady strengthening of regard on her side and quiet friendliness on his. Of his deeper feelings she knew nothing and began to wonder if the love he had confessed for her back in Thrushton days, had disappeared or declined into dependable friendship. That moment when she had been so sure, misted with doubt as the weeks lengthened into one month, two ... and then it was December and Christmas Eve.

'Oh for God's sake, can't you get it right?' Alfred wiped his sweating forehead and ran easing fingers round the neck of his shirt. 'Miss Redmayne, surely you know about not masking another actor? I asked you to lead the chorus round the *back* of Mr Sullivan, not in front. We can't have all you buxom beauties cutting out the view of the "Prince", even if he is behaving more like a Wandering Willie than anything else. More fire, Mr Sullivan ... passion ... intensity. Get back in the wings and try again. The village maids can remain off stage I think. Now then, Mr Jerrold, *if* you please ...'

Frances with the village maidens and James retreated to the wings prompt side, and Grimsby took up his original position in a dwarfish crouch.

'Who dares to storm my Beauty's Bower?
None but a Prince may at any hour
Come within four feet
of her bed,
Or else his puny life he forfeit.'

Grimsby grated out the words and leapt from his stool with a harsh cackle of laughter, beckoning with crooked finger on crooked arm.

'Come then you creeping, peeping Tom
I'll coax and wheedle you ere long
And then impale on hedge of thorn
Till life and limb from you be torn.'

More harsh laughter as James walked through the open doorway of Charlie's carefully constructed castle wall, and tiptoed to the bed where Celia lay, hands crossed over innocent bosom in endless sleep. But before he reached her the muscles of her face quivered and she let out an enormous sneeze. Alfred ran despairing hands through his coxcomb hair. In the wings, waiting for her next cue, Frances sniggered nervously.

A dress rehearsal of the pantomime was an occasion rarely indulged. Most rehearsals were barren affairs with sketchy stage direction that leaned heavily on each actor's experience and a great deal of last-minute invention. But for this pantomime it was different. Alfred had put a lot of hard work and harder cash into the production. He was determined not to be cheated of triumph.

'Mrs Sullivan, can't you restrain yourself?' Formality abounded during working hours.

Celia raised herself on one elbow, felt feverishly for her handkerchief, sneezed again twice and looked at the actor-manager resentfully. 'I card helb havig such a bodstrous cold id the head!'

'Well for all our sakes may heaven preserve you from sneezing tomorrow! All right, we'll break now for ten minutes . . . time for one swig of gin but no more. I don't want you on stage like oiled herrings.'

Alice Douglass, Queen of the Night in shimmering black satin, her crown aglitter with black and silver spangles, stalked through the crowded wings sniffing contemptuously at the idea that anyone . . . ANYONE . . . should suggest she might take a drop too much.

'Her ladyship's feelings are hurt,' Charlie said to Frances, looking up from the prompt script.

'The gent says gin, so who am I to disobey!' Lizzie, in a feather-light ballerina skirt, opaque white face with exaggerated eyes, waved a bottle at Frances.

She would rather have had water, but accepted a quick swallow and was glad of the glow that it brought. Standing in the draughty wings on this icy afternoon had chilled her to the marrow.

'There's a nip in the air all right,' Kate Cumberland came in shivering. 'Oh, Frances . . . your admirer is round at the stage door.'

Brother more like, Frances thought. But she could not be depressed and ran from the wings along the frosty passage. John was standing just inside the door with Joe, who looked extremely uncomfortable, as if he were astounded to find himself in such extraordinary surroundings.

'We've come for Christmas,' John said with a grin as big as a half moon.

Frances was delighted but flustered. 'Where will you stay . . . when do you have to get back . . . Joe as well?'

'We're staying at the Pheasant for two days . . . starting work again after Boxing Day.'

'Splendid . . . splendid,' said Alfred, who overheard as he was passing. He stopped and slapped John on the shoulder. 'Join the party tonight. It's at the Pheasant . . . the more the merrier!' Christmas jollity beamed from him even when he switched to more practical mood with: 'Back on stage now everyone . . . time's up!'

'I'll have to go,' Frances said. 'You will come tonight, won't you? Joe too . . . or Lizzie will be disappointed,' she added with a spark of devilment.

Joe shuffled his feet and looked at his brother.

'We'll be there,' John said.

Frances was glad when the dragging rehearsal was over. In spite of the lengthy preparation things kept going wrong and Alfred became irritable again. It was a relief when they packed up and walked round to the Pheasant. John and Joe were already there, sitting by a roaring fire in the specially prepared room. Frances eyed the long table lavishly spread with food: a barrel of porter at one end. It was a far cry from last Christmas Eve and yet that had been celebrated too, with less abundance but as much enthusiasm. The room was thronging with actors, gabbling, laughing shrilly, spreading eloquent arms to the company. Sitting at the table beside John, Frances asked:

'Can you come to the first night of the pantomime?'

'I wouldn't miss it for the world . . . Joe neither.'

She was not sure if she was pleased or sorry. Secretly she had hoped that the next time he saw her act it would be in a more worthy role. But she could not remain uneasy for long. Wine and good food saw to that! As the evening wore on, faces grew flushed and laughter came in great gusts, blowing goodwill through the air to twine round them all.

'A song, Lizzie, give us a song . . . yes a song . . .' The request came from all sides. Alfred swung her, protesting, onto the table, clearing a space with a sweep of his arm, spilling cutlery and wine. A cheer

spiralled up with the pipe smoke. Lizzie, fluttering eyelashes like moths, smiling seductively began to drawl, leading to her well known chorus:
'I ... told ... him ...
Courting down below stairs ...'
They joined in, summoned by her hands: 'I ... told ... him ...'
Lizzie swept her skirts high, kicking in a froth of lace petticoat frills. Glancing at Joe, Frances saw open admiration in his face. She caught John's eye and realized he had seen as well. There was an exchange between them that spoke of their own relationship. With a tightening in her throat, Frances knew that if he understood, he would recognize as she did this minute, that she loved him. Or was it the wine loosening tightly controlled loneliness, to weave into their established friendship? Suddenly she wanted to be away from this noisy overheated room stuffed with sweating flesh. Her surging emotions made her almost faint.

'More ... more ...' Clapping for Lizzie; the cheers turning to shouts.

Lizzie was smiling, hands on hips, provocative. She winked at Alfred who needed little encouragement. With a whoop, he heaved himself onto the table, pulling her close with a smacking kiss. An OO of approval from the company.

'Give us a tune then and we'll give you a dance,' Alfred shouted, but he had overlooked the spilled wine. With a kick of one heel as a prelude he came down in the wet patch. His foot skidded across the table, racketing through the crockery with a truly alarming noise as he lost his balance, clutched at Lizzie and fell with a crash, pulling her on top of him.

People leapt up. Alice, who happened to be closest to the accident, lunged forward and grabbed Alfred by his coat collar, sliding an arm under his head for support. Lizzie was scrambling to her feet, none the worse after her first yell of alarm. But Alfred was less fortunate. He was groaning amid the ruins of the table.

'Ouch ... no, let go ... for God's sake, my ankle ...' He pushed off all help.

It was broken, so the doctor said after Kit Cox had fetched him. The wreckage had been cleared away and a subdued company lined the walls.

'Not badly so,' added the doctor with hard cheeriness. 'Just a small bone. A few weeks with your leg up and you'll be as right as ninepence.'

At that moment Alfred looked as though it would take a lot more than ninepence to make him right. With the swollen ankle strapped, he lay back in a chair, green and shaking. Nell gave him a glass of brandy provided by an anxious host. He took a gulp and his face warmed to white.

'My God, what about the pantomime . . . that damned trap!' he moaned.

Everyone knew he was thinking about the entrance he made as Demon King. He might be able to arrange his other sequences to exclude movement, but nothing could smother the physical effort of the rushing trap which must shoot him high to make him land hard on his damaged ankle.

Frances' mind raced, sliding through scenes, sorting, shuffling, working out times and entrances. 'I could do it for you,' she said. 'Not the Demon King . . . I couldn't be that . . . but a gnome, a hobgoblin, one of your minions.' No one actually scoffed and Alfred was looking at her blankly but not frowning. Gathering enthusiasm she rolled along: 'If you could be seated behind a gauze painted with flames, it would only need a careful light change to reveal you at the moment the goblin shoots through the trap.' She hoped her suggestion would be accepted in the spirit she intended, not wanting to push herself. It was the performance that mattered, not an individual player.

'Of course we don't have to have a star trap entrance at all.' Celia's voice cut the thick silence like a hot knife. It was an unfortunate bid.

'Of course there must be a star trap entrance! It's expected,' Alfred said, hoarse with pain. 'I like it . . . needs some careful polishing, but the basic idea is good. Charlie, could you work out the lighting and get the gauze painted in time?'

'It'll be ready if I have to work all night.'

'Good man . . . now if you don't mind, the party's over friends. Rehearsal Christmas afternoon, three o'clock sharp. Sorry (in answer to the groans), it can't be helped.' He was sweating now and Frances felt weighed down with pity and exasperation.

John put a hand on her shoulder. The first informal contact since they met in Warfield. 'Clever wench,' he said. And it was the best praise she had ever been given.

She pulled a face to cover her pleasure. 'So much for Christmas Day! I know just how it will be ... costume fittings, practising the trap entrance, working over the script. Good-bye plum pudding and roast goose!'

'No it isn't. I'll see you get your share if I have to serve it up backstage myself,' John assured her.

She smiled at him, watching the good-humoured lines crease round his eyes in response, and felt fierce love flare up. It was real after all, she thought with astonishment. Loneliness might have been the match that set it alight, but it had been built back in the country days and had secretly smouldered ever since.

'I'll see you home and then Joe and I'll bed down in the stable . . . it's all we can afford!' He looked at her anxiously. 'I hope everything will turn out all right? It's a wretched piece of luck.'

Wretched? It was miraculous! And then she remembered he was talking about Alfred's accident. Even that had acquired a bloom of stardust and raised excitement in her at the prospect of shooting through the trap. John had fetched her cloak and slipped it round her shoulders.

'Come on,' he said, and they left the Pheasant together.

10

'THAT SHOULD HOLD IT,' SAID ROSIE, SNAP-
ping off the cotton with her teeth. She stuck the
needle amongst the tucking on the bodice of her
dress and held out the costume she and Frances had
worked on all Christmas Day. It was contrived from a pair of fleshings
and an old long-sleeved vest belonging to Grimsby. Between them
Frances and Rosie had cut, darted and gusseted the vest into a second
skin, and dyed it and the fleshings black. Over all was stitched one
hundred black spangles which were intended to catch the stage lighting
in flashes of hellfire. Frances had also made a mask from two layers of
sugar paper covered with a piece of black satin and edged with tinsel.
With that and the tight-fitting black cap, she would be covered almost
from head to toe.

'Try it on, me duck.'

She looked at Rosie, hesitating.

'Down to your skin . . . I'll turn me back if you like.'

'It's not that,' said Frances, already in underbodice and cotton
drawers. 'It's so cold. Besides, if I take all my clothes off I shall flop
about. Goblins don't flop.'

'Here, we'll strap you with this ribbon. It's broad enough.'

It was a struggle getting into the costume; they had fitted it so well.

'I'll never have time to change,' Frances said despairingly. 'All those
village maiden petticoats and my underclothes to take off and then get
into this and rush under the stage . . . in six minutes!'

'If I make the opening in the back a bit longer . . . how about that?'

'But it will never be ready!' The theatre had already opened its
doors and the rustle of the audience seeped in with the draught.

'Don't panic, me duck. You've been grand all today. Tell you what
. . . if you wear the goblin costume under the village maiden clothes,

then all you'll have to do is strip off and add your cap and mask. It would be much quicker.'

'The black fleshings will show through the pink ones . . . oh, and I've not finished my make-up,' Frances said a tone higher, feeling panic rear up without knowing why. She always had butterflies beforehand, but never this awful fluttering void with her insides feeling as if they had melted.

'They'll be fine . . . try it!' Rosie said soothingly, helping her to roll them over her legs.

Lizzie came in, swinging a pair of black dancing slippers.

'Oh, you angel!' Frances said gratefully, feeling worse than ever. What else might she have overlooked?

'Your locket is too much of a lump,' Lizzie said.

It was true, but she did not want to take off the charm that watched over her performances. Reluctantly she untied the black velvet ribbon.

'Pretty, isn't it?' Rosie said, pocketing it, then tying the tapes of Frances' blouse.

The call boy was ringing his bell. Frances heard her name and hurried to take up her position in the wings. A roll of the drum and the band changed from the jogging overture to a blare of trumpets and a squeak from the clarinettist, who had caught Celia's cold, then slid into a gay country tune. The curtains rose taking Frances' stomach with them . . . and then she was on, dancing round the village street with the other half-dozen supernumeraries, clapping hands in rhythm, circling the stage several times and skipping back into the wings where she could hear Alfred growling curses as he hobbled behind the gauze hanging at the back of the stage.

Charlie's mate was holding the horse and pony ready for the Prince to ride across the stage with his young page following. The page was Frances, goblin in disguise. A last minute addition by Alfred who had hired them from a travelling circus act down on their luck. The pony was frisky and Frances soothed him with murmured nonsense.

'Come on, me duck, or you'll not be changed in time,' Rosie was calling.

Breeches this time, shirt and waistcoat. Hair tightly coiled under a feathered cap. Frances got onto the pony, feeling him quiver beneath her weight.

'Quiet, boy!' She patted his neck, thinking this would be the most curious ride of her life. A slow trot round the stage twice; alight; some conversation, then on again with a jump which was easy as the pony was small. James looked uncomfortable on his white horse, but managed well enough as they trotted out into the sparkling light. For a moment Frances thought the pony might object to the appreciative cheers of the audience, but he was a circus pony and only tossed his mane like a trouper.

More costume change; village maiden . . . and back again as page. She hoped fervently that the mask would be effective when the time came. No spare moments for elaborate make-up. A touch of antimony powder on her hare's foot would be all she could manage. The goblin part had swelled her lines considerably and she wanted to speak them well. What if she fell from the trap? Actors had been known to enter badly . . . lose their balance.

'Cheer up, love. You'll soon be dead,' Lizzie said, passing through on her way to the dressing-room. 'Got a bottle of madeira for after, just to celebrate.'

'I could do with some now,' Frances said fervently.

'I've heard of soused as a herring, but never soused as a goblin!'

'Fool!'

She was on again and the germinating ideas were smothered in the adventures of the Prince and the dreams of the Princess, caught in soap bubbles that winked and burst under a silver-blue light.

Back into the wings; Rosie waiting. The frantic job of removing skirt layers and peeling off fleshings made the sweat pour from her and she did not dare think about the effect on her make-up. Thank God for the mask! Narrow curved stairs took her into the underworld beneath the stage, where new-fangled gas had yet to penetrate. Candles in sconces drew flickering shadows between the cumbersome shapes of trap machinery, turning them into dancing ghouls stinking of mildew and tallow. Frances saw Charlie's mate, a wizened monkey, cap rakish on the back of his head, crouching over the lever that would release the counterweights of the star trap.

'Ready, miss?' His voice rasped out. He cocked his head on one side, listening for three blows from the Demon King's staff which was the prearranged signal.

Frances climbed onto the rigid platform slotted into grooves between four stout supporting posts. The counterweight chain with its descending row of iron balls hung from the pulley above her head. She looked up at the leather-hinged wooden flaps of the star trap, hoping that the bruise on top of her head, memento of the practise run, would be protected by the pad she had sewn into her cap.

Charlie's mate sniffed, rubbing a grease-blackened hand under his nose. Frances began to quake. What was the cause of the delay? Surely she had never had to wait this long in rehearsal? Perhaps Charlie had forgotten the fuse that would set off the blue fire which was to coincide with her entrance? No, he was perfect efficiency . . . most times . . . perhaps . . .

Three hollow blows! No time to jump off, though her legs were like junket and her stomach knotted and sour. No time at all!

Charlie's mate released the lever and with a tremendous jerk the platform shot towards the stage, fractionally slowing as each ball-weight came to rest on the floor below. In the split second before she rocketed through the trap, Frances saw again the unknown black clad figure shooting out onto the empty stage. The Demon King . . . Alfred Bowstock, kind and familiar . . . the company . . . herself. Out she catapulted through licking blue flames and acrid smoke; afire with a myriad glittering black stars. Behind her a wall of light; in front Prince and Princess, Dwarf and Queen of the Night, changing with all the artistry Charlie could muster as he faded frontal lights and brought up ones behind the gauze to reveal a truly devilish Demon King on his throne of hellflame.

Frances landed, neat as a wren, arms outstretched, and full-bellied cheers from the audience cocooned them all. Lost in the dream of it she spoke her lines, using deep notes that shivered into harsh goblin croaks:

'Here oh Master, King of Hell,
Summoned by your midnight knell,
Come I, Grumbler Grodwinkell,
Bringing singing charm and spell.'

There was more of that, and more. The pantomime spun its web of fantasy that enmeshed her by the sheer professional team work that was making a resounding success out of tinsel words and gossamer scenery.

A new dimension, she thought. And it had been there all the time!

She removed her mask before the dressing-room mirror, peeled off her cap and took out the hairpins, letting her bush of hair drop over her shoulders. To be so dull not to see what lay in front of her nose! But that was the queer thing ... she had always known that theatrical productions were the result of concerted effort, not a single star shining out in lone perfection. The difference was that what she had coldly known was now warm reality. The star trap had acted like a catalyst, changing the ordinary into something plain as the nose on her face, retaining everyday connections but completely altering her attitude. There was so much to be thought over and compared in the light of her new understanding, but as the dressing-room filled with gossiping supernumeraries she abandoned all idea of contemplation.

'Heard the news?' Lizzie said, coming in with a whirl of tarlatan.

Frances dragged herself away from lingering thoughts. 'What?'

'Mr Mercer Simpson was in the audience tonight. What do you think of that?'

Frances tried to look suitably impressed, but could not begin to imagine who he might be. Lizzie burst out laughing.

'Don't try me with your "Oh-fancy-that" act. Admit you don't know who he is!'

'I don't know,' said Frances obediently.

'Manager of the Theatre Royal, Birmingham!' said Lizzie in a voice that would have paid homage to royalty.

Frances was really impressed. Her pulses raced. 'Looking for talent?'

'Shouldn't think he's here for his health.'

They exchanged glances. The Theatre Royal, Birmingham ... the place that was a stepping-stone to greater things.

'Don't hope too much,' said Lizzie. 'But I thought you might like to know. Now where's that madeira? I feel like a kipper, dry and shrivelled. Are you coming to the party? Alf's laid it on at the Pheasant.'

Another party? Frances was reluctant. She wanted time to absorb her new vision, enriched by Mr Mercer Simpson's visit. And there was John. Before she could form an excuse, the call boy knocked and shouted through a crack:

'Gentleman to see Miss Redmayne. At the stage door.'

Frances's heart missed a beat. Was it the Birmingham manager? No, he wouldn't be just a 'Gentleman at the stage door'. It must be John.

She caught sight of her reflection. What a fright! Never mind, she would slip on her cloak and dash out for a few words before the tedious task of removing make-up and changing into day clothes. Someone had turned out the gas jet in the passageway. A futile stab at economy. A single light outside the dressing-room did little more than reveal movement at the far end. She ran over the bare wooden floor, calling:

'John, I'm so glad you are here. Did you enjoy . . .'

She stopped abruptly and the words dried on her tongue. The man who came to meet her out of the shadows bore no resemblance to John.

'Good evening, Fanny. So . . . I've run you to earth at last!'

She could not speak. She could not think. She could only stare in fear and disbelief.

'Well, have you nothing to say to me after all these long months?'

'Papa!' The name whispered from her sticky throat.

'I'm glad you recognize me. Had it not been for the sound of your voice, I would hardly have known *you*!' A ghost of a smile touched the gaunt face and pulled at heartstrings Frances would have gladly cut. Out of her first shock came another. How had he known where to find her? John would not betray her. Mr Hartlipp? But he had promised . . .

She stood like a stone, waiting to be told what to do. All the years of subservience walled round her.

'Are you well? I can't tell what lies under that mask of powder.'

'Yes, my health is . . . good. And yours?'

'Tolerable.'

A heavy silence fell between them. With a little trickle of surprise, Frances realized she was not going to be ordered about . . . not yet. She snatched at her wits.

'Forgive me, Papa. I wasn't expecting you or I would have . . .'

'Ah yes! This John . . . you thought I was he?' Sir Oliver interrupted. 'And who pray is John?'

'Just a friend,' she managed to croak out, terrified he would press for further explanations.

'I have a private room at the Goat and Compasses. Will you dine with me there?'

Astonishment on top of astonishment! To be asked instead of ordered! The novel idea that he felt obliged to feel his way instead of

resorting to curt direction, crossed her mind leaving a trail of mystifica-
tion that was wiped out by the alarming thought that any moment
now John would come in through the stage door. Whatever happened
she must not let him be confronted by her father. She was in enough
trouble without having to explain how she came to reopen her
association with the farm boy turned engineer.

'Of course. I will join you directly I've changed. Don't wait for me
here, it's too cold and you can see how long it will take me to remove
all this make-up!' She smiled tentatively.

'Very well. The innkeeper will show you to my room.' He was gone
with no pretence at niceties, leaving her with a churning stomach that
was worse than the panic she had felt before the show began.

She lingered for several minutes, unable to face the backchat of the
dressing-room and while she was still standing there the door opened
again.

'John!' In a flurry of gabbled words she told him about her father's
arrival and begged him to reassure her that he had not been the one to
tell where she was to be found.

'As if I would!' John looked at her with reproachful eyes.

'I didn't think you would . . . then Mr Hartlipp . . .' She left the
question in the air.

He shrugged. 'I wouldn't have believed . . .'

'I'll have to go. I'm so sorry. I was looking forward to our meeting.'
In the dim light it was difficult to read his expression. She wanted to see
real disappointment, anything that would tell her he cared as much as
she did, but it was impossible. She wanted to suggest tomorrow. There
would be time to meet before he had to catch the stagecoach for
Birmingham.

'Tomorrow then?' he asked, and she was delighted.

'Come round for me. I shall be up with the lark.' Who cared about
threatening trouble! She would not let Papa interfere. Somehow she
would gain this last single day of freedom. A bitter chill crept over her
as she recognized that by next week she might well be back in
Thrushton.

'Frances!' He had his hand on the door.

She paused, turning back. 'Yes?'

'I just wanted to say if you have to go back home . . . I . . .' Words seemed to desert him. He came back very quickly, put his hands on her shoulders, gently kissing her cheek, and was as quickly gone.

Overwhelmed, Frances stood in the passage, then with a skip of joy, ran away towards the wings where Charlie and his mate were striking the last flat. They were too occupied to notice her and she was glad. She wanted to savour this strange overflowing moment in silent solitude.

The stage was bare and almost dark. A couple of gas jets hissed. The sour sweet smell almost dominating the odour of size and dust and trailing scent memories left behind by the actors' sweat and make-up. She walked out onto the stage. The curtains were still raised and she stared into the dim auditorium which such a short time before had been teeming with life.

Every second since she set out all those months ago had been worthwhile. Not a single instant would she willingly relinquish; not even times of anguish and despair. John's kiss was the final drop in her cup of happiness. She hadn't been mistaken after all and the way she felt in return was an extraordinary explosive tranquil joy, with the theatre part of it all. She spread her arms wide as if to embrace an invisible audience. No longer an outsider, a foreigner fruitlessly struggling to find a niche; she belonged!

When the explosion came she was totally unprepared. The force of the blast flung her face down across the apron of the stage. Stunned and terror stricken, she rolled over trying to sit up, and saw a wall of flame stretching up into the flies. Her head was spinning and everywhere seemed blanketed in sickly choking smoke, making her cough and splutter. More flame and more; in front and behind. There was no view into the auditorium, no view anywhere. Fear clutched her. Dizzy and bewildered, she at last dragged herself to her feet. Which way to go? In the dense fog she ran in mortal terror anywhere to get away from the killer that surrounded her. She was in the wings. Less smoke there, but intense heat growing all the time, scorched through her costume. Time ceased. Tears streamed, blinding her eyes. Mucus poured from her tingling nose. She coughed and coughed again.

Oh God! How to get out? Someone was screaming above the roar of hungry flames. Footsteps running. The dense smoke thinned briefly revealing the small prop room which lay between wings and passage beyond. Through there! But before she could reach the door there was a rumble that grew to tremendous proportions as a roof beam gave way, crashing to the floor in a shower of needle-hot sparks. The whole theatre was a gigantic tinder-box. Ancient dry worm-eaten wood was perfect fodder for this enormous bonfire. In an extremity of terror she backed away and fled ... anywhere that took her away from the flaming flying wood.

She ran hard into a dark shape, banging her already painful head, which had the odd effect of scooping up the remains of her common sense. It was the door leading from the wings into the gallery behind the first tier of seats. She pulled it open, fanning the fire with this new draught and heard a fresh explosion which shot kaleidoscopic flames that darted singeing tongues at her body. She did not stop. The gallery stank of acrid smoke and burning rag. Wooden benches in the pit glowed and smouldered. She did not see. Her eyes were stinging so much she could not open them and stumbled along by the feel of the wooden wall, curving in a semicircle towards the double doors and merciful safety. So wrapped was she in animal self preservation she did not hear the running feet. Suddenly she felt herself caught and lifted. She flung her arms round the unseen neck, clinging for her life.

'Frances ... thank God!' Charlie said. 'I knew you was out on stage.'

He did not say more and she was past speech. In a swimming haze she clung, feeling cold frosty air bite her cheeks as Charlie ran into a blaring clamour of sound in the cobbled street.

'Who's missing?' A man's voice asked.

'Dunno ... Lizzie Masters I think ... maybe one of the supernumeraries,' Charlie said, lowering Frances onto the pavement where waiting arms prevented her from falling.

'A feller ran in to look for her.' The man's voice again.

Frances retched, coughed and retched again. Her head seemed filled with smoke. Dazed, she tried to open pain-racked eyes. Through a film of bleary tears she made out a seething mob of bodies who pushed and jostled round her, shouting, weeping, waving helpless arms at the terrible conflagration that bombarded them with heat.

'Where's the parish fire engine ... a bucket chain while we waits ... Kit ... where's Kit Cox?'

Frances rubbed futile hands over face and eyes, trying to take hold of herself. If only she had some water! Her mouth felt parched as a desert but any water was needed to try and put out the fire.

'Oh Frances, you're safe! We were so afraid . . .' Nell had pushed through the crowd and crouched down in the bedraggled remains of her queenly robes, hugging Frances to her in a frenzy of relief.

'Lizzie?' Frances managed to croak. 'Someone said she was still inside.'

Nell said nothing, but an agony of uncertainty communicated through her loving arms. Frances tried to struggle up.

'No . . . no . . . they're looking for her. There's nothing you can do.'

Frances felt a scream mount inside and fought to keep it from escaping. Before her horrified gaze the fire writhed and spread in monstrous hunger. Tongues of purple, orange, green and gold poked through every aperture wildly to burst and roll on beds of smoke. There seemed no end to its animal appetite. Slate, plaster, brick, wood, all were consumed. And somewhere in the heart of the furnace was Lizzie. The thought was unbearable. To have to sit helpless while Lizzie died the most ghastly death . . . no, she could not do it! She wrenched away from Nell with her remaining strength and tried to fight between tight packed bodies. In the distance a bell began clanging.

'Merciful Lord, it's the fire engine at last!' said a fat woman and burst into a flood of tears.

Hazy with shock, Frances did not recognize Rosie until she seized her arm.

'Fried to a cinder he was . . . fried to a cinder . . .'

'Rosie?'

'My Grit . . . they brought him out . . . fried to a cinder.'

Frances saw the staring red-rimmed eyes and heard the cry of distress as a distant echo. There was no room for anything in her mind but Lizzie. She had to find her. Angrily she threw off the clinging hands, pushing towards the scorching heat.

'Look out! The roof's falling!'

Screams burst from the watching mob. Frances felt herself lifted and swept away down the street, crushed ever tighter as the people squeezed together until she thought her ribs must surely snap. The bell clanged louder. The rumbling fire changed voice. In the crackling smoke-filled air the animal burst all bonds; its immense energy shooting flames fifty, a hundred feet towards the impartial stars.

Two snorting horses pulling the water pump, canvas hose coiled along one side, came down the street. Spittle frothed as they chewed on their bits, tossing nervous heads, but the driver steered them firmly through the crowd. Three other firemen were already amongst the people, pushing and urging:

'Make way . . . make way, or the whole street will be ablaze.'

To get through . . . how to get through? Frances glimpsed the alley leading down one side of the theatre, ablaze with light. No way there, even if she could reach it. Desperately she dug her elbows into her sides, trying to ease the pressure on her groaning ribs.

'Make way I say!' One of the firemen waved his hands angrily.

The crowd shifted and spread. Frances seized her chance, sliding, squeezing, twisting and turning eel-like through the mass. Away from the fire and down the street, past the cattle market and along the lane. She took the long way round that led her back to the rear of the theatre. A crowd here too, but thinner. Easy to slip through. Her head was swimming and she ran on legs she could not feel. A group of onlookers thickened into a second crowd; staring. What was in the centre? Scratching, elbowing, she strove to get there.

Lizzie lay on the ground, protected by a piece of sacking someone had spread over the cobbles. Frances shoved through, squatting beside her.

'Lizzie!' she begged, gazing at the pulpy face and blackened hair.

Lizzie opened terrible bloodshot eyes that flickered a moment's recognition. 'Never fancied the part of a . . . kipper,' she whispered, barely audible. 'Looking for you . . . tell you about the offer . . .' Her eyes rolled up.

Frances looked beseechingly into the face opposite her.

'Unconscious,' Alfred said. 'My poor gal . . . my poor gal!' Tears streamed down his grey smeary cheeks through his drooping moustache to drip onto his filthy shirt.

'Get her away from here,' Frances shouted. The scream she had held back would not be controlled. 'Get her away . . . away . . .'

Someone seized her by the shoulders and shook her roughly. 'For God's sake stop that racket! If you can't help then go away.'

Shocked out of hysteria, Frances stared blankly at Charlie's stern face. Queer how he seemed to be everywhere. In the smothering atmosphere coloured lights revolved before her eyes. The buzzing of a thousand bees hummed relentlessly, and for a single puzzling moment the scent of wet loam existed and was gone.

She did not fall. There were too many people huddled round. She knew nothing of lying on cobbles wet with muddy water, or being lifted and carried away from the stench and heat of the fire.

At the bottom of the street lit by flaring firelight, John Gate stopped abruptly.

'You?' The voice said, harsh and disbelieving. 'Give her to me!'

John looked at the Squire. 'She'm hurt,' he said. 'Let me pass.'

'Give her to me!'

'This ent the time for quarrels. I'm taking her back to her lodgings for sleep and care.' He walked forward.

Briefly they faced one another. Sir Oliver was the one to step aside. He did not remain, but followed in close attendance, the firelight playing over the ruts and hollows of his face, making an arid landscape; betraying nothing.

Part 3

1846

★ ★ ★

THE NEW WORLD

II THE SNOWFLAKES HAD SETTLED IN ARCS, TURNING the small square windowpanes into portholes that looked out onto a wedding cake street. Pale January sunshine reflected from the snow, illuminating the bedroom with a bright fresh light. From the ceiling a single cobweb undulated with every movement of air, waving high as the door opened and Frances came in. Under the white honeycomb quilt on the narrow bed Lizzie lay asleep. Even though four weeks had passed since the theatre had burned down, Frances could never look at the long dressing on the left side of Lizzie's face without a shudder. The horror of that night still visited her in terrifying nightmares. Her own lesser burns had healed, though her right hand was still tender with new pink skin across the palm. Her memories of the fire were fuzzy and she would have known nothing about being carried home by John if Rosie had not told her.

'Your dad with him an' all,' Rosie said. 'Ever so icy . . . never a word between them, and your dad's face! If looks could have killed, poor John would have been dead as a doornail.'

He might just as well have been dead if his absence was anything to go by. Sliding days and nights joined hands into a lengthening silence. Neither Rosie, Lizzie nor the landlady knew why, and Papa she dare not ask. Her own indifferent health and Lizzie's desperate state prevented her from travelling to Birmingham to see him and she found herself pining in a most humiliating way. She longed for John and was given instead the company of Papa, who payed for the lodgings, hired Rosie as nurse and smothered Frances with his frequent presence.

Lizzie stirred and opened hollow eyes underlined by black smudges. With skin stretched taut and yellow over evident bones, she was a thin shadow of her former self. But she was alive! Three weeks of intense fever had failed to kill Lizzie's unquenchable spirit.

'How are you today, Lizzie?'

Lizzie smiled faintly. 'Living . . . how's yourself?'

'All right.'

Rosie bustled in with a tray laden with breakfast. Gruel for Lizzie, a boiled egg, toast and tea for Frances.

'Your dear father was a heaven sent blessing,' Rosie said for the hundredth time. 'Where would we have been without his bounty?' She set down the tray on the small table beside Lizzie's bed. 'There's good news this morning. Nell Hampton dropped by with Charlotte . . . my how that child does grow. I declare she's half an inch taller since Christmas . . . anyway, Nell and Charlie have got a place in York with work for the kids as well. Isn't that grand?'

'Better than Birmingham, and that's saying something.' Lizzie looked at Frances. 'Not that I'm scoffing.'

'And what's more,' Rosie went on, 'she told me that Alfred's been in touch. He's trying to get another company together to play at a little theatre Northampton way that he's managed to lease. He's got spirit, I'll give him that! With all the scenery and props lost in the fire *and* every last penny gone in paying off debts, he still knows how to raise a loan to get started again! Course the Town Council were very reasonable. There's many a theatre owner would have had him in court for negligence, but there you are, I reckon he was just lucky it wasn't owned by one man. Not that it was his fault . . . all due to that nasty gas. Dangerous stuff if you ask me, and not half as romantic as candles and no one'll ever be able to convince me otherwise.'

'Now you've got two chances,' Lizzie said to Frances. 'Alf 'ud snap you up if you say the word. So if the Birmingham offer comes to nothing, you won't be out of work. Have you made up your mind yet?'

Frances shrugged. 'How can I?'

'I know!' Lizzie said. 'All this generous spending has got to be payed for.' She moved restlessly between the sheets. 'I'm that grateful, but . . . well if it weren't for me lying here like a rag doll, you wouldn't have so much to pay back.' Tears welled into her eyes.

Taking one view she was right. Frances knew that no money was expected in the tacit transaction between herself and her father. The debt would be payed when she was fit enough to travel by returning to Thrushton. She stood there, silent and miserable, unable to reassure Lizzie.

'Breakfast is what you both needs.' Rosie was ever practical. 'A warm lining to your stomach does wonders for the spirits.'

'Do me dressing first, or I'm likely to spew it all up again,' Lizzie said.

Frances turned away and stared down into the street while Rosie changing the dressing.

'That's it, me duck,' Rosie gathered up the rubbish. 'Now eat up the pair of you or it'll all be cold as a stone.' She hesitated, looking at Frances. 'I'll be back directly,' she added.

Frances sat on the edge of the bed and divided her time between the egg and spooning gruel into an exhausted Lizzie.

'Gawd!' Lizzie remarked when the last drop had gone. 'Shall I be glad when I can look after meself again! As soon as I can get up I'm orf home to Ma. Rosie'll see me there . . . stay awhile too, I daresay. She's in a bit of a pickle now that poor old Grit's dead.'

Frances felt suddenly abandoned. 'I thought you might be coming to Birmingham with me if I go. You had an offer too, don't forget.'

The old shrewd look was in Lizzie's eyes. 'Face facts!' she said. 'Even if you manage to get your dad's consent, I'm in a different boat. I've looked in the mirror. No make-up is going to disguise that little lot. Two professions blotted out by one sweep of fortune.'

'Two?'

'The stage and . . . the gentlemen.' Lizzie gave a curious snort. 'Don't get all upset, love. I'll make out. I always have. I'll be giving Ma a hand. Maybe I'll take over the house . . . she's getting on you know and her legs is not what they used to be. Veins have swelled up and knotted something dreadful. She can have a well earned rest.'

With a sudden rush of compassion, Frances took the thin hand and pressed it to her own cheek. 'If I ever become a leading lady I shall need a personal dresser, and if I don't I shall be badly in need of a companion.'

Lizzie tightened her grip. 'Go on!' she said gruffly. 'You'll be a star all right, but you have a year or two to go yet and it won't be easy. The money'll be scarce with none for luxuries like a dresser. But I'll be waiting. Now you've said that, I shan't let you orf the hook. Like a limpet I'll be . . . clinging!'

'Finished?' asked Rosie. She pushed the door to and stood with her hand resting on the brass bedrail. 'Now your spirits is raised I've got something for you, Frances. Nell gave it to me this morning . . . said she hadn't brought it before because . . . well you'll see.' Rosie held out her plump work-roughened hand and Frances saw her missing locket. A mockery of her locket! Blackened and twisted with no trace of the ribbon, it was obviously a victim of the fire. 'Must have fallen from me pocket in the rush to get out of the theatre,' Rosie said. 'Nell kept it till you was over the worst. Kit give it her. He picked it up when he and Alfred went over the ruins the next day.'

Frances took the locket and prised it open. The buckled hinge snapped under pressure. Inside, all that remained of her mother's portrait were some smudgy marks on the brown cracked surface of the ivory. Frances gazed at it bleakly.

'Your Ma was it?' Rosie asked sympathetically.

Frances nodded. 'Lucia Fabricci.' The milk and honey name was all that remained for her.

'What's that you said?'

'Lucia Fabricci.' Frances looked at Rosie, hearing the surprise in her voice.

'Well I'll go to the foot of our stairs! Lucy, of all people . . . your Ma!'

Frances was suddenly terrified of learning about her mother from a first-hand description. She had longed for such an opportunity but now it had come the impact was too real to be borne.

'Did you know her,' she asked, scared out of her wits.

'Know her? I should think I did! There can't be two with a name like that. We was in more than one show together. She was a high kicker if ever there was one. Better than our Lizzie, and that's saying something! Got a nice voice too, deep . . . like your's now I come to think of it. Fancy you never saying before! She was a sharp one. Knew which side her bread was buttered, but a heart of gold. Never turned anyone away who was down on their luck. Not that she ever had much to share . . . went through money like water through a sieve. She was that fond of finery. Always buying new clothes for her act. I remember once she spent ten pound on ostrich feathers for her costume and all they covered was a large fan and a split overskirt . . . had to be split for the high kicks you see. But there, I'm running on. You must know all this.'

Frances could not even shake her head. She was stunned. Something of her inner chaos must have shown for Rosie said anxiously:

'Sore memories are they? If I'd have guessed, I wouldn't have gone on so. I'll stop me chatter and get on with some work.'

'No!' Frances caught her sleeve. 'You have to tell me all you know about her.' To have the image of her mother shattered without any pieces left to fit together was intolerable.

Rosie looked uncomfortable. 'Well me duck, that's a tall order and it's a long time ago. Course when she got married she stepped out of the theatre world and didn't come back for four years or more, so I lost touch.'

'Come back?' The words grated in her throat. 'How could she, when she was dead?'

It was Rosie's turn to look astonished. She opened her mouth as if to speak, then thought the better of it. But Frances would not be put off. Too much was at stake to have the matter hedged over.

'You have to go on,' she ordered.

'She left your dad . . . ran off with a feller from Italy . . . one of her own countrymen . . . ever such a bobby dazzler he was, with curly black hair and eyes to melt your soul. He was part of a travelling circus . . . did a breathtaking turn on the tightrope. She joined him in it, so I heard. Never did see for myself.' Rosie looked at her, hard. 'No one told me she left a kiddy behind.'

There was nothing inside Frances but icicles and despair. All the years of devotion had been no more than the idolizing of a shadow . . . less than a shadow.

Lizzie, who had said nothing throughout Rosie's chat, raised herself on one elbow. 'You don't need a prop,' she said. 'You've got talents of your own.'

Frances was too drowned in self pity to do more than store the comment. Sudden anger swept through her. How dare Papa delude her all these years; allowing her to have illusions about a great actress cut off in her prime! No wonder he had been like a clam. It was not grief, it was shame! The sacred Redmayne name had been desecrated. Her anger spread to the mother she now felt she had never known. Cheated . . . fooled . . . led by the nose! So much for her romantic fantasies! Lucia Fabricci had been nothing but a cheap dancer! But conscience would not let her get away with that.

What else was she, Frances, but a cheap actress on the face of it? Fodder for melodrama. And Lizzie; was she a cheap dancer too? Frances stood up. No one, not even her father, was going to stop her achieving the peak of her profession. If it took her until she was an old lady she would strive and work until she reached the top.

'Mutiny there,' Rosie commented, as Frances went out of the room. 'She looks that mad. I would never have said a word if I'd have guessed.'

'Don't take on,' Lizzie said. 'She's a tough 'un. She'll get over it. Besides, she's got that determination nothing can quench, and with her voice, when she learns the rest, the managers will be fighting for her.'

Rosie grunted, only partly agreeing. 'She'll need to be tough then,' was all she said.

The anger lasted until Sir Oliver arrived at the lodging house. In the dark overfilled parlour, Frances' spirit quailed; defiance when Papa was absent was quite different from when they were face to face. As he sat down on the buttoned black leather chair, she knew that this was the moment of reckoning. He had his thick eyebrows drawn above his jutting nose in something that was less of a frown than an expression of great determination.

'And how are you today, Fanny? Well enough to travel?'

The words struck her with cold alarm. 'Yes . . . but where to?'

'Home, of course. Where else?'

'You know about Mr Mercer Simpson's offer to take me on at Birmingham?'

'I had heard. But there is no question . . .'

'Oh yes there is! A great big question . . . a huge, gigantic one,' she interrupted, driven by nervous desperation. 'I've made my way this far goaded by a lie.' She remembered Lizzie's words. 'I don't need props any more. I'll achieve my goal with my own talents. And no one is going to stop me.'

She was really shaking with fear. They had clashed before, but she had never been so uncompromisingly defiant. The pulse in his forehead was throbbing and she knew that for a warning sign. She closed her eyes, waiting for the storm to burst.

'All your life you've been headstrong and self-opinionated and full of half digested ideas. You talk of achieving your goal as you call it. Though what you mean by "Goaded by a lie" is a mystery. But have you ever stopped to consider that goal in the light of cold hard fact? I am assuming we are talking about the same thing – acting.' His voice was chilly and detached.

'What do you mean?'

'You must know what I mean. Though we have never discussed your progress since you ran away, I have learned enough from your so-called friends to know your thespian life has been anything but easy. I would go as far as to say it has been squalid. And the rest is likely to be as bad if not worse.'

'You can say that when your own wife . . .' She could not bring herself to name her as 'mother'.

'We will leave her out of it.' The cold precise tones heated, and she was glad.

'Because she's dead,' she sneered.

'Because it has nothing to do with this present situation.'

'How can you be so hypocritical?' She was past all restraint now. Anger and hurt throbbed out. She was not conscious of past or future, though both affected the present battle. All she knew was the blessed, brassy relief of raw truth being spoken. 'She's not dead, or not that anyone knows. At this very minute she's probably prancing round some circus ring.'

The silence was more devastating than her words. In a panic, Frances wondered if he were going to hit her. She dared not look.

'She is dead,' Sir Oliver said at last, without expression. Almost as if he were commenting on the state of the weather or the condition of a particular horse. 'She left, as I see you know, but one year later died of a putrid throat. Her . . . friend wrote to me of the death.'

What was there to say? Frances felt as if a hurricane had battered and blown her from one extremity to another. Now its energy was spent, as was hers. She sat on a rocking sea of vacuous thoughts that made little sense and were no help at all. If only John were here! She needed his quiet common sense and support more than ever before. But John was not likely to come. The truth was that she had allowed expectations of growing affection to build up, when really all that had developed were *her* dependence on him, *her* love for him. And now this!

'Papa . . .' She looked at him through eyes blurred with tears. How to explain; to spin that delicate thread of understanding? 'I've only just learned . . . I didn't know . . .' It was true as John had said. Her father looked as if he were carrying a great weight. Was she that burden? Did she matter that much? In these restless floating weeks she had resisted any sign that might have been a token of regard on his side. Money for doctor and lodging was returnable in some form; but affection? Dare she believe in that?

Sir Oliver stretched out a hand and touched hers briefly. A light cold brushing of winter leaves.

'I have to explain how much being part of the theatre means,' she went on. 'It isn't a whim. I have to do it . . . to prove I can, because . . . How can I explain? It's a need in me. To do something bigger than myself. It's flying instead of being shut up in a cage.' She gave a humourless laugh. 'I'd be hopeless running a house and playing hostess . . . no, perhaps I could do that part. You see? Everything comes back to acting in the end.' She smiled hesitantly, not wanting to seem flippant.

He got up and went to look out of the window at the blanket of snow patterned by footprints; hands clasped under coat tails. Frances wished the conversation would flow. Sir Oliver coughed and eased his shoulders.

'There is a gulf between us, Fanny,' he said at last. 'It seems to me it has ever been so. As to the fault . . .' He shrugged, turning to look at her. 'Perhaps there has been some on both sides.'

Frances could not believe her ears. This was surely not an apology? It couldn't be! Whatever it was it differed from anything she had expected and she was left floundering in doubt.

'I cannot ignore your plea,' he continued. 'I would be dull indeed not to recognize a ring of truth when I hear it. But to concede . . . that is another matter.'

Frances seized the frail straw. 'Papa, I must go to Birmingham. I must at least try. Don't you see, if I didn't and went home with you, I would be miserable and . . . and useless. Everyone has their dreams . . . you did! Can't you remember what it was like when Grandfather opposed your passion for the new railways? Mine is a passion too. Oh, it's not had much satisfaction yet, but don't you see that makes me all the more determined to try even harder. It's the only way, isn't it . . . to keep trying and trying at whatever you want to do? Then if nothing comes of the effort, you have only yourself to look to . . . no laying the blame at other doors.'

Seldom had she seen so much response in his expression. Never, in fact! The battle was won. She sensed triumph. The elderly face wrinkled into a smile and she was torn by the knowledge her actions had aged him, just as John suggested. The spring of affection she had so carefully tried to close, flooded her with spontaneous love. Impulsively she jumped up and went to put her arms round him, but as she reached him he put a hand on her shoulder. Whether the movement was intended as a rebuff, or was the demonstration of tenderness expressed by a reserved man, it effectively crushed her intention. Stubborn will saved her from giving in to a sudden desire to cry. She spoke with difficulty:

'I can go then?'

'For one year,' he said. 'If your efforts prove successful then everything will lie at your feet. If you are no more advanced than when you begin in the company at Birmingham's Theatre Royal, I shall expect you to return home without fuss. Is it a bargain?'

'It is.'

'And now I must go. I have promised to meet Mr Hartlipp and discuss the progress of the railway. Having sunk a considerable sum in the venture I like to keep a keen eye on the financial side of things.'

It had never occurred to her before that Papa had any personal interest in the Warfield railway. 'So that's how you came to be here,' she said. 'And I thought . . .'

'What?'

'It doesn't matter.' In the pain and disorder of the past few weeks, she had been so occupied with her own worries and her deep anxiety for Lizzie, that she had not given a thought to the puzzle of her father's presence at the theatre. He had read the playbill, just as John had done, and seen her name.

'Before I leave, tell me how is Miss Masters today?'

'Miss Masters continues to improve,' Frances said primly.

'Good! Tell her to hurry back to full health, but not to be concerned over domestic affairs. They will be taken care of.'

'I'll see you out.'

She was touched by his kindness and it annoyed her. There seemed to be no solution to the enigma that was her father. After he had walked away down the street it came to her that they had still not exchanged a word about John. She felt angry and frustrated, as much with herself as with either of them. They all seemed to be taking part in a strange charade which consisted of totally ignoring the existence of the thing which affected them most . . . the relationship between herself and John. John's silence was a tacit way of joining in the absurd game. She was not going to play any more! Today she would go to Mr Hartlipp's Warfield office and see if anyone was going to Birmingham. If there was, she would send two messages, one to John and one to Mr Mercer Simpson. With growing excitement she closed the door and ran back upstairs calling out:

'Lizzie . . . Rosie . . . I've made up my mind. I'm off to Birmingham just as soon as I can pack.'

12

FRANCES CLIMBED FROM THE STAGECOACH INTO the grey slush which lay over the cobbled forecourt of New Street Station. It had been a tedious unpleasant journey from Warfield with the snowy road almost impassable in places. Once they had been stuck in a drift and had to climb out; waiting in the freezing wind while the coachman, horses and two obliging farm workers heaved and strained to release the snow-trapped wheels. If only the new railway had been finished the journey would have been vastly improved. But work was delayed by the heavy snowfall.

She looked round for John. People were gathering their luggage, stepping gingerly through the slush, skirts lifted, coats pulled tight against the raw biting cold.

'Your bag, miss!' The coachman held out her shabby carpet bag and she took it from him.

Her first sharp disappointment at John's absence hardened into annoyance that was not dispelled by the thought that her message had probably never reached him. The old doubts about whether he cared for her in the way she did for him, returned, cancelling out much of the settled nature of their Warfield meetings. Another of those all too familiar plunging moods dragged at her heels. She resorted to common sense, telling herself it was, after all, a working day so there was no point in waiting, and began walking away from the station towards the theatre. Three o'clock had been the time given for making herself known to the prompter. The coach should have arrived in Birmingham at twelve, but all sense of time fled with the laboured journey. She felt more alone than since that first awful night when she discovered Miss Pringle had left London. A pony and trap passed, throwing up a spray of dirty snow which splattered her skirt and, as she instinctively drew back, she bumped into a man walking in the opposite direction. Discomforted, she hurried on. There was no point in going straight to the theatre. Better find the lodging house Rosie had recommended. The note of introduction was safe in her reticule.

Left at the theatre . . . first right then right again past the Three Hands tavern and then . . . Frances slopped through the slush feeling damp and miserable. Water had seeped between the seams of her worn boots and wetted her stockings and feet. The lodging house looked mean and grimy when she finally found it. The front door led straight off the passage which connected two streets. An odour of stale cabbage wafted out as it was opened by a small girl about twelve years old. Her hair was tied up in rags and a shawl hung from her bony shoulders.

'Is Mrs Beecroft in?' Frances asked, holding out the letter.

'Ma . . . a lady to see yer . . . one of them theatre ladies,' screeched the girl.

Frances followed her into the entrails of the house where a sleezy woman in rusty black, sleeves rolled up to the elbow, was busy stirring something in a large iron pot on the kitchen range.

'You'll be from the theatre then,' she said, taking the letter but not looking up. 'Attic room meals in the kitchen breakfast and high tea dinner separate arrangement no smalls to be left in the bedrooms to dry washing done on Thursdays sixpence extra any questions?' The information streamed out and she cast a needle-sharp glance from boot-button eyes.

'Er . . . no . . . that is . . . what are your charges?'

'Five shillings basic, with the extras if you choose.'

'Thank you,' said Frances.

'Wet boots off and dry your feet. There's tea or gin . . . take your choice.'

Frances chose tea. In spite of the unblinking scrutiny of the girl and the offhand manner of Mrs Beecroft, she felt an underlying kindliness there. If nothing else she had found a temporary home. Somehow she had got to learn to stand alone. It was the first venture without Lizzie and she felt rather insecure. She drank the scalding tea then followed the girl up lino-covered stairs to a bleak attic room.

*   *   *

The smell that met her as the stage door opened was strong and musty; more like an unkempt stable than a theatre. Frances stepped inside, spoke to the doorman and waited for him to find Mr Gavin, the prompter. A great deal of noise issued from the gloomy depths where the wings must be: voices, the whinnying of horses, iron-shod hooves scuffling on wooden flooring. A door clanged.

'Faugh! It's like a cess-pit in there, not a theatre . . . manure steaming on the floor!' The man who was complaining came up to her and peered through steel-rimmed spectacles. 'Gavin is the name . . . and yours?'

Frances introduced herself and shook hands.

'Horses,' said Mr Gavin in total disgust. 'Donkeys . . . monkeys . . . and an *elephant*! Wrecked . . . utterly wrecked.' He scraped at his tufted grey hair with harassed fingers.

Frances tried to imagine what must be wrecked. The stage she supposed, probably with the weight of all the animals. 'Mr Herring's Mammoth Equestrian Establishment with Wild Animals Tamed and Trained by Himself Alone!' She had read the playbill thoroughly before braving the interior of the theatre. Herring, she felt, was hardly the right name for the proprietor of a troupe of highly skilled riders. The troupe was large, but not large enough for 'Mazeppa' it seemed. Lord Byron's play was certainly a step in the right direction. Being a Tartar horseman was better than nothing.

'You don't like horses?' she asked.

'All right in their place. The theatre isn't their place . . . slavering and messing everywhere. Excuse my manner of speaking, but I'm deeply disturbed. Only this morning part of the floor gave way. The elephant!' He breathed the word as if he were speaking of Satan himself. 'I've put a stop to that!'

Frances felt vaguely uncomfortable. They had progressed half a dozen steps away from the stage door. She supposed he was taking her to collect her script and receive instructions for any rehearsal, also to meet Mr Mercer Simpson. But Mr Gavin seemed more preoccupied with his emotional reaction to the intruding animals. One or two actors hurried along the corridor with interested glances at Frances. The noise of hooves increased. Mr Gavin shook a fist in the direction of the stage. 'Ruin . . . ruin!' he shouted. He gripped Frances' arm, pulling her closer, wagging a warning finger. 'Mad, I tell you . . . obsessed by spectacle. Wrecks on the High Seas, Death by Drowning, Avalanches . . . and now ANIMALS!' Shaking his head he let go of her arm and seemed to lose his indignation in remembered responsibility. 'Ah yes! Miss Redmayne . . . Miss *Frances* Redmayne. This way. Your script is waiting. Mr Mercer Simpson asked to see you just as soon as you arrived. This way . . . the greenroom . . .'

*   *   *

Frances slid off the piebald pony. The Tartar trousers were marvellously comfortable. When she had first put them on she had expected the voluminous folds to hamper movement, rather like a skirt, but she had been mistaken. She waxed out the ends of her black moustache and felt the spirit gum tweak her skin where the hairs stuck between nose and upper lip. The pony twisted his quarters, bumping into her. She pulled on the ornamental bridle, patting his neck. The smell was rather overpowering, mixed with all the other smells of the theatre, but she liked it. A horsy, homely smell, that brought back old memories, a little too poignant for comfort.

'Well done, lass. A touch more speed coming down those steps if you can . . . but don't break your neck, nor Gideon's neether.' Mr Herring nodded at her encouragingly. He nodded all the time, reminding her of one of those porcelain figures with suspended heads; a likeness which was strengthened by the turban he wore, which gleamed red and gold under the gaslight.

The rehearsals had gone well enough and 'Mazeppa' opened to an enthusiastic house. Frances shivered uncontrollably before each performance. It was stupid to feel so nervous. She had no lines to speak, being part of crowd scenes; two separate roles, shepherdess and Tartar warrior. The only special thing she did was a piece of trick riding which had come about more by accident than anything else. During one rehearsal the rug, which served as saddle, slipped. In her efforts to adjust it she had slid off. Praying that she would not be noticed, she had adjusted the rug, then taken a leap onto Gideon's back just as he changed position, the result being she had gone flying over his rump in a most athletic manner, surprising herself as much as Mr Herring and the other onlookers. Doing it to order had been more difficult, but she had managed.

Frances handed Gideon's bridle to one of Mr Herring's grooms. The audience was still cheering, but she would not be required for any curtain call. As she turned to go to the dressing-room she was engulfed in sudden loneliness. Around her in the wings actors and horses jostled, but the very closeness of all the life and movement accentuated her feeling of solitariness. It gave her a queer closed-in sensation, as if she were invisible. Although she had been part of the Birmingham company for four weeks, she still felt an outsider. What was the matter with her? Wasn't she doing the very thing she had striven after? No big dramatic roles had come her way yet, but time was on her side. A chance must surely arrive. But no matter how she tried to rationalize her position she kept coming up against this wall of misery. If only there was someone to talk to . . . not passing the time of day, but real talk. Someone like Lizzie, or John. She stared hard at her reflection, concentrating on removing the make-up to stop herself brooding.

'Have you heard about David Gerard coming?' A shepherdess made her way into the crowded dressing-room. The other supernumeraries looked up, commenting, bandying hope and laughter.

'You'll be lucky to get the smallest walk on part . . . he's got a reputation for rough handling . . . catch me being his leading lady . . . Mrs Faucit was a mass of bruises someone told me . . . rubbish, that's sour grapes, nothing more . . .'

The conversation echoed Frances' swinging reactions. David Gerard, famous and formidable . . . coming here! Hope sprang up only to be quenched by the feeling that such luck could not possibly be hers. She wrenched off the remains of her moustache, finding a sharp satisfaction in the prickles of pain, knowing she was in danger of dropping into one of those troughs of depression which dogged her. Hurrying through the routine of dressing, she hardly exchanged one word with any of the other actresses, pushing out into the friendly shadows of the passage.

'Good night, miss.' The doorman nodded cheerfully.

'Good night, Bob.'

Outside, a sharp frost had crisped the remains of the snow and a light wind cut her cheeks. Overhead, a coal-black sky watched with a multitude of sparkling eyes as she crossed the street and crunched along the cobbles on her way back to the lodgings. In the chill of her empty room she was in two minds whether to go to Mr Cowper-Donkin's workshop in the morning. It would be Sunday, when people either went to church or stayed at home, but she guessed that John's enthusiasm would probably compel him to work. Pride, which had kept her away, seemed futile after all. Anything was better than facing this hard gripping loneliness. Even the humiliation she felt trickling in at the edges of her decision, was more bearable than inaction. She crawled into bed. Everyone had to face moments of depression in their lives, she told herself. But it wasn't just that, there was something else. She hadn't come to the point where she was afraid to go on acting . . . was it another side of her? Everything was mixed . . . confused . . . she wanted . . . Nothing crystalized, and uneasy dreams were all that filled her sleep.

*   *   *

Frances thought at first that the yard in front of the workshop was deserted. She stepped through the gate, closing the small door behind her. In the silence of a Sunday morning the place looked ill at ease. One of the big double doors into the workshops stood ajar and as she went towards it an elderly man in a stained cap and trousers tied at the knees with string, came round the side of the building.

'Looking for someone, miss?'

'John Gate. Is he here?'

'Oh him . . .' The wrinkled face creased into a smile. 'He's never at home. Lives at his bench! I'll take you to him.'

'It's all right, I know the way, thank you.' She slipped inside and stood looking at the iron heart of the workshop. At the far end someone was stooping over a bench. She knew who it was. He did not look round as she walked quietly across the floor. The pieces of machinery lying in front of him absorbed all his attention.

'Hello, John!' she said.

He spun round as if he had been shot, completely ignoring the carefully poised arrangement of rods and levers which collapsed with his sudden movement. She saw many things surprised in his face. Things she had longed to see; that he had kept hidden.

'I thought,' she said with a touch of waspishness, 'as you were obviously too busy to call all these weeks, I had better come and find out what kept you away.'

She still smarted under the lash of having to humble herself. Elements of her upbringing had warmed half forgotten attitudes into life. Without framing them in words, she had the feeling it was his place to seek her out, rather than the other way about. She wanted to punish him. After all it was nearly two months since the fire.

'I can see you are *very* busy!'

It had all gone again, the joy, the delight; wiped away, leaving a guarded expression.

'Frances, I . . .' He came towards her, then stopped, catching sight of the thick smears of grease on his outstretched hands. 'All this time and I can't even offer you a hand to shake.' He looked at her anxiously, wiping his hands on a rag. 'You are well again? I did come to see you. Didn't you get my message?'

Frances was taken aback. 'No one told me.'

'The next day, but you were too ill to have visitors, Squire said. I came again the following week, but he still wouldn't let me see you . . . said the doctor had given instructions you weren't to be disturbed, so I gave him a note for you and said I'd wait until you sent for me.'

Bitterness rose up, overwhelming the newly-developed affection. What a fool to have trusted Papa! The ugly truth that he still looked on John as a highly undesirable friend for his daughter was sickening. But out of this crushing disappointment came the warm comfort of knowing John had never abandoned her. Impulsively she caught his hands, moving towards him.

'It's honest dirt,' she said. He smelled of oil and sweat and something else that belonged to him alone. She wanted to say so much, but words after all were such useless things. How could she find any that could express the depth of her feelings? Yards and yards and hours and weeks and months of them, and still they would not be right. Yet somehow she had to tell him. Releasing his hands, she put her arms round his neck and hugged him, standing on tiptoe in order to reach.

His response was total, breaking through barriers of reserve before he hesitated; drew back.

'Frances?'

She kissed him then, tenderly, knowing that the seeking had to be all on her side because of the way their lives had been in the past. It was a curious shifting of position. She was quite certain that his feelings for her were stronger than ever, but she knew equally certainly that he would never express them if she didn't force him into it.

'I love you,' she said simply. And when he stared at her in absolute astonishment, added: 'Quite as much as you love me, so don't argue!'

He burst out laughing, and, forgetting all about his dirty hands, picked her up and swung her round, kissing cheeks, eyes, mouth.

'You'll do!' he said when he stopped for breath.

She had joined in his laughter, understanding only that she had succeeded.

'I don't know when it all began,' she said.

'I do.'

'When?'

'The moment when I picked you up out of them thorns and the mud, when Bastion tipped you over that hedge.'

'Oh! And I thought you were just another farm boy. I was more interested in me.'

Her honesty made him laugh again, but it was full of open tenderness that made her happier than she had ever been. How strange life was, full of unexpected twists and turns.

He lost the laughter and held her away. 'Frances . . . I don't know the words to say, but no matter what happens I shall always love you.'

There was a chill edge to his seriousness that filled her with foreboding. Happiness fell away, frightening her. She looked up at him with equal seriousness, absolutely determined not to let anything divide them.

'Nothing stands between us now . . . neither money, nor position, so what is to stop us being together the rest of our lives?' She paused and darted a questioning look. 'Unless you have objections to such a doubtful prospect as me. You know what they say about actresses!' It was an enormous relief to see a smile chase the desolate shadows from his expression. He gave another snort of laughter.

'What, and me an ex-poacher! Think of all them rabbits o' yourn I snared! We'm a pair of no goods and that's a fact.'

Hearing his speech lapse into Worcestershire burr made her smile too, but the shades still hovered.

'Squire won't like it,' he said.

She did not need to be told. 'He's not stopped me yet, and I don't intend he should start now.'

'You always was pig-headed!' he said admiringly, and hugged her again.

For a long time they said nothing more. The sensuous delight of touch and the deeper joy of being together in a way that would go on broadening and strengthening, filled their world.

'We'm feasting on dreams,' John said at last.

'Dreams?' Frances could only think of dreams that were to come true and there was a touch of melancholy in the way he spoke.

'Neither of us have thought about all the practical things.'

'Those are simple! We earn our own livings and everyone knows two people can live more cheaply together than apart.' She was glad to see him smile again.

'But our work is likely to take us separate ways and what would we do then?'

'John Gate,' she said, exasperated. 'Here we are together . . . loving each other . . . *together*! And you have to start being cautious about something that might never happen. I can invent things too you know. I might get a place in one of the London theatres and you might get a job in a London workshop. What do you say to that?'

But he would not commit himself and she had to be content with knowing she had pushed away the gathering problems at least for the time being. She certainly could not remain solemn for long. Happiness kept bubbling up, making her want to run and laugh and skip about. The dreary grey mood that had pressed down for so long had dissolved and inanimate objects like John's bench, the pulleys and chains overhead, an old broken stool in the corner, even the grimy windows, changed for her, throwing out an aura of well-being. It was something she had noticed before. When times were black in her mind then the mood stretched to the things surrounding her, threatening with their presence. Happiness brought a glow to the world. She lived in a smile. It was like that now. She wanted to tell John how she felt, so that he could share with her. But there was no need. He knew already.

157

'It's like living twice as strong,' he said, opening his hands as if he wanted to say so much more but could not. 'Words!'

'I know! There are some things you just can't say.' Understanding flowed between them. She grinned. 'I'm so hungry!'

They went into the drawing office where Mr Hartlipp had been sitting the first time she visited the workshop. A fire burned in the small black stove in the corner of the room and a kettle was singing gently.

'I brought a slab of bread and some cheese,' John said. 'I thought as how I might get caught up in my work. Lucky I did!' He took a jug and basin from the shelf, poured out some water, adding a little from the kettle, and began to wash his hands.

It was like being in the hut all over again, sitting by the fire, sharing time together. They ate lumps of soft new bread and John made tea in a cracked brown pot, pouring it into a tin mug which they shared. She knew he was thinking of the same thing. The world had been waiting for them then, full of dismal threats. Now there was more hope, but she was glad of temporary shelter, knowing that John was right. There would be many problems to face; Papa being the greatest.

'How's Joe?' she asked hastily, backing away from the thought of her father. It was not a good choice.

'I don't know what to do about him,' John shook his head and looked worried. 'He'm that unhappy.'

'What is there to be unhappy about?'

'It's the work really. He just ent fitted for this kind of life. He misses the fields and the trees.' There was a breath of longing in John's voice as if part of him missed these things too.

'Why doesn't he go back then?'

'You know my dad!'

'That doesn't stop him from getting work on the land somewhere else.' As soon as she spoke she knew it was a foolish remark. Work was scarce enough for farm workers living in their own territory. Strangers would never be welcomed.

'He'm hungering for Thrushton.'

'Is that why he came back from America?'

'That and bad luck. He caught the cholera when he was travelling down the Mississippi river on one of them paddle steamers. A lot of folk died but he recovered. He said it was never the same after. All the time he was ill he longed for home. It was like a maggot eating at him.'

Frances wished she could help in some way. She might have suggested speaking to Papa on Joe's behalf. As things stood she knew any plea of hers would be doomed to failure. Some of the golden quality went out of the day. She stood up and went to look out of the window. Outside, a thin tabby cat walked along the top of a broken fence with fine judgement. It paused for a moment, then leapt into obscurity behind a shed. The sun parted the clouds and brought a breath of spring, making diamonds out of a beaded cobweb on the windowpane.

'Let's walk somewhere,' she said. 'I'm too restless to stay still. Or should you be working?'

'Work? As if I could! It's not every day I agree to get wed, even if we haven't named the day,' John said, tweaking her nose.

She blushed then, the plain way he spoke bringing home the intimate relationship that had been born.

I3 FRANCES WAS STILL WALKING ON AIR THE NEXT
day, when Mr Mercer Simpson called her into his
office. Another person was there already; a swarthy
stocky man with a face pock marked and coarsened
from years of theatrical make-up.

'Frances, I want you to meet Mr David Gerard. I am sure he needs
no further introduction.' He turned, hand outstretched. 'This is the
young lady of whom we have spoken, Mr Gerard.'

Frances looked at the visitor with renewed respect and some
amazement.

'Ah, Miss Frances Redmayne, is it not? The lady with the
Voice!' David Gerard said, his own voice unusually mellow and
varied in tone, contrasting with his unremarkable appearance.
He was looking at Frances with eyes vividly alive. 'Sing!' he
instructed.

Already bewildered by the unexpected interview and the awe that
the great actor inspired, she merely stared at him.

'A snatch of anything you please,' he insisted.

Gathering her scattered wits she took a deep breath and launched into
a popular song she had heard Lizzie singing: 'I'd be a butterfly born in
a bower . . .'

'Capital . . . capital!' He clapped his hands when she finished. 'Now a line or two of speech.'

'Wilt thou be gone? It is not yet near day;
It was the nightingale, and not the lark,
That pierc'd the fearful hollow of thine ear;
Nightly she sings on yond pomegranate tree.
Believe me, love, it was the nightingale.'

'You were right . . . absolutely right, Mr Simpson. She will suit admirably. Of course I shall advise and polish the rough diamond, but I am sure the basic material is there.'

Hope, breathless excitement, doubt, all sprouted together leaving Frances in a jellied quivering state. She wished the man would explain himself instead of talking in half riddles.

'. . . not much time for rehearsal,' he was saying. 'But then I don't need time . . . I've played the role on so many occasions.'

'Please . . . what is this all about?'

A smile broke up the pitted face. 'Ophelia, my dear; a difficult role, maturity of thought required. I want you to play her to my Hamlet. What do you say?'

For an incredulous few seconds she stared at him, then the whole room warmed towards her. The floor shone, cracks in the ceiling beamed and even the walls wore a special smile.

'Yes . . . oh, yes!' she said fervently. No matter what happened in the future, nothing would ever be able to dull the glory of this moment.

In the jealous rehearsal days that followed, she walked in a protective haze. There was no time or attention to spare for envy or petty spite. The few idle moments brought a wondering surprise at the extent of the change in herself. Girlish, romantic pictures of theatre life had crumpled with the paper illusions of her mother. In its place had come a genuine concern for the craft of acting. All her energies went into learning how to breathe life into the characters she played, so they would reach out across the whole house, from pit to gallery. Deeper than that, the preoccupation defied capture. But she knew that at long last she stood independent and calm.

* * *

'Say you? Nay, pray you mark.
He is dead and gone, lady,
    He is dead and gone;
At his head a grass-green turf,
    At his heels a stone.
Oh . . .'

The notes lifted out of ripeness into a thin plaintive cry. Frances, held in the lost passions of Ophelia, knew nothing of the silent watching people beyond the footlights. The stage was draped and shadowy. Limelight shone with sweet brilliance onto her white shift bound with blue ribbon crossing between her breasts and caught the trailing wild flowers pinned in her loosened hair. She could hear her own voice speaking words that were burned into her brain. Every inflection, every movement she made was the fruit of intense thought and practice, yet they flowed out of her as if born on the moment. It was as if her mind was in layers. Fear, joy, a sense of the rightness of performance beneath the skin of Ophelia herself. And the words . . . the golden beautiful words that echoed despair and distraction. She knew how it felt to be despairing, she had touched those depths and she put all that she had learned into the words that were hers and yet not hers.

The Queen was speaking: 'Alas, look here, my lord.'

Frances' mouth quivered and genuine tears welled in her eyes as she pulled at the flowers in her hair:

'Larded with sweet flowers;
    Which bewept to the grave did not go . . .'

The King, Laertes, messengers, moved in and out, weaving the pattern of the play. Ophelia returned, stroking cold fingers down her cheeks and picking at the broken flowers.

'. . . He is gone, he is gone,
    And we cast away moan:
    God-a-mercy on his soul!
And of all Christian souls, I pray God. God buy you.'

Coming into the wings peeled back the skin of Ophelia, but even so Frances found it difficult to become herself. She lodged in a no-man's land, her part in the play over. But she felt compelled to watch the angled view of the stage as David Gerard strode through the graveyard scene. There was much she did not like about his performance. Gestures that would have been more at home in a melodrama; a tendency to revel in the music of his voice, but in spite of this and the fact that he must be nearly fifty, she had to admit there was a magnetism about him. He had only to be there, on the stage, to pull attention to himself. Star quality. A little frightening, very awe inspiring and certainly difficult to pin down. There was not much physical attraction about him. Short and rather stocky, he was hardly the right shape for Frances' conception of Hamlet. But once he began to act, those drawbacks melted and ceased to exist.

The play had reached its peak; the stage strewn with bodies. She flattened herself against the wall behind the proscenium arch to let Fortinbras and a group of soldiers march onto the stage.

The first night was over. Waves of applause spread through the theatre. In a dream Frances felt herself taken by the hand and led, by Laertes, to the apron of the stage. She curtsied with all the grace of much practice. It was difficult to think at all. She could only feel. Expanding emotions squeezed against the wall of her skin, pushing tears into her eyes and blocking her throat. In the wings again, she burst into inconsolable sobs as Hamlet bowed and bowed again, a silver figure in the solitary limelight.

'You caught their hearts, love.' Laertes put a hand on her shoulder. Other actors passed with smiles and sympathetic pats; jealousy forgotten.

As the storm of tears quietened, she retreated to the dressing-room and sat looking at the wreck of her face reflected in the mirror, utterly exhausted. At the further end of the dressing-room the Queen was moaning over her bruised arms.

'And I have to go through it all again tomorrow,' she complained. 'Look ... red marks where his fingers gripped me! Everything they said about that man is true.'

Frances silently agreed. David Gerard had certainly been rough in handling the poor Queen, throwing her violently away from him at one point, so that she caught her shoulder on the bedpost.

'I'll be black and blue tomorrow. How can I go on stage with great purple marks all over my bare arms?'

Frances nodded in sympathy, a little amused by the rainbow-coloured descriptions. She unscrewed her jar of pomatum, scooped out a generous amount and began cleaning her face.

'Tell him not to be so rough,' she suggested.

'What, and have my head bitten off!' The Queen was scandalized.

'Oh, he's not such an ogre as all that . . . just a little thoughtless.' Rather like Papa. In the afterglow, not entirely extinguished by fatigue, her fears seemed groundless. She decided to tell Papa that very evening that she and John were going to be married. The idea must be eased into his mind, for even now the prospect of speaking out was unpleasant. Choose the right moments . . . slip each fragment of information obliquely into place . . . there would be no need for blunt words . . . a delicate subject to be treated with finesse.

'I suppose a bruise or two must be accepted as the price of rubbing shoulders with the famous!' said the Queen, rolling down her fleshings.

'All in the cause of Art!' Frances smiled and began brushing out her hair, coiling it into a bun and securing it with half a dozen hair-pins.

Frances was still turning over ways of approaching her father as she passed David Gerard's open dressing-room door. He came out into the passage, still in costume, his face grotesque with make-up.

'Miss Redmayne! How fortunate . . . I was hoping to see you. A private word if you please. I know you will spare me a moment. Come in . . . come in . . . sit down there!'

She was swept into his dressing-room which was thick with cigar smoke, the scent of attar of roses and a curious animal musk.

'Forgive the muddle, but I did want a *private* conversation.' He was pacing about with all the restlessness of a caged panther but without its lithe grace, sweeping the air with his hand. 'You may have heard that I am planning to visit America?'

It was news to her, and nerve ends knotted under her ribs.

'By invitation you understand, commencing in New York and playing in all the major cities; travelling south. I intend taking a select company with me and am persuaded that you would be an excellent choice.

The season will not begin until September and should last four months, perhaps five ... we shall see. What do you say?'

What could she say! A thousand fragmented thoughts hopped about in confusion. She knew she ought to sift them carefully and weigh up every aspect of the offer, but all she could think of was the fact that she would be parted from John. And yet how could she refuse? It was the chance for which she had longed. Speech was impossible and she could only nod her head while her heart cried for John.

'Splendid ... splendid!' He rubbed his hands together with beautifully executed satisfaction. 'You are the first member of my company. The others are yet to be recruited ... not from this theatre alas. I fear there will be some broken hearts when the news travels.'

He really was rather conceited, she thought with a flicker of surprise. Perhaps this was another facet of star quality. Did you have to see yourself as something exceptional in order to achieve the heights? It was all so confusing. No matter how much she pondered, there seemed no positive answer.

There was a pause in the monologue and she realized that the interview was over. She stood up, faintly embarrassed; aware that she had fallen into the old trap of losing herself in her own thoughts rather than listening to what was being said.

'Thank you, Mr Gerard,' she said, torn by the choice she had made. Conscious that something further was required, she held out her hand. 'I can't express how honoured and grateful I feel. I will do my best to see that you never have cause to regret your decision.'

He shook hands enthusiastically, unaware of her inner conflict; bowing as she left him, then breaking into a rich baritone which echoed down the passage.

Frances walked towards the stage door where she knew her father would be waiting. She had chosen America and separation! The idea left her sick and hollow. How cruel of Fate to present her with such a choice.

'You are looking very solemn, Fanny. Not the right expression at all for one who played Ophelia with so much perception,' said Sir Oliver as she reached him.

That was praise indeed, but her warm smile came from a sudden resolving of all her problems. There was no choice after all. John could come with her! They would be married secretly and travel over the high seas together. America was a very long way from Papa's wrath. Besides, there was plenty of work for good engineers out there. She had heard Mr Hartlipp say as much in the days when he stayed at Thrushton Hall and had talked endlessly about railway affairs with Papa over the dinner table.

'I'm tired,' she said, and realized it was true. She felt drained of every last drop of energy.

'I am sure some good food will help to change that. I have ordered dinner to be served in a private room at the inn.'

In the warmth of the small room, with its mellow panelled walls and comfortable seating, Frances felt some of her fatigue seep away. The table was laid with a clean damask cloth and sparkling silver. She looked across it at her father, speculating whether this was the right moment to speak out. There was much she ought to say, but it seemed a pity to break the eggshell peace that surrounded them. It could wait, she thought.

The words were still unspoken when the meal had been eaten and it was time for her to put on her cloak and bonnet. She had not even told him about Mr Gerard's company and the visit to America. They had talked of other things, most of which had to do with the boom in railway building. He seemed to skirt any reference to theatre life as if it were still too sore a subject.

She stood up. Now was the moment! Gripping the back of her chair, she tried; but she could not say anything about John and had to be content with explaining about America. He listened with a calmness that surprised her.

'America is a very long way from England.'

'I know, but it will only be for five months at the outside,' she urged.

'I can see your heart is set on the venture.' He looked at her with a strange expression which might have been sympathy. She waited in an agony of suspense. If he refused to let her go . . . She dared not think further than the moment.

He rubbed the tips of his fingers together. She noticed that the joints had thickened, another mark of age.

'What do you propose doing during the summer?'

She had not thought about it. Travelling perhaps . . . the summer circuit?

'Whatever you wish. I could come home.' Now why had she said that? She added hastily: 'For a holiday at least.' Summer in Thrushton. She could ride Mistral . . . spend time really conquering Bastion . . . go to London to visit Lizzie; better still have her to stay. With the railway almost within walking distance of the Hall she could travel anywhere she chose . . . even to Birmingham! It would be sweet to taste freedom again for a brief period. The thought brought a train of guilt and hinted at self deception. Freedom was hardly the word she would have applied to her previous life in Thrushton! This time it would be different. At least she would know there was an end. And what an end! Life with John.

'It would be very pleasant to have you home once more, Fanny,' Sir Oliver said. Collecting his top hat and opera cloak seemed to be an all absorbing occupation. He picked up his cane with the silver knob and twisted it between his fingers. Frances could feel the air heavy with some unspoken feeling. It was torture having to stand quietly, waiting for his decision when so much hung in the balance. After a long time when he appeared to be struggling with himself, he said:

'You really want this more than anything?'

'Yes,' she replied. A lie that was not a lie.

'Very well . . . I agree.'

She did not make the mistake of going to kiss him as she had done before. The joy that she felt beamed out and kindled a response that was quite unexpected. He took her hand and dusted it with his lips then put it away from him.

'I've missed you, Fanny,' he said.

'Papa . . .'

'No, don't say anything. I learned years ago that recriminations bring nothing but anger and bitterness. It is enough that we have reached a position of better understanding. We will go on from there.'

She felt guilty at deceiving him. None of her previous rebellious thoughts mattered any more. Presented with this sudden deepening understanding, she was disturbed by having to be such a hypocrite. If she had any honesty at all she ought to tell him about John without further hesitation. But that would wreck everything. His attitude would change in a flash and she would be ordered home. There would be no trip to America and certainly no wedding. All she could do was bear the pain of deception. Why did life have to be so punishing? Nothing was ever straightforward and simple. No sooner had she smoothed one relationship and found happiness, another tangled up. There seemed no hope of unravelling them both. They seemed destined to spoil each other.

'There are only two more weeks of the season left,' she told him. 'I'll see Mr Mercer Simpson tomorrow and explain that I shall be leaving the company then.'

*　　*　　*

The train rattled rhythmically over the iron rails, forcing Lizzie's song to revolve in Frances' mind. 'Courting down below stairs . . .'. She hummed under her breath. Beyond the carriage window a pale sun shone over an April landscape where primroses bunched under hedgerows mossed with a first stirring of green. She responded to it, feeling the effect of spring running in her own veins. Four months of country summer. It was a marvellous thought. She had not realized how much she had missed the scent and sight of it all; being part of living things.

'We shall be reaching the junction shortly,' said Sir Oliver. He sat opposite in a corner seat with his back to the engine. They had the carriage to themselves all the way from Birmingham.

Frances smiled uneasily. She still had not plucked up enough courage to speak about John, and soon they would be meeting him at the junction, where the Molesbridge branch line joined the main Birmingham–Gloucester railway. John, Mr Hartlipp and Mr Cowper-Donkin would all be there for the final testing of the brake system John had worked on for so long. Yesterday she had thought the coincidence of the test with the journey back to Thrushton an excellent one. Today she felt less confident. Time was escaping . . . in fact there was no time at all to tell Papa before they reached the junction where they were to change trains. She would just have to warn John not to say anything. Not that he was likely to; he had disapproved of the deception and had been outright alarmed at the idea of eloping to America. The trouble was he always saw too deeply into everything and his natural caution prevented him from launching into schemes he dubbed 'outrageous'. Their parting had been scratchy, marred by tensions that had erupted into argument.

Frances concentrated hard on the swiftly moving fields and hedges. No point in going over such thorny memories. Today was the important thing. Papa was bound to be interested in the brake test. Anything to do with railways was guaranteed to please him and might provide a stepping-stone to better understanding between him and John. The test had been planned to take place in a siding which branched from the Birmingham and Gloucester line just before the junction was reached. It was a convenient place, out of the way of main line traffic, but not too far from Birmingham to make the journey impracticable. Facing downline, Frances could already see the signal in the distance. The red flag was down, indicating a clear line. In a moment they would be passing the siding and she would be able to see John. She stood up, intending to go and sit in the other corner seat to get a better view.

'Be careful you don't lose your balance when the train . . .' began Sir Oliver, thinking she was preparing to leave the carriage. But he never finished the sentence. There was a violent lurch and a hideous screaming of tortured metal. The carriage seemed to rear up, hang suspended, then topple with a roaring crash. Terror sprang out.

'Papa!' Frances shrieked as an agonizing pain tore at her arm and extended in waves across her shoulder and neck. 'Papa!'

In the disintegrating carriage, wood and metal were torn from position with the ease of ripping tissue paper. Splinters of glass flew in the air slicing her hands with fine cuts she did not feel. In the tumbling confusion and terror of the moment she was flung about and did not know whether she stood or lay. Floor and ceiling ceased to have any meaning. The only reality was the excruciating pain across her right shoulder. Fighting to overcome its all embracing hold, she was deaf and blind to her surroundings. Only gradually was she able to struggle up out of the mists and try to take stock of the situation.

There had been a crash, but she could not begin to understand the cause. All she knew was that she had to get out. Whatever had happened it was all over. The terrifying movement had juddered into stillness broken only by screaming and shouting coming from somewhere

169

outside. She tried to find out if she was capable of moving. As far as she could tell, she was lying in a twisted position half on her back. The pain was terrible and she could only move her left arm, the right one seemed useless. Try to sit up . . . try . . . try . . . Surrounded by the shattered wreckage of the carriage she could place nothing. But she had to move . . . had to get to Papa. Since that first awful moment when she had cried out, he had said nothing.

'Papa, are you all right?'

No answer. Outside was a confusion of noise which isolated the silence of the carriage. A piece of torn upholstery fluttered and settled like a ragged moth on the back of her hand. She shook it away, trying to force her body into a sitting position, but pain and something weighing across her legs mastered her and she fell back with tears of frustration, but not before she had glimpsed her father spread-eagled in a lumpish awkward fashion somewhere below where her feet should be.

'Papa . . . Papa . . .' she called desperately. In the answering silence her control broke and she yelled: 'Help me . . . someone help me!' Again and again she cried out, gripped by terror. At last her strength sapped and the panic slumped into shivering misery. Sounds from outside joined with the brash sunshine crashing through jagged spaces in the broken carriage. They were not distant sounds, but close at hand. Someone was working to release them. She called out again. The sounds increased and a voice asked:

'Are you hurt bad?'

'I don't know. I can't move . . . something pinning my legs. But it's my father; he's unconscious.'

Above her head the wreckage of the door was prised open by a crowbar. A face peered down.

'Hang on, miss, and I'll get you out quick as I can.' The man disappeared shouting: 'Give us a hand over here.'

Her relief was enormous. She began pushing again and as she turned her head, saw John leaning towards her through the gap. He didn't speak. The horror and concern mirrored in his face said everything.

'You seem fated to pick up the pieces of me,' she said.

He strained to move the buckled seat which lay across the lower half of her body. The older man, who had first found her, wormed his way into the broken carriage and eased round towards the back of the seat which now rested on the floor. He grasped the part trapping her.

'When I lift, miss, see if you can move from under this lot. John'll give you a hand.'

'Papa?'

The man nodded at her soothingly. 'You first, miss. One at a time.'

She had never known such agony, but she clenched her teeth hard together. The weight had gone from her legs and bit by bit she hunched into a sitting position. John had his hand under her good shoulder, the other lifted her, gripping her skirt.

Lying on the embankment in a hazy fog of semi-consciousness, she felt she was floating somewhere just outside the real world. Her eyes opened onto a scene that did not make sense. Two carriages had jack-knifed and remained poised in a pyramid, while others lay on their sides across the track. At the far end two locomotives were joined in a steaming heated embrace.

'I'll have to leave you, Frances, just for a while . . . if you ent too hurt? There's others trapped.'

'Of course,' she managed to say. 'But Papa . . . did you get him out?'

He cupped her face in his hands. 'He'm dead.'

'Dead?' It was foolish to repeat words that meant nothing.

'He couldn't have felt anything. The impact broke his neck.'

So life ended in the time it took to snap one's fingers. Papa was alive and a second later ceased to exist, except for the useless envelope of himself. She closed her eyes, overwhelmed with fatigue.

'Frances . . . my love . . .' Sunlight glistened on tears sliding over his cheeks.

She opened her eyes, not wanting to have to think about the emotions that troubled John or anyone else. There was not enough strength in her for anything at all.

'Go and help,' she whispered. 'I'll wait here.' In her head the words turned:

> 'He is dead and gone, lady,
> He is dead and gone . . .'

14

SIR OLIVER REDMAYNE'S COFFIN LAY IN THE ornate hearse, covered with white lilies. Four black horses in front were dressed for the occasion with black plumes mounted on their heads. The coachman was equally decorous in sober black; top hat draped with a mourning scarf. In the following carriage Frances sat alone. Behind, other carriages stretched in a long line down the lane; mourners from town and country, reflecting Sir Oliver's interest in railways and the county of Worcestershire.

Frances could see the red gravel drive leading to Thrushton's small grey stone church. On either side of the drive the villagers stood waiting in silence. Polly was there, round as a dumpling, with a comically fattened Wilf. John was with them, standing a little apart from his parents. Even at this distance she could see that he was watching her. It was incongruous having him out there, instead of sitting in his rightful place at her side. But a funeral was no place to flout convention. She smoothed the folds of her dress with her free hand, sitting straighter so that her injured shoulder no longer touched the back of the seat. The movement of the carriage made it ache and she tried shifting the position of her arm in the grey silk sling.

The hearse had entered the church grounds. As Frances' carriage passed through the open gateway, she was reminded forcibly of the last time she had followed one along this same path, four years ago. John had been there, although at the time she had been unaware of him. It seemed more like forty years of living than four. She felt a good deal older than the untried rebellious girl who had accompanied her father to her grandfather's funeral. Perhaps she was wiser too; certainly her position was vastly changed. There was no one left to threaten her ambitions. A few remote cousins she hardly knew, were tucked into the following carriages. Apart from them she was the sole representative of an unbroken line of Redmaynes who had lived at Thrushton Hall for three hundred years, and was the last to bear the name. Whatever life held now, it was the end of a dynasty.

The carriage stopped. Climbing down from his driver's seat, Jim Prescott opened the door and helped her out. The attendants, who had travelled with the hearse, had already shouldered the coffin. She marvelled at their easy management of the load, though she could not accept the fact that her father lay inside the polished oak box. The idea was absurd! She shied away from the memory of him neatly packed between the velvet walls of the coffin, like a grotesque parcel. It had been her first sight of death. The cold inescapable fact that her sleeping father was no more than a husk, empty of response or feeling, had confronted her with a battering array of emotions. Fear and regret had been there, grief as well, but a sense of freedom edged in, lifting her spirits. Astonished by her own reaction, she had turned away without touching the corpse. To have felt lifeless flesh was more than she could stomach.

Inside the church the coffin lay on a purple-draped plinth before the chancel step. Still alone, Frances sat in the Redmayne pew. Mr Hartlipp and Mr Cowper-Donkin sat behind and were joined by a tall hairless man with a beak of a nose who was Mr Culpepper, Sir Oliver's solicitor. As the organist played a few doleful chords, Mr Farthing, the parson, emerged from the vestry preceded by a server in a freshly laundered surplice and ruff.

The little church was packed to capacity. Hymns and responses cannoned round the nave, but Frances could not throw off the curious detachment which had been with her ever since she had returned to Thrushton after the crash. In front of her she could see a spider spinning across the corner of a choir-stall. Sun shone on the silken tracery of the web and reflected from a small pool of water beside the vase of daffodils on the chancel step. But she really ought to pay attention! Mr Farthing had begun his address. The trouble was that she could not reconcile the fact that her father was dead, with all the shrouding sorrow, and this growing relief that she was liberated. More than anything she wanted the ritual to be over; the burial, the funeral meal and the reading of Papa's will – so that she could go and find John.

The coffin bearers had lifted their burden and were solemnly moving down the aisle. Frances rose. Mr Hartlipp slipped a hand under her elbow as they left the pews.

'Are you all right?' he asked, noticing her pallor.

She nodded and walked steadily past the staring eyes, out into the spring morning. The rest of the ordeal moved by in a dream; watching the coffin lowered on ropes into the waiting family tomb, returning by carriage with no more than an unsmiling exchange of glances with John; later still the dreadful meal in the long dining-room where every mouthful choked her.

'Please be seated,' said Mr Culpepper.

Frances, the cousins and a group of Sir Oliver's friends, beneficiaries under his will, sat down at the table in the library. Half a dozen servants, also beneficiaries, remained standing. A good log fire burned in the grate, taking the chill from the air. Through long windowpanes the sun poured in, polishing the dome of Mr Culpepper's head to a gleaming perfection and picking out the gold tooling which decorated the rows of leather-bound books. Mr Culpepper cleared his throat and took a pair of pince-nez from his coat pocket, perching them on the end of his nose. Then he extracted a thick document from his briefcase and broke the seal. Looking over the top of his pince-nez, he said in a dry unemotional voice:

'Sir Oliver's will is clear and to the point. The bequests are directed simply and were arranged according to his desire immediately following his inheritance of the estate. However, of recent months he added a codicil. I explain this before I begin reading because I know it was his intention to alter this codicil, but the lamentable accident intervened.'

He did not look directly at Frances, but she felt a rush of alarm. She sat rigidly in her chair wishing he would hurry instead of wasting time wiping his nose and fiddling with the parchment. The other listeners were impatient too; the quiet room was disturbed by the sound of their shuffling feet and nervous coughs.

Mr Culpepper smoothed his bald head twice and began to read. Small and medium sized bequests were dealt with, including ones to the waiting servants who were then given time to leave before coming to the bulk of the estate. When Frances learned that all of it, land, house, money and an enormous quantity of railway shares were left to her alone, she was stunned; even though it was the logical expectation. Mr Culpepper was to be her legal guardian until she came of age.

'And now the codicil.' This time the solicitor looked directly at her. There was a touch of reticent sympathy in his expression that mingled with reserved disapproval. 'I, Oliver Elliston Redmayne, being of sound mind on this day 30th of August 1844, do state that the above bequests stand as I have ordered, except for that to my daughter Frances Alice Mary. She shall inherit my estate only if she agrees to leave her present occupation or any future occupation she may have embraced and return to live at Thrushton Hall and make it her business to deal with the affairs of that said estate; unless she be married with my consent. If she refuses to accept these terms, then I wish the whole of my estate to be sold and the proceeds to be used to endow a school of railway engineering under the direction of Mr James Hartlipp, with five hundred pounds only to be given to my daughter.' Mr Culpepper folded the parchment and pocketed his pince-nez. 'And that, ladies and gentlemen, concludes the late Sir Oliver's will.'

A hum of excitement mixed with the scraping of chairs on polished floorboards.

'Congratulations, my dear,' said one of the cousins.

Frances looked at his stoop shoulders and straggling grey hair. What a strange remark!

'You are a fortunate young lady.'

'Very fortunate ... my sympathies are with you of course, but ...'

'You will be staying on at Thrushton, I suppose? If ever you wish to have a change of scene, my home is always open to you ...'

The cousins were clustering round her like a flock of crows on a cornfield. In a gap between two cousinly heads, Frances saw Mr Hartlipp talking earnestly with the solicitor. He must have known about the engineering school for a long time. It was a splendid idea, but she was disturbed by the thought that Thrushton Hall must pass from the Redmayne family forever. Not that there was any choice. Her American tour was settled, Papa had approved, and yet she was sure he would not want the estate to be sold, even to provide for something to which he had been so passionately devoted. How much she needed John to help her out of the muddle, but there were guests to look after.

Some were staying the night, some had to be put into carriages or taken to the station to catch the afternoon train. The duties of hostess weighed heavily.

'Frances, my dear,' Mr Hartlipp said as she began walking towards the library door. 'I hope you don't feel I conspired against you in any way?'

'Of course not.'

'Not that there is any choice I know. Life has a curious way of changing one's whole approach to living.'

'You expect me to stay?' she said wonderingly.

Mr Hartlipp did not reply but his expression said that he did.

'Don't make any hasty decision,' Mr Culpepper intervened. 'Take as long as you wish. My time is at your disposal.'

'You are very kind.' Frances wanted to seem responsible. 'I will delay my answer until I am convinced I have made the right choice.'

'Any advice you may require, you have only to ask.'

'Thank you ... thank you.' She went through the motions of politeness, returning to the cousins, seeing to their needs, giving Mrs Drayton, the housekeeper, orders for dinner. And all the while part of her was laughing at the incongruity of it all.

It was two hours or more before she had time to do anything about contacting John. She wanted to ride over to the cottage where Polly and Wilf lived, where he was staying, but her troublesome shoulder would not allow it. Instead she sent for Jim Prescott and gave him a message, telling John to meet her in the park where the elm trees bordered the meadow. Jim Prescott's face was expressionless as she gave the instruction, but his disapproval was plain. Well, let him think what he liked. She was Squire now, if there was such a thing as a female Squire. And if she decided to go walking with one of the villagers on the day of her father's funeral, or any other time for that matter, it was nothing to do with him.

Out in the park, with the breeze gently billowing her cloak, Frances breathed in the sweet scents of new green growth. The light wind seemed to be blowing away any clinging strands of formal grief, freeing her spirits. She walked towards the cluster of trees and bushes, the spongy grass glistening with moisture, drenching her shoes and the hem of her skirt. The sharp air was exhilarating. It was impossible to feel gloomy on a day like this; there was so much to look forward to and discover. The excitement of living was already crowding out the rites of death. She reached the edge of the copse and went to lean against the great trunk of a single oak that ruled the elegant elms. Overhead a flock of rooks wheeled and called in harsh voices as if they were already preparing to nest. Soothed, she stared up through the weaving birds into the sky.

After a time she grew impatient. What was keeping him? Jim Prescott must have delivered the message some time ago and it would take no more than ten minutes, fifteen at the outside, to walk from the village. She scanned the park and saw John pass between two of the beech trees lining the driveway and walk purposefully across the grass. There was a manliness about his stride and in the carriage of his body that brought a smile of pleasure. She stood quietly savouring the delight of seeing the gap between them close.

'What took you so long?' she called. 'I thought you must have gone back to Birmingham,' intending a joke, but as he came nearer she was brushed by unease. Even at a distance he seemed unresponsive.

He stopped deliberately a yard from her.

'Hello, Frances.'

There was a shadow of a smile, but he was looking at her in a way that nipped her happiness; implied restraint.

'John . . . what's the matter?'

'Everything's changed, hasn't it?' he said.

'Some things,' she admitted cautiously.

'You know we can't go on.'

For the second time that day she was stunned, and it smacked her into anger. 'No, I don't know. Explain yourself!' No kiss, no sign of affection, no words of sympathy, just a blunt statement. What was he trying to do . . . say that he no longer loved her? One look at his agonized appealing expression drove that idea away.

' 'Tisn't easy for me, Frances. You knows you mean more to me than anything in the world, but we can't go against facts.'

'Facts . . . what facts?'

'Can't you see the position? Me a villager, and you'm Lady of the Hall. How can we be man and wife?'

She wanted to shout and stamp her foot and yell out that he had no right to come and shatter all her hard-won happiness . . . that it was cruel to abandon her just because of some inevitable social snobbery, but all she could say was: 'What nonsense!'

'Is it?'

Everything she valued and understood seemed to be rushing away from her as she looked into his face and saw his deadly seriousness. 'It is . . . it's utter ridiculous nonsense. We don't belong *here* any more. We aren't marrying each other's families, only one another. So don't bring up all that degrading claptrap about being a lesser person because of an accident of birth. You should have more dignity.' The ugly unfair words struck out and shamed her, but her mood was so tormented she wanted to shock, even destroy . . . anything to break through his desperate calm.

'Frances . . . please . . .' He was deeply hurt.

'Well, it's true,' she said with less conviction, then shouted: 'You make me lose faith in you,' because her mood still made her cruel.

The injustice pushed him into anger. 'If I ent able to forget my father were only a labourer . . . you'm no better, for all your talk,' then immediately caught her hand. 'Oh love . . . I shouldn't have said that . . . it ent true . . .'

But nothing mattered except the feel of his rough jacket as she stumbled against him. His arms came round her, gently, as he rubbed his cheek along her hair, speaking her name again and again, apologizing.

'It's me that should be saying sorry,' she said, her voice muffled. 'But you frightened me so. Say you don't mean it!' Then before he could answer, pulled away and gazed earnestly at him. 'You don't know about Papa's will. It makes a great deal of difference. The estate is to be sold unless I agree to live here and spend my time running it. The money will endow a school of railway engineering and I shall receive five hundred pounds. So you see we shan't be destitute after all. We can go to America. There's plenty of railways to be built over there, and I have the tour. What's to stop me from staying on afterwards. I might even launch my own company.' She was tempted by a gorgeous powder puff of a daydream which vanished when John spoke.

'You ent really changed, Frances; not with all your travelling. Can't you see there's others involved? You'm responsible now for the village and all the folk hereabouts. They depend on you. What do you think would happen if a stranger took over? There's been Redmaynes here since living memory and long before. You can't give it away like an old coat.'

'Me . . . responsible?' She was struggling to understand his concept of her role.

'Yes! Who controls whether they work or starve? Who do they look to for protection against the world that's already broken through with the railway? A bad Squire would make a living hell, and a strange one could bring fear and suspicion that would need a deal of tact and understanding to straighten. They'm simple folk, Frances. They need you.'

Her world twisted back into a lunatic shape, but she hung on with bitter determination to the threads of her driving will.

'All right then, if I stay, you stay as well. You know far more about farming than I do. You'd run the estate splendidly.'

'Oh Frances! What would I be doing as Squire? Having Mam and our Polly bob a curtsy and Dad and Wilf touch their caps . . . as for the folk in the village, they don't even accept me for myself, so they ent going to take me as their master.' He looked at her with such tenderness she felt she could not bear the weight of so gigantic a love. How could he contain it and put outsiders first? But they weren't outsiders. She knew that what he said was right, though she could not bring herself to agree and was filled with despair.

For a long time silence hung between them. He had released her and they both moved away from each other as though by mutual agreement, knowing that touch could only bring a flood of blind emotions that would leave no room for clear thought. There *must* be an alternative to the bleak future stretching ahead. If she could not see it plainly now, she would search until she did. All the toiling years which had at last held the promise of fulfilment in her work and her love for John was not going to be allowed to slip from her grasp. She tightened the muscles of her jaw, almost bullying happiness to come back.

'I won't let it happen,' she said. 'Promise me that if I find a solution you will marry me after all?'

She had forced a smile into his face though his eyes were still sad.

'You never give up, do you?' he said, with the promise lying in the tone of his voice.

She kissed him then, not caring about the pain in her damaged shoulder as she pressed against him. Afterwards she ran away across the grass, leaving him to return to the cottage.

'Ah, there you are, Miss Frances! I was hoping for a word.' Mr Cowper-Donkin coughed his way across the hall as Frances came in through the front door. 'Mr Hartlipp has just explained your dilemma.'

For a split second Frances thought her conversation with John in the copse had been overheard. She looked at him in some surprise.

'The content of your father's will, m'dear.' He smiled at her with disarming frankness. 'Rather conflicts with your acting career it would seem ... and your ... um ... romantic attachment!'

Before Frances could reply, Mrs Drayton came into the hall carrying dry shoes.

'Is there somewhere a little more private we can go?' he asked, with a sidelong glance at the housekeeper. 'I have a proposition to put to you.'

There was something about him that reminded her of a cheerful gnome. Round and jolly with distinctly impish tendencies and a suggestion of intelligent perception. She changed her shoes and allowed her cloak to be removed, then led the way into the small morning room next to the library. Late afternoon sun made a jewelled pattern through diamond leaded panes onto a richly-coloured carpet. It was warm to the eye as well as the skin in here, in spite of the empty grate, and she felt in need of such comfort. Events were beginning to move at a rather alarming rate, leaving her floundering.

They sat on either side of the fireplace.

'Now then!' Mr Cowper-Donkin held up his left hand and began ticking off a list of points on his stubby fingers. 'You cannot inherit if you stay on the stage ... right? If you decide to do that, the money will go to a school for aspiring railway engineers ... a subject very dear to my heart I must add. On the other hand everyone expects you to take control of the estate, run the farm and so on. But ...' He paused and looked hard at her. 'What no one seems to have perceived is your other little problem.'

She fully expected him to say 'John Gate', but instead he said:

'Your real vocation as an actress.' There was an emphasis on the word 'vocation'. 'I've had me share of opposition and trials of that sort, m'dear. I know what it is to have to face misunderstandings, even downright antagonism. So being a bit of a devious feller, I've thought up a plan to scotch the lot of 'em. Shall I go on?'

She nodded . . . speechless!

He rubbed his hands together. 'I'd thought of offering to rent the Hall and estate from you . . . sort of tenant farmer, but that wouldn't do because of the limitations of the will. So how would it be if I were to buy from you . . . and then make you my heir? Got no descendants you see . . . crabbed old bachelor whose doctor says "Country air or you snuff it"!' He grinned at her. 'Always gives me pleasure to score off these lawyers. I know your Papa was going to alter that codicil. So why shouldn't you and I alter it for him? That way we all get what we want. You, your beloved acting . . . me, the chance of getting some life into these poor old bellows.' He tapped his chest. 'And seeing a project I've thought about for years turn into fact . . . I'm talking about the engineering school. On top of that Thrushton is within striking distance of Birmingham, so what could be more convenient? Don't look so shocked, m'dear.' He began to laugh at her expression, with little bursts of sound like a locomotive pulling away.

What could she say? It was as if someone had lit up the stage of her life. One moment everything was gloom and shadows, the next moment the future was bathed in brilliance. The tears she had restrained when she was with John began tumbling down her cheeks. Mr Cowper-Donkin looked alarmed. He pulled out an enormous white handkerchief and offered it to her.

'There, there, m'dear . . . perhaps I should have waited . . . not the right day for . . . forgive me . . .'

Frances blew her nose and smiled through the folds of linen. No words could express her gratitude. She got up and went to him, putting her uninjured arm round his shoulders so that she could give him a squeeze while she kissed his forehead.

'Oh, dear me . . . dear me . . .' He was quite flustered, his face purpling and his breathing growing more agitated.

'I'll never be able to thank you enough,' Frances said at last. There was still the problem of John. Dare she ask that he be released from his work? There was nothing like asking, though she felt nervous, knowing how devoted John was to his engineering. And what would Mr Hartlipp say? 'There was one small thing,' she said tentatively. 'It concerns John Gate . . .'

'Ah, the romantic issue.'

Frances licked dry lips. 'We had planned on being married before . . . all this. We still can, now that you have made such a marvellous arrangement. But you know about my tour of America in the autumn with Mr Gerard . . . I . . . we thought of being married before then and going together.' She felt she was explaining things very badly and hurried on: 'Would you and Mr Hartlipp let him go?'

Mr Cowper-Donkin pinched his chin, looking at her seriously. 'Well now, that is a thing for consultation with my partner, and for John too. Have you talked it over with him?'

'Yes . . . but . . .'

'Don't let your own desires cloud your judgement, m'dear. If you push him along the path you have planned instead of choosing together, it may come between you for the rest of your lives.' A fit of coughing attacked him, leaving him gasping for breath.

Frances was full of concern. He was quite right in every way, just like John. How could she have been so blind and selfish? Everything lay before her. What was five months separation, if that was John's decree! They would be married as soon as she returned. This odd fatherly little man could not look into the future with the same confidence. She had the premonition that his life span was limited, in spite of his cheerful talk about the benefits of country air.

'I'll talk to John,' she said.

It was dusk when John arrived. Frances had learned her lesson and had sent Jim Prescott with a message asking him to come to the Hall that same evening. Mr Drayton, the butler, announced him with subtle scorn to Frances, who was sitting alone on the little sofa before a crackling fire in the morning room. She waited until the door was closed, then took his hand and pulled him close so that there was no chance of any constraint building between them.

'I've something very important to ask you,' she said. 'Whatever the answer is, it must be decided by us together.' And she told him all about Mr Cowper-Donkin's proposition and the fact that both he and Mr Hartlipp had agreed that John must be free to decide whether or not he left their employment. If he wanted to go with Frances to America, then there would be a letter of introduction for him to take to an engineering company with English connections.

'And you want that I should go?' John asked her.

Frances closed her eyes, mortally afraid that her new resolution would collapse if she looked at him. 'I want what you want,' she said.

'Then we'm both of a mind.'

She opened her eyes, joy flooding in. 'You'll come?'

He shook his head. 'How can I with my work half finished. When that addle-headed pointsman forgot to switch the points and sent your train into the siding to crash into the other locomotive, those braking tests hadn't been made ... still haven't. I can't leave such work undone when so many lives may depend on it. Don't you see?'

She shut her eyes in defence and did not answer. He went on with a touch of desperation:

'What happens now in a real emergency? They put the locomotive into reverse and try to use the carriage brakes. It isn't enough. A new system is long overdue ... I can't abandon that! Another thing,' he added, touching her cheek lightly, 'I can't walk out on Mr Hartlipp ... wouldn't be right. I owe him a lot. He's been a good master to me.'

Bewildered, she opened her eyes. 'But I thought ...'

'You could stay in England ... go back to the Theatre Royal in Birmingham, then we wouldn't be parted,' he said gently.

She stared at him. There was a hint of mockery in his face and she realized he was making her accept that they both faced the same choice in their different occupations. But she could not give up the chance of playing with David Gerard. It might never come again. She could spend a lifetime in a stock company, working from Walking Lady to Juvenile Lead and back down the slope to First or Second Old Woman as age claimed her, with never a taste of those coveted parts like 'Portia' and 'Juliet' on the great stages of the world. She put her hands to her face.

'It ent the end of everything,' John said, pulling them away, tilting her head so she had to look directly at him. 'I'm taking on the problems that'll face us when Mr Cowper-Donkin dies and you own Thrushton all over again.'

She smiled then, the lump in her throat making talking very difficult.

'It may be years,' she whispered. 'And our children . . . they can inherit. Gate is a splendid solid English name.'

'Squire Gate,' he said, considering the title gravely . . . then burst out laughing.

15

A ROSE AND GOLD DAY BLOWN ABOUT BY A blustering autumn wind swept the quay where Frances stood with David Gerard and the rest of his company, waiting to board the high-masted sailing ship that was to take them to America. All around was a hum and a bustle. Sweating porters ferried piles of luggage up the gang plank; passengers said hurried good-byes to friends and relatives, while on deck the crew ran here and there completing last minute tasks.

Frances looked round at her own group of friends who had come to see her depart: John, Mr Hartlipp and Mr Cowper-Donkin, with Joe hovering in the background, waiting to travel back to Thrushton with the new Squire after the ship had sailed. Mr Cowper-Donkin had offered him employment, working the land on the Thrushton estate. He was going home and was overjoyed.

David Gerard suddenly pushed between the waiting people and began fussing over a pile of cabin trunks. 'Labels,' he said in a thunderous voice. 'Where are they? I told everyone to make sure there were at least a dozen to each piece of luggage.' He began waving his arms, making incomprehensible signals.

Frances sighed. He might be an excellent actor, but she could see that he was going to be an exasperating fellow traveller! 'The trunks are well labelled,' she said. 'Look!' Pointing to various pieces of white paper pasted on the sides.

John took her hand, quietly sharing her smile of resignation as David Gerard grumbled his way towards another member of the company who had made the mistake of equipping herself with a new parasol. 'Blow inside out . . . the winds . . .' they heard him exclaim.

'Do you think he will be like this all the time?' Frances asked.

'There's always thorns,' said John. 'He'm only a small prickle!'

'Five months of it though!' Frances groaned in mock dismay.

'I'll miss you that much,' John said with quiet intensity.

'Me too!' Oceans of tears were swimming about inside her. Enough to float a ship as big as the 'Gay Galliard' which rocked before her in the harbour. She fought them back, turning away so that the sight of him would not be able to shake her resolve. As she did two figures appeared at the end of the quay; disappeared behind a jumble of wagons heaped with boxes, sacks and barrels, and reappeared with streaming skirts as they scurried towards her, leaning against the wind.

'Lizzie!' Frances cried. 'And Rosie . . . oh, how good that you came.'

She was enveloped in wet, warm embraces that smelled of gin and lavender and were as heartening as a summer day.

'We couldn't let you go all that way across the water without so much as a wave of the hand, could we, Rosie?' Lizzie said, glimpsing Joe over Frances' shoulder and putting a hand up to shield her scarred cheek.

Frances ached for her. Pretty vivacious Lizzie, who looked as she always had until she turned her head. The papery scar puckering the whole of her cheek, pulled the eyelid down and the mouth up in a permanent grimace.

'A bit of old England for you to take on your journey,' Rosie was saying, holding out a small bunch of heather. 'Picked it with me own hands when I went up to visit me old auntie in Yorkshire last summer. It's a bit dry now, but the smell is still there . . . OOO!' Her voice ascended into a shriek as a gust of wind tipped her jaunty hat and would have whisked it away but for two sturdy hatpins well anchored in her freshly reddened hair. Lizzie broke into a fit of giggles and even Frances could not restrain a grin.

'Come along now . . . come along . . . time we were getting aboard.' David Gerard had returned, shooing his company before him like an oversized mother hen with her chickens.

'Hark at the old fusspot,' Lizzie said in a loud whisper. 'You'll have to watch him, Frances, or he'll be tucking you up safe in bed every night and your John won't like that!'

John put an arm round Frances' shoulders. 'He'll have me to answer to if he tries it on,' he said jokingly. Then: 'You'd best be going, my love.'

Frances turned to shake hands with Mr Hartlipp and Mr Cowper-Donkin.

'Good-bye, Frances. Success be with you.'

'Take care, m'dear. You're a wise child . . . we played a good trick on those legal gentlemen, didn't we?' Mr Cowper-Donkin chuckled.

Joe was looking at Lizzie and started slightly as Frances took his hand. She kissed his cheek lightly and said in his ear: 'Good-bye Joe . . . don't pity her. She would hate that.'

He looked down at her with eyes that were so like, yet so unlike John's.

'Ent what I was thinking at all, miss . . . Frances. 'Twere something much more pleasant. She'll more likely take me now.'

'Good luck then,' she said.

And John was left.

Rainbows trembled on her lashes as the gusty sun caught involuntary tears. She returned his kiss and pressed him close to her for a long moment. He held her away and the expression on his face warmed and chilled.

'I'll be waiting,' he said, and paused, then added: 'No matter what happens.'

She knew that this moment must be the finish of their old lives and that John was saying good-bye to his home and family, the rolling hills and apple orchards, the hop yards, the colony of rooks untidy and ragged, ringing Piper's Wood . . . all that was his childhood and adolescence. There would be no going back. The future lay before them, a play yet to be read.

And then he smiled, pulling strings of bewildering sad happiness in her that tightened her conviction that they would never be divided. When she returned in five months' time, they would be married.

It was an end.

It was the beginning.